ALIGN THE STARS

BOOK III

IN THE

Journey Series

C.E. HAUPT

Align the Stars
Book III in the *Journey Series*

v2.0

Outskirts Press, Inc.
http://www.outskirtspress.com

ISBN: 978-1-9772-5661-4

PRINTED IN THE UNITED STATES OF AMERICA

My third book is dedicated to my brother Chuck, who with me, was enthralled about space and the Universe. I hope you have found another universe where you can be peaceful and with a happy existence. My heart is always with you dear brother.

To all my children Jay, Mike, Jessica, Jonathon, Kathy, and all the students I may have taught over 37 years for one or two of those years, who were my 'kids' for that time.

I can't forget those who have read and enjoyed my fanciful tales of a world that could possibly be true. To you, I applaud your patronage, your support and your positive feedback. I take it all in good stride and it helps me stay grounded.

Other books by C.E. Haupt

Journey Series

Book I - Journey to the Blue Planet

Book II- Alternate Routes

Acknowledgements

To Jim, I could never do this without you. Your computer knowledge is so helpful, your ideas are usually spot on and your patience is outstanding. I just need to help you get over your fear of the vacuum cleaner.

In our world today, I also owe a debt of gratitude to readers everywhere. To all readers and writers, your pleasure encourages me to write more. Your freedom to be able to purchase and read my stories makes me grateful for the freedom that gives me to write. May you have the freedom to write and read stories and tales, both true and fictitious without fear of oppression or banning original ideas and the ability to use those ideas to expand our minds and imaginations

National Geographic continues to be a source of information and new mysteries presented or solved almost every day.

Wikipedia gave me useful sources for Proton therapy and positronic and fusion engines; fuel research as well as knowledge concerning space, moons and planets, to try and keep it real.

NASA, as usual, gives out enormous amounts of information concerning space and our Rovers, The Hubble and

Webb telescopes and promised voyages of other robotic travels from many countries. Thank you to Jessica Lu, for her knowledgeable article on Einstein and his theories

Thanks to Outskirts Press whose guidance helped me arrive at another milestone.

Cast of characters-Book I - Journey to the Blue Planet

Council **of 15** (in alphabetical order)

Acacia Mikel, Professor of Archeology and Paleontology at the Berkeley campus in Los Angeles

Alyssia Angeles, replaces Egan in Book II and III, former mistress of Quimby Papadakis, wizard at Math and computer Sciences

Agatha Anastos, first lead member of the committee, age unknown

Cornelia Lovett, 'family' and wife of Senator Jaxon Lovett

Egan Filbert, partner of Petrus in life and business; they run investigative offices under the auspices of NSA and MI6 in England

Evangela Acivedo, wife of Raul Acivedo; both professors at the University of Madrid, she in Mechanical Engineering

Francis Asazi, second lead member of the committee, former pilot and survivor of *Mauritius,* a starship landing from over 150 years ago

Kiefer O'Brian, in charge of finances, spending and expenses

Leander Barbas, Attaché to the Ambassador of France, husband of Willow Barbas, father of sons, Tegan and Phillip

Nikos Kostas, general counsel in DC courts, father of Cloe Kostas, husband of Isabel Kostas

Petrus Alecho, partner of Egan Filbert, Replaced by *Cloe Kostas,* undersecretary to Secretary of State in D.C. daughter of Nikos Kostas

Quimby Papadakis, CEO of a large, multinational leverage firm, husband to Marian and father to twins, Tyson and Isaac

Raul Acivedo, Professor of Languages/ Linguistics in Madrid Spain; husband of Evangela Acivedo

Suri Callas, third lead member of the committee, president of a multi-Conglomerate which includes armaments and munitions factories

Tegan Barbas, son of Willow and Leander Barbas and teacher of the children in the family compound, new member

Willow Barbas, wife of Leander Barbas and mother of Tegan and Phillip. A navy Jag lawyer, once stationed in Belgium

Incursion #2-1610 B.C.E Akrotiri, Greece, Island of Santorini

Lucius- using tool to cause a volcanic eruption near Santorini

Cordova- helping Lucius to perform task to hide their presence here

Other Characters in Book I

Akel, concierge at Santorini hotel,

'Bellboy,' (Anthony) works in hotel in Santorini

Rodane Arcos, Archaeologist, teaches Antiquities

Sophia Arcos, daughter of Rodane, lives in Va.

Caroline Arcos, ex-wife of Rodane-lives in Va.

Iona "Oma" Cosmas Arcos, mother of Rodane Arcos – home in Va.

Addison 'Addie' Arcos, Rodane's father, stabbed to death

Adam Porter, boyfriend of Caroline Arcos

Cassandra 'Cassie' Arcos, sister of Rodane Arcos

Animals in Book I

Max, the cat

Silas, the dog

Beaker-Sophia's dog

Gunny, dog at Arizona farm

Greece

Sabina Carter, PhD in Volcanology and Geology; Archaeologist

Captain Andreas Ignacio police in Santorini

Sergeant Christoph Acurus- police in Santorini

Helene-security for Sabina Carter

Eugenie 'Genie'- security for Sabina Carter

European team

Theras Gallo, survivor of starship *Mauritiu*s, enemy of the committee and 'family' members

Acteon Hanas, works for Theras Gallo

Renata Kappos-works for Theras Gallo-sent to Naples, daughter of *Father Pietro,* priest of the parish

Tabor Doukas- works for Theras Gallo-sent to Naples

Aldora Spiteri, hidden sister of Rodane Arcos, works for Gallo

U.S. East Coast team

Zoe Martin-works for Theras Gallo

Lexus Fira, works for Theras Gallo

Principal Belva, Principal at Sophia's school,

Zoe Martin's family

Anthony 'Ducky' Martin, *Zoe's* brother, a state detective

Jennie, 'Ducky's fiancée

Edie Martin, mother of *Zoe Martin*

Charlie, son of *Jennie*

Naples, Italy

Amber Windom, helps Eugenie save Rodane from attack

Teddy Scalia, rescues Eugenie and Rodane

Doc, treats Rodane for his injuries

Flossie, nurse who takes care of Eugenie and Rodane

White House etc.

President Sheamus McAndrew, president of the US,

Lori McAndrew. Wife of the President, and 'family'

Senator Jaxon Lovett, husband of Cornelia and father to

Hallie Lovett, best friend of Sophia Arcos

Secondary characters_

'Nurse Ratched' ,hospital nurse

William, 'supposed' tech in hospital

Pierre, Guard at Amiens, France

Franco, Guard at Amiens France

Margo, President's Executive Asst

Fuller Cork, Lawyer for Adam's Estate

Taffy, works for Kieffer O'Brian

Simon, works for Kieffer O'Brian

Myrna, housekeeper in Arizona

Cloe Nikos, daughter of Nikos Costas and Isabel Costas

Ed Tolson, Provost of University of Montana

Tara Porter, Adam's sister

Mrs. Floyd, Caroline's neighbor

Eliana Nicolau, substitute for Rodane at UofM

Isabel Kappos, sister of Renata

Marco, son of Isabel Kappos

Flora Kappos, Renata's mother

Officer Flint, protection in the hospital

Officer Cochran, protection in the hospital

Marty, gym instructor

Actual characters-Book I-

Christian Barnard, South African doctor of heart Transplant

Johanna Gabrielle Ottilie "Tilly", a German-American paleontologist and the founder of paleoneurology.

Additional Characters in Book II- Alternate Routes-

Incursion #4-8022 CE

Aho-lee, leader of the tribe

Anchee, second leader-engineer and technician

Saha, wife of Monee

Monee, husband of Saha

Sida, wife of Anchee

Tanatu, a woman of the tribe

Kata-hee, tribal member

Towhee-tona, raped Saha and made her pregnant

Malia, four yr. old tribal child

Tuckahee, guardian of the children,

Moneata, Saha's baby boy

El Salvador Tribe

Nala, survivor of plane crash, 'family'

Eduardo, 'Eddie', survivor of plane crash

Carlo and Gustav, died in crash

Patrick, Scully's brother; died in the crash

Zoata, Nala's friend

Aluna, friend of Nala, has a baby

Botapua, chief of the tribe

Other characters in El Salvador

Eliana, sub for Rodane, works for Theras Gallo

Rusty, pilot for the plane for Rodane and Sabina

Generale, hunting for Nala and Eddie

Batu, Rusty's crew leader on the ground

Incursion #5- Petra Jordan, 4th/ 5th Century, period of the Parthian Empire

Mannawat, goddess of the sea, death

Al Uzza, goddess of war, mistress of heaven, sister to Mannawat

Allat, goddess of moon and love

Al Kutbay. Scribe, storyteller

Deshares, god of Nabataean Pantheon

Al Qaum, god of war and blood sacrifice

Levinius, dock master

Other Characters

Senator Lindley Gorham

Senator Orel Hitchen

Real Characters - Book II

Ferdinand and Isabella-reigning monarchs of Spain

Martin Luther, one leader of the Reformation-Germany

Thomas More, Humanist during the Reformation-died in

Tower of London

Phillip III, Expelled Muslims from Spain

Alphonse, Emperor of Rome; built Roman temple found under Shrine of St James

St James the Apostle, Place of burial: Cathedral of Santiago de Compostela, Spain

Pelagius, lived in Galicia, 'wandering hermit'

Sir Francis Drake, English buccaneer

Aula Palestrina Emperor of Rome

Priscillian, Bishop of Germany, tried for witchcraft

Benedict Arnold, traitor in Revolutionary war

Additional Characters- Book III- Align the Stars

Commander Ernst Haller, chief Officer of *Asternum II*

Captain Devin Socrat, Starship *Asternum II*

Piri Cassel, passenger on *Asternum II*, extrasensory abilities

Lieutenant Cliff Stanoff, engineer trapped in *Mauritius*

Lt Forbes, member of *Asternum II* crew

Characters on the 'Dig'

Ritchie, team member

Claudia, team member

Cosimo, team member

Professor Wilfred Schultz, team member

'Andy', team member (Andrew McCarty)

Additional characters- Book III

Jacob, Cassie Arcos' friend, law enforcement

Miranda, Jacob's sister

Dr. Francesca DePenier, doctor treating Iona Arcos

'Misery' keeper and abuser of Marian Papadakis

Elsa, cook at the compound

Solana Pappas, hired by McCarty to find Aldora

Ivan, technician; builder of the Bathyscape *Stellae*

Marjorie, student in the compound's classroom

Joe Jordan, working for former President McAndrew

Gerard Fowler, working for former President McAndrew

Bruno Zowalski, discovered a cave In France

Claire Fowler, wife of Joe Jordan

Grace Jordan, wife of Gerard Fowler

The Calm Before the Storm

Incursion#6-
Four Corners of the US-
1000 C.E.

The Lander had entered the atmosphere with no glitches or failures. Those within remained inside for a seven-day Earth week to test for safety and livable atmosphere. First chore was hiding the lander and it took some time to do that in the dense trees they used for shelter. Once outside, they set up a perimeter guarded by laser, cloaking device and they viewed the surrounding area from the internal camera monitoring system. They had been there for three months at that point and still had not seen any of the local natives or any neighboring tribes

They dragged out all the equipment and tools they couldn't afford to have found. They would be away exploring the area and it protected their presence if for any reason anyone could break through and get in. A small overhang of rocks had been turned into a bunker where they stored all these and sealed it with a false front covered with thorns and thistles that could only be opened by their tools. They had begun some forays into the wooded areas and spread out over the weeks to other areas more open with drier desert in soil and topography. Soon after, they had experienced their first losses.

The other two members of their team of four had died during that time, one of whom died from a rattlesnake bite soon after landing, despite the medicines they carried on their ship. It was ironic that it was the first meat they had tasted since landing. They buried him. The other team member had fallen off a steep cliff they were exploring when the soft dirt and pebbled surface gave way. She tumbled down, hitting a boulder on the way and broke her neck. They had no cures for that and had a second burial. They might have burned the bodies to follow their own rituals but were worried a neighboring tribe might see the smoke and come searching for the source.

They needed more time to acclimate to this new world before they exposed themselves, especially since they now had two less for protection. They buried her and made note of both graves. They gathered all their tools and divvied them up between them and made notes for future families who would be expecting and examining records. Their notes were getting longer and longer with more details as they discovered new animals and new… everything, not taught in their own lessons back home. Home was so distant from this strange planet and they knew they would most likely never hear from them again or see any of their own.

The camp was set up deep in the forest and four wild mustangs had been spotted on the open plains, miles away to the west and rounded up with their electric prods: two for riding and two pack animals. They had set the prods on *gentle* because they didn't want some angry or scared horses trying to break out of their camp before they had learned to ride them, introducing them to their smell. Smell was distinctive and once the horse was bonded to the rider, it was loyalty until death, and they could be trained to do just about anything. It took a while for them to make the reins strong enough, using materials from the Lander and much practice riding bareback.

Both men had easily learned how to make campfires, finding plenty of flint along the sandy shores of rivers. They also had meat for their meals though they cheated to run them down and kill them with their own stunners set on *kill.* For the first month they ate the rations loaded in the lander but soon tired of the blandness and lack of variety as well as monotony of the texture that left them wanting more. They would have time enough to practice, using the weapons they would learn to make and use, in obtaining their own meat in the way the natives did it. When they had killed and skinned two deer as they had been taught at home, they ate venison many days and nights and learned to like it, as well as how to dry it into jerky for their travels. They scraped their hides as clean as they could, used their own urine to tan them soft and smooth. They used their multiple use tools with razor thin laser beams to take bone fragments, cut and sew pieces of hide into a rough assimilation of a pair of leggings and short- sleeved leather vests using the dried tendons and sinew for sewing them together.

Their ceramic tablets were loaded with geological sites and more information on early American tribes' culture and societal behaviors, using their communication devices to tap radio waves coming from space. These would be collected in the Lander's back up cells and provide energy to allow for use of the holographic directions and filed away in the memory cloud built into their tablets with unlimited storage.

Watching the holographic tutorial of using the smaller pieces of tanned leather, they fashioned a quiver to hold arrows. Their next move was to set traps in the early morning in dense brush to trap pheasants and grouse. They could use the meat from the birds for their meals and some was dried into jerky for their explorations abroad for miles or days. They discovered they didn't care for the gamy taste of birds as much as for deer.

Most importantly, they would have the benefit of all their feathers for arrows, made for higher and more accurate flight. Arrows, notched and whittled from the yew's thinner tree branches, were then bound with metal tips formed in the Lander with thongs made from sinew and tendons or thin strips of leather, drying and twisted into tough strings. They were wrapped as tight as they could manage onto the arrows. They then carved bows from those thicker branches that were stout and strong and practiced for days to gain accuracy and distance.

All this they had learned from their lessons back home before they even set out for their perilous journey to this Milky Way Galaxy. They used their ceramic tablets that taught them whatever they had a need to learn. They spent whatever time they had left in the day to reinforce the lessons they also had to depend on for keeping themselves hidden and secure. They sent daily messages back home on the back of the cloud, using infrared and solar beams that powered their tablets. They retained hope something would reach home to let them know they were here and safe. They knew those messages would take years and might never reach home as they hoped. But hope was a small thing that kept you from losing heart or a desire to conquer the bigger things.

Finally, they decided to set out on a journey to investigate the surrounding areas. They took their weapons and tools to scout the geography of the area as well as protection if they should come upon natives that might view them as enemies. They made sure their lander was secure and well camouflaged and protected by stun circuits around the entire perimeter to a mile. Heading north into the northern most part of what would become Arizona, they passed through wooded areas tall and thick; stately sentries guarding those traveling through, near streams and dry gullies. Woods were thick with aspen and pine as well as some cypress and oak.

The horses plodded along through more canyons that were present in every direction. Following those canyons, they continued north until they realized the walls were meandering around steep edges and gorges that carried running water that flooded with unexpected rainstorms, floods that could carry them and their horses away if they didn't prepare to avoid them. Often, the skies threatened and then opened to instant deluges, with little warning at times.

During one of these forays into an unknown canyon, Asa looked ahead at Dimas, gently prodding his horse to continue through narrowing folds of solid rock, walls with horizontal streaks, layers of red, brown, yellow and rust, that rose higher and higher. His horse's flanks twitched and shivered as the rising sides seemed to move closer and closer to his flesh. The horse he had named Cinnamon, from his rust red color, finally balked at a curve that was almost 90 degrees and refused to move further. He began to back out one step at a time. As Dimas put more and more pressure on his flank, he whinnied sharply and bucked while Dimas hung on tightly then released the pressure and dismounted from him, holding the reins loosely.

Asa also dismounted, "Maybe this is a bad idea. We could take the lander and fly over the area or even use one of the sleds and see where all this goes. Much safer than getting caught in a place where we can't find a way out. Our horses might decide not to listen or might escape in terror, given the chance."

Dimas was skeptical, "Taking the lander up or even using a sled might cause more problems if there were any natives around to witness it."

"Yeah" Asa agreed, "You're probably right and that could cause more damage than scoping out the land by ourselves. We might stumble on valuable things of use to us and maybe in time, meet up with some others."

Dimas thought for a few seconds, "I can't see any other way out except to forge ahead or turn them around and go back to camp. That's over a half mile back out, just to the entrance."

They both agreed but Asa was still thinking. He looked ahead then looked behind as he pointed, "Know what just occurred to me? If we go back to camp and take the Lander up high enough to record data and create maps to graph this territory, it could come in very handy for us to begin unloading our supplies at spots along the many trails. We could use these canyons to make them our bases for taking off and landing anytime we chose."

"We could leave maps for those who come after us." Dimas agreed,

"But wouldn't we be seen? That could cause possible interference."

"It would be a safe way to use our Landers" Asa said, "if they were so high up without being visible and with our sleds moving so quickly. We would have plenty of warning if people were near and it would be so much easier than having to carry packs on horseback every time we want to explore somewhere farther away."

Dimas shook his head slowly, "We'd have to first make friends and become part of a tribe in order to have that luxury." Dimas studied his partner, adding more logic, "It could only be for those for whom we had absolute trust, not to either faint, have a heart attack or run and tell everyone. We'd have to let them in on our arrival and…"

"No" Asa grinned at Dimas, "We'd have to convince them we were leaders or chiefs or…" He waited for the thinker to realize his point.

"We'd be their Shamans or medicine men!" Dimas exclaimed. "I'm beginning to see some possibilities here. If we found a tribe and were welcomed as medicine men, or even better, Shamans, there would be a chance they would eventually trust us with decision making and pronouncements in the Kivas at their councils."

"It would have to be a Navaho tribe or a Shoshone tribe" Asa added, "Those are the languages which both of us became fluent, and the others are too different to convince them we are friends. We'd have a much better chance of finding them friendly and willing to take in strangers."

Asa knelt on the ground with a stick and dug lines in the sandy soil. With a piece of charcoal from the campfire, he drew outlines of the canyons they had already scoped out,

"Look here. See all the divides in the canyon walls along the way? They could become bases with a little excavation and fortifications once we knew where they lead to."

Dimas scowled with his mind racing, "We couldn't expect them to agree to this building and sculpting until they had completely come to look to us as their Shamans. The outcomes must be partly 'their ideas'. Dimas was now engrossed in thinking ahead and planning which was his strong point. Asa's was creativity and new ideas.

"It would take months to build and create those bases unless we used our tools. Think that would be possible?" Asa sat back on his heels and waited while Dimas thought,

"I don't see why not." Dimas got up and began pacing, thinking rapidly, looking toward the stars, "We train a few men we can trust using our tools, explaining that they are great and powerful magic. They could not be used in the presence of any others of the tribe if they wanted to keep the magic strong and useful just for themselves" He looked over at Asa and grinned, "Gets them every time, if the lessons are accurate."

They ended up having to back out only a quarter of a mile to where they entered that canyon and returned home to graph their journey. They stayed up half the night designing plats of directions and distances and spent the rest of the night going over their plans for how to reach a native tribe. They were no longer bored with trivial chores and reviewing lessons from their ship. They took weeks to make up a detailed plan with every eventuality and then set out on the first of many journeys through the area.

Becoming Navaho

For the next two years, they journeyed southwest and east in a vast desert of open flatlands, canyons that diverted in all directions, mesas that spread out for hours of walking to reach a way down to their next stop where they set up camp. There were mountains that reached as high as 13,000 feet. They would eat whatever they had managed to trap or kill with their much better aim, even to take down anything from rattlesnakes to huge bison.

Sitting each night at a campfire, they worked on projecting the route they had taken that day and saving it onto their expanding collection of maps and directions on the tablets. They would go to sleep to the '*screech*' of owls, probably sweeping away a young unaware rabbit or killing desert animals out hunting for food. The first time they heard the howls of coyotes it made their skin crawl, and they added more wood to the fire. The rustle of mice, as well as other small, unknown creatures around their camp equipment, kept them awake until they learned the various calls. They got used to them after many nights in the open, under the stars.

They spent days searching for rare birds and even found a dead carcass of a young condor, far from home as well as an injured, dead eagle in the desert. They gathered all the bones, feathers and claws as well as rabbit, fox and a couple of porcupine carcasses, still fresh when discovered in woods filled with mixed hardwood trees and pine. Two skulls were found with the other bones strewn about, one of an elk and one coyote skull, a real find for their designs of headdresses. They took turtle shells from the mud of lake beds. Skinning fresh carcasses at the fire, with their feet sore from walking and knees aching from bending and digging, they left the remains of the animals that were not rotted at the campfire during the day, knowing it would give a meal to many different animals.

Both got very good at scraping and tanning the skins in record time but Dimas was happy that Asa didn't mind so he did more than his share. Dimas, however, became quite adept at sewing the tanned skins into the finished products, hoping they would use them to impress and convince whoever they lucked upon or who found them to be of importance. They were making a very impressive number of native headdresses, dreamcatchers from strong willow and beautiful, significant breastplates for men and colorful, delicate ones for women.

When they finally arrived back at base camp after months on the trails, long nights of labor were spent at the repro-printer in the lander with their finds. It was a copy machine, 3D printer, reproduction tool, bake-oven combined, that redesigned whatever was programmed into it with the materials placed inside and came out exactly as it was programmed. They made many mistakes at first but got the hang of it after a few failures, ruining two valuable skins and a batch of beads that melted after too long in the oven. Failures, led by necessity and practice, became successes. There were treasures in this world they were now a part of, that amazed them when the finished products came out as they should.

Their machine, from another world and time, produced beads from the dozens of small, round pebbles gathered from streams and from shorelines, complete with holes after baking and larger rocks found at the base of mountains that required some grinding and some stonecutting. After spending hours upon hours learning what they could be and how they were left there on beaches and in riverbeds, they searched those same rivers and streams for more hours.

They uncovered chunks of quartz, minerals with hidden beauties in the stones, not unlike what Michelangelo saw in that huge boulder that turned into the statue of David. There was an abundance of gemstones; opals on the beach and agates as well as garnets, jade, obsidian that reflected light off the black, opaque sharp edges, turquoise for the taking, as well as quartz that became known much later as 'Pecos Diamonds' in the desert of New Mexico. Everywhere they looked, there were rock-strewn areas at the base of mountains. Their packs were heavy with their finds and necessary for their entrance into a tribe, when or if one was found. The horses carrying them wouldn't have agreed they were needed, but they didn't complain, well… not so much.

Some journeys led to dead ends and many with a maze of possible routes taking them out and on to other areas. Once, they got lost in a deep, winding canyon that amazed even them with towering, majestic, jagged cliffs and pathways that were extremely narrow going straight down to a swift, rushing, white-water river with a deadly drop of over six miles. They rose one morning early enough to watch this sun rise on a strange but awesome planet. The colors were vibrant; sun flashing off reds and browns, golds with fire in the rays, purplish hues in the layers of rock etched there from millions of years. There was every shade of brown imaginable, the air still, and the sound of the various birds floating on the air currents with their '*screes*' and '*caws*' breaking the silence. They had volunteered to come to this magic land for the rest of their lives. It didn't seem too much of a burden, but time would tell.

At one point in trying to reach the bottom of an enormous canyon that stretched as far as the eye could see and beyond, they had to take their horses by the reins. They led them gingerly downward and around narrow curves that followed another swiftly flowing white-water river with huge boulders scattered in the fast current. It was a very perilous, dangerous, sloping hike that had their hearts racing, their stomachs tossing and their breath held for each slip of a hoof or stumble of one or the other.

When they made it to the bottom, they set up camp and strolled along the beach. They searched for more treasures that were hidden behind the dull, grey, outer layers of rounded rocks, protecting the beauty inside. They filled two leather bags with precious and semi-precious stones with huge chunks of jade and agates. The sharp, putrid smell led them to an eagle carcass but the only things salvageable were the claws and a few feathers not scattered to the winds. They stayed there for three nights and left at dawn the next day and headed back to camp.

More weeks passed when they finally decided they had found enough and made some gorgeous pieces of Indian jewelry from gemstones and leather pieces. They hid the lander once again and set out to find a tribe near to where they had decided was a good place. They saw it as perfect for their ideas of bases and hidden compounds if things turned out well for them.

Then, they became part of a tribe. At camp one morning,

after traveling for three days, they were surprised by three visitors on horseback at the top of the hill to their right. It was far enough away for them to prepare for anything, a fight or a visit. They used hand signals to hail them and waited for the visitors to make it down the hill and come slowly to their campsite. One of them stepped up to Asa and asked in Navaho, which made him let out a breath of relief without too much attention,

"You travel far through our lands?"

"We seek a new land for hunting and fishing. Our tribe was…a small one and they are all in the spirit world with their ancestors from a disease that ran through our camp like a pack of hungry wolves. They were taken in days, while we were spared while out hunting. I am Asa."

The one who asked questions looked over to Dimas, "This is your…brother, your friend?" He waited and Asa could tell he was confused by Dimas' dark skin, thicker lips and tight, curly hair.

Asa smiled, "He is my friend…my companion, my blood brother, from a far-off land, faithful to me as I am to him. We travel together now for many suns and moons. It was time to find a new tribe; to let us live and hunt and fish as our ancestors have done for so many suns and moons. We have put away our grief and moved on."

The Indian spoke while watching Dimas, "Your… companion does not talk? Is he of sound mind? They call me Ahiga and it means…"

"Fighter" Dimas answered and stepped up to Ahiga, "It is a strong name and I think it must be that you are strong and brave." Dimas waited for a response.

Ahiga looked to Dimas and took a few seconds to respond,

"You had no other tribe close to you that would have taken you in?" He tilted his head and looked from one to the other while Ahiga's other two companions stayed a little back and watched silently, with bows and arrow still out of reach.

Asa glanced at Dimas before he answered and Dimas nodded his head so slightly that only Asa took notice or so he hoped, "They would not. It was too dangerous for them to do so."

Ahiga and the other two reacted sharply, with one reaching for his bow and Ahiga stepping back with a scowl on his face and his hand on his leather sheath for the knife in it.

"You speak words of danger. Yet you look to pose no danger. Your… companion finds it difficult to greet us and that makes us wonder but we do not see any danger here." All three visitors looked all around them, alert and tense. Their horses shuffled in the dust and whinnied softly, pawing the ground. The two holding the reins looked even more anxious.

"Do you bring your disease with you to bring us and our children death?" His voice had a very hard edge to it.

"Not at all" Asa put out his hands open and palms upward. "Our weapons are not of bow and arrow or knife or lariats to take down your horses. We offer no disease or threat."

Dimas spoke, "My brother in blood speaks of the threats they felt in having more than one medicine man among them. It was decided that even if they could accept one, two would be too much of a temptation to the dark spirits to cause discord and jealousy among them."

Ahiga looked back at his two companions who had wide eyes and an expression of confusion and anxiety while they looked from Asa to Dimas and back again to their spokesperson.

"You are both medicine men? You are Shaman?"

"We are...but you have nothing to fear from us. Our magic is strong, but our wishes are for peace and a place to lay our heads and live a peaceful life and help whoever decides we can live among them."

After more conversation, they were invited to accompany them to their camp. There they presented the chief and all his head councils with some of the beautiful headdresses and breastplates they had so painstakingly fashioned over their months alone. They offered the women dreamcatchers that were *oohed* and *aahed* over; headbands that sparkled in the sun from the beads sewn in tiny, intricate rows and started learning circles with the youngsters, teaching them how to make them as well.

They remained there until disease and a 50-year drought of the year 1130 CE forced them almost to extinction from starvation. By this time, they had spread to many camps and became widely known as A*nasazi, 'THE ANCIENT ONES.* So, it came to be that they took up residence with a large tribe who had made their home in the desert on top of a huge mesa now known as 'SkyCity' in New Mexico, looking out over a vast land of sharp-peaked mountains in the far distance.

They were close to some of the canyons for which they had created detailed maps and had investigated a few of them for themselves. Their reputations started spreading far and wide. Their trails became known as the Chaco roads that covered over 180 miles of desert land and were approximately 30' wide to accommodate the sleds and the lander they built that were hidden along the routes. Some of those tracts led to lakes, mountain tops and pinnacles, with easy access for cooling water for their engines and signposts for their landings. There was no ideology as was supposed by archeologists who study the Pueblo people, who mistakenly attribute these roads to trade and religious gatherings.

It was the great North Road to Pueblo Alto, even now seen as a cultural link between tribes throughout the deep west. Their grand pueblos were meeting houses for their small group; all in connection to each other and the other members they found over the years from other starships having arrived earlier or discovered after they searched them out. They kept tedious, coded, exact notes to leave behind for the others who came after, hidden both with code and buried deep in the walls of deep, unexplored canyons and caves.

They formed a large cadre of native Indian companions who swore their allegiance to them and then took them on journeys to those canyons where they carved out homes using their 'magic' under cover of night. Weeks and months were spent forming whole levels of homes built into the mountain sides and creating kivas for their meetings and their pow wows. The Indian youths that revered them at this point, made strong ladders out of thick tree branches and rope made from lengths of yucca and horsehair that was braided and tied into knots, for reaching those unreachable cliff homes. Their technology and their tools allowed them to finish them in weeks instead of months and the doorway lintels were raised to accommodate their taller height while the design of the interiors allowed for open space, doors for privacy, insulation for cooling and rooms big enough to allow for entire families to be together.

The atmosphere was one of peace and hard work. They grew vegetables like squash, maize and beans and added their own seeds brought from their old home to make hybrids that would last for eons if necessary. They sent hunting parties out for fresh meat. Their lives were full and happy as they took wives, had children with long lives and large families. They became legends of a strong people who had great knowledge and lives rich in food, trade and 'magic' that led to stories and tales that lasted for thousands of years.

The lander was used sparingly when they could go on their 'spirit journeys' into the canyons. They were alone to explore, fly high into the skies to graph, map and make observations. They wrote these observations in their own language to save for their own kind when more arrived. Those became petroglyphs and pictographs found all over the canyons painted and carved into rocks and the sides of cliffs as signposts, some seen from far above for taking off and landing in the dead of night.

With time, they grew old and feeble. They made sure their faithful followers placed their tools, deeply hidden, into canyons and caves for others of their world to find them. Their times then changed to centuries, when others arrived with more knowledge to understand the clues left behind. They studied and learned the stars in this galaxy and drew their calendars and plotted their lunar and solar eclipses. There are monuments all over parts of the world they had been directed to, which are studied in Archeoastronomy today, wondering at their advanced knowledge of mathematics, architecture, agriculture and scientific expertise. They were grateful for a well-lived and fruitful life. The stars had most definitely aligned for them and those they lived among for so long.

Chapter 1- The Party's Over

Bruniquel Cave- South of France

Created 170,000 years before Stonehenge-

Two people were sitting in beach chairs, wrapped in large fluffy towels at the edge of a cave on the side of the beach. Most other people had left as the sun had pretty much gone behind the high rocks and taken all its warmth with it. Clouds gathered and waves tumbled to shore and began their high tide. The time on their imposed vacation was almost over and both were anxious to return to France.

Agatha had left Rodane Arcos a cryptic message the day before and told him to be prepared for a nice surprise when he returned home. Both he and Sabina Carter were anxious to visit Eugenie in the private nursing facility where she had been moved to see any improvement for their selves. Rodane was eager to go back to spend more time with Sophia. He understood that Phillip had come to France to spend some time and Sophia, Rodane's daughter, was over the moon with being able to see her favorite hero and friend and delve into new Manga books and drawings. What was that about?

Rodane turned to his partner and asked, "Sabina, do you

remember any of the history that you studied when you were young, about how far back 'families' had come or when they had come?"

She thought about it for a minute and answered hesitantly, "Well…I remember that hundreds of centuries ago there were caves everywhere…" she pointed behind her to the small cave opening that was roped off, "and one cave that we found when one starship first arrived on Earth about… oh maybe fifty thousand years ago. There were hundreds of stalagmites all broken up and they were arranged in pieces in cryptic piles on the floor of the cave. If I remember correctly, there were two stone rings, one very large and one was smaller inside of it and there were several piles scattered around containing charred rock. Nobody had discovered this cave before and the only reason we had was because the travelers had been given a map with which to locate it. They had instructions as to where it was and the fact that it had been used by 'family' in a previous period. The original inhabitants of the cave may have used it for holding a religious ceremony or maybe they just needed a place to cook away from cave bears and other animals."

"Was it a field trip, some kind of test, part of your training?"

"Well, it was extremely cold outside. It remains kind of confusing because the 'family' never told us anything other than we would find things inside the cave."

"Maybe they left some kind of code or hidden message?"

"We weren't sure what that really meant. We haven't been back to investigate for a while. Because it's in the deep south of France and that's now a very well toured area. We don't want to make ourselves well known or find ourselves under observation. We do know that it was about 176,000 years ago, then used by Neanderthals."

Rodane mused, "That would make that cave the oldest hominid construction that's ever been found. I know what you're referring to now. It's called the Bruniquel Cave and it was the first to be used by early humans, even before Stonehenge in Britain."

"It's not the most sophisticated among all the places our family used then. Our documents let us know that it's been investigated by them. It does provide the latest addition to a growing pile of evidence even in your own records, that the Neanderthals that lived in that cave and elsewhere, were much smarter than we once believed. It's not just proof of evolution. We were given instructions for finding that cave and there must be a reason we haven't uncovered one yet. It's just that with those incomplete instructions, we all know the cave was discovered..." she thought a bit and paused, wrapping herself tighter in her towel.

Rodane added, "in the early 1990s by a teenage boy, fifteen years old, named Bruno Zowal...ski...something like that" and he grinned again, enjoying himself too much with this. She smiled at his excitement as he continued grinning at her.

"You and your eidetic memory" Sabina elbowed him gently in the ribs as he continued, "He spent years by himself, hauling away rocks and rubble from the hillside before he even told anybody. Then he found a passageway that was so tight, he went and got a member of the Spelunking club who was skinny enough to get through. He was determined to see what was there."

"You're enjoying this story, aren't you Rodane?"

"I've always dreamed of finding a cave somewhere on the

beach and going inside to find treasure. Makes me remember how much I loved 'Goonies'! That story entranced me even more."

"Goonies? What in the world was that?"

"I'd have to show you before you would understand." He grinned widely at her, protecting his ribs.

"I'll hold you to that Buster. Well, it was so narrow only the thinnest member of the local Sri Lankan Club could even squeeze through. Remember I told you that anytime there are digs or research into new finds, there's always someone from the 'family' that goes there or finds a way into the group?"

"Yeah, makes sense if you had someone who you could trust let you in on the information found and maybe a heads up when something big was discovered."

"Well, not only was our skinny caver one of us but they sent Paleoclimatologists from the Laboratory of Climate Sciences in France and they decided to go and investigate this pile of rubble that a fifteen-year-old had been taking out of this cave for… I guess months, maybe years."

Rodane added, "I think it was about three years but don't hold me to that."

"They decided to go in and examine it." She sat up straighter, "They made their way through the roughhewn tunnel and past the piles of animal bones and mineral formations and then they arrived at a chamber that was 300m deep and they found an extraordinary construction inside."

Rodane was remembering more information from his eidetic brain as they continued their conversation. This was his field, his life from so many years of being immersed in archeological findings.

"The experts and an archaeologist used radiocarbon dating to determine the age of the material based on the carbon atoms. They estimated that a bit of burned bear's bone found on one of the stone structures was about 47,000 years old, making it almost as old as modern humans and their presence in Europe but it didn't go anywhere. The head of the expedition died before anything further could be done and everything was left to just settle and subside. No other scientists were convinced to look any further. At least that's all I remember."

Sabina turned her head as she continued telling him what she knew, "More than a decade later, someone, maybe another Paleoclimatologist was putting a team together and decided to go back and investigate this cave a little more since she now knew the dates or suspected them from the radiocarbon dating. It wasn't even precise at the best of times so along came new technology of Uranium Series Dating, as applied to non-organic matter. That let them know almost the exact date when those stalagmites were broken off and placed in circles. They formed their little team and when they got inside the cave, they couldn't believe that it was such a secret for so long. 'It was definitely made by people,' that was the verdict."

"Was this ever recorded in journals that you know of?" Rodane looked mystified. "I don't remember any of this." He was intrigued that only now, they were finding out more about something not generally mentioned in any current journals.

Sabina shook her head and continued with her tale, "I only remember because it caused such a stir that they tried to employ a research team immediately. It took a lot of money and persuasion to keep them away and from following through. It was bad enough that their findings indicated that the stalagmites were broken off…I guess around a hundred seventy-four thousand years, long before humans had come there. They didn't find any evidence of cave bears in the spot where their bones had been located. It wouldn't explain who broke them off or who built the fires for light. It could only have been created by Neanderthals who lived in this cave or so they determined."

At that statement, her face was tilted toward him; her expression one of teasing out a mystery, "Scientists long believed that such structures as complicated and as sophisticated as these, went beyond the capacity of the Neanderthals and now they had to recalculate and redesign their arguments to absorb some semblance of respectability. That generally happens to scientists who are proven wrong."

"Hey, maybe because we're seldom wrong!" He tweaked her nose.

"Well, when they are…when *we* are" and she gave him another soft dig in the ribs… "*they* can't live it down and they will argue their position till the cows come home. Well, they aren't coming on this one." She shifted in her seat, "What they do know for a fact is that nothing from the prehistoric past has been found anywhere as old and as dark and deep a mystery as this one…now they just need to admit this was somehow done by unknown innovators back in time. We just won't ever tell them who they were."

Rodane also shifted his seat to form a new hollow in the sand and ease his scratchy bottom, "Why was it so necessary to throw them off? Was there something that could lead to you?"

Sabina brushed off the air-driven sand from her legs and shifted to lean more toward the lowering sun, "If they were allowed to dig, they would have found particles of the minerals we used for making light inside the cave. No one had carbon filament lamps in those days so it's a pretty good guess that would have confounded them and put them on the hunt for more. They would have found more."

"Really?" Rodane grinned again.

"Digging into the base of the cave was not an option so we sent two of our best R&R people to go in and clean up the site. It took all night and they left right before dawn and arrived home with bags of dirt and pieces of bone that would identify them as anything other than Neanderthal along with those that were. Our 'silver thingy'…" he smiled at her, thinking of their first introduction, "sort of…would have been a dead giveaway as well as DNA present in so many spots.

Well, we found the 'silver thingy' (his term referring to the tool he had first seen when he met Sabina while she was digging for one) was not there but the DNA was, so we still got off scot-free." She pulled her towel closer around herself.

"Sabina, when this is over and everyone is safe, if it ever happens…"

She squeezed his arm in hers, "Rodane, it will happen, we're getting closer each time someone gets a little too greedy or someone else wants a bigger piece of the pie or…someone acts out of rage and the desire for revenge. Every one of our bad guys has a weakness we can exploit. They think they can do the same with us. We've proven them wrong time after time. Let's go shower off and look over our plans for the trip home. What did you want to do when this is over?"

"Would you go on a dig with me to a really, nice site? I'll even let you pick, anywhere in the world, just to have fun and not have our lives on the line."

"On one condition…if you ask Caroline to let Sophia go with us. I'll pick a place I know she will love! That's if she wants to go."

"Maybe. She's been begging me for years. I think Caroline might not be too ready for it after their latest incident. Maybe not ready to let go a little yet." He shrugged his shoulders. "We'll have to test the waters."

They rose at the same time, brushed themselves off and both ran from the drizzling rain they had been sitting in for over a half hour and headed for a warm shower.

"Have you talked to Aldora?" Agatha looked hard at Rodane. He and Sabina were speaking to her from their joined pins rather than cellphones for security's sake, letting her know their plans to return home.

"Yes, I have. We've agreed to meet somewhere halfway between here and… wherever she tells me and iron out some very sticky problems that our new…relationship poses." His relationship with a previously unknown sister had just reached a point where they were ready to share past lives. His ex-wife, Caroline, was still adjusting to being single again after Adam's violent death.

"Good! We can get down to work as soon as you return.

That's if you care to." She eyed him on her messenger face to face, quietly questioning his sincerity and that was it.

Agatha disconnected and everyone remained sitting down at table in their conference room; turned off their printers, closed the monitors on their computers and waited. Agatha turned to all of them and raised both hands for any comments. They looked around at each other and Nikos asked, "Do we hit him with all our news as soon as he arrives, or do you have something else in mind?"

Chapter 2

The Boat has a Leak

Quimby stood on the pier of an island where all the past days' events had ended. Too many things were happening at once for him to take it all in. He put his hand in his pocket and felt the small pin that had been given to him by the captain of the *McCain*, waiting at anchor for the remaining men from shore so they could make their way back to Guam and port. Terrence Gurlow, once Theras Gallo was dead, completely, utterly dead. Quimby's wife, Marian, was on her way to a hospital to be checked out, treated and her condition would be assessed. He didn't know how he felt about that at this moment. He was somewhat numb from the past few months. Hell, he was numb from the past few years.

He and all his family had been on a roller coaster ride for quite some time, and he knew it was not over by a longshot. He needed answers from one Emmanuel Duncan, the engineer that had designed the plans for the bathyscape, *Stellae*. It now rested atop the reconstructed battleship, the *Neptune*, now under control of the Coast Guard. All the people from the bunker had been removed to…he didn't even know where and Duncan was waiting off to the side of their decking, hands and feet shackled and apparently asleep or lost in thought. He'd better be thinking of coming clean on questioning if he ever wanted to see daylight, blue seas and sun again. That also was not a given.

The pod was entering the Earth's atmosphere at incredible speed and all the men alive on board were expecting to die in a hideous fiery death at any second. Some had already vomited their stomach contents over their boots and the smell of that plus the sweat of fear, the loosened bowels, the urine expelled, hemorrhaged blood and bile was a horrific testament to how much fear even the most tested and prepared people could experience under these circumstances. The heat inside had been building faster as their speed continued unabated. Breathing was becoming more and more labored for the living scrunched among the dead or dying. Instruments were shorting out once the water with salt in it had flooded the cabin up to their seats as sparks flew everywhere, some singing their suits.

Suddenly the pod lurched and bounced from side to side as it leveled out, came to a second's standstill, and then proceeded at a slower and smoother pace toward the sea of blue below them. They had just gotten a glimpse of it from the tiny porthole when it was visible to them during one of its last gyrations.

{how stupid was my decision to come on this one-way journey}

It splashed down with a mighty heave to the side, which sent two careening through the pod with unhooked seatbelts. He had been ready to do the same, to exit the pod before it sank and him with it. Only the staunch fortitude he could muster kept him from doing that. The hours following were filled with fear and dread of drowning, those escaped from the pod trying to aid those who were injured. They were still able to recover some of the canisters they had been allowed from the starship, with survival gear and tools. They left the dead to the sea, along with the pod filled with nothing but death and a few remaining canisters they could not retrieve once it had begun to sink to greater depths.

There were three other pods which had left their mother ship as well as the drop of sleds and landers that had been released into the atmosphere with a timetable to recover them when they had made it to land. They had no idea where the other pods had landed but they needed to set up a perimeter for protection and set up camp until they could assess the damage and look for those remaining two pods.

They burned their dead (two did not survive their injuries from being lashed back and forth in the pod during the final moments of splashing down in the sea). All the survivors were kept busy for two weeks doing all they could to ensure their safety as well as their anonymity among the people of this world. Eventually, they went on a trek using the coordinates given by the sleds and landers upon arrival and located each one that was still viable or in good enough shape to use for parts. They hauled them back to their camp on sleds during the night and hid them under brush and tarps until they could locate a suitable place to start building their first compound on this world of water and land and people so behind them in technology that they could only imagine what would happen if someone stumbled upon them.

"Uh…Mr. Papadakis…we finished sir, with all the paperwork and cleanup and we wondered if…"

Quimby was startled out of his dark reverie by the two guards charged with watching Duncan and doing last minute clean up from the gruesome wreckage left behind from Theras Gurlow's death.

"Thanks guys, I'll take it from here. Thanks for all your help and you understand of course that you can't..."

"Yes sir, we've already taken the oath and you won't hear a word from us sir, ever."

They still looked a trifle pale from the last few hours after the *Stellae* had been recovered from the depths. The helicopter team had saved the drowned woman and most had seen the interior of the bathyscape. The decks had been cleaned of all the vomit that was spewed by those of weak stomachs and the men had been arrested from the bunker and the labs. They were carted in three trips onto the ship lying offshore with the Coast Guard crew. Those left behind would be loaded onto the dinghy and returned to shore where they would be offloaded.

"Carry on men" and Quimby moved toward Duncan while the men tried unobtrusively to watch and see what would happen next in this unbelievable day at sea. Duncan looked up and over to them and they turned away and started toward the dingy waiting for them at the dock to take them back, along with the two guards in the office.

He stood over Duncan for a moment, said nothing and then decided how he would handle this. He moved over to the railing "One more question and I need an answer from you before we begin with my other questions, my wife..."

Duncan looked up, startled, "What about her?" I don't really know anything other than what I already told you."

"The videos we received of her during her capture, the statement she was forced to read on camera..." His eyes had taken on a glitter of rage and anger,

"Did you hurry that along or even come up with the statement or promote it?"

"I had nothing to do with that. I didn't even know who she was or why she was being kept on the ship." He looked down, ashamed and scared. "I swear to God I didn't'! I was never involved in any of Mr. Gurlow's personal movements or plans." A long, silent pause had him looking up at Quimby, then he looked down grimly at his restraints and asked,

"Think you will ever trust me to walk the ship, Quimby?"

"You are too much of a quandary for my people or me to make that decision now. You know too much, and you have a…history."

"Is that your way of saying I'm a liability and may never see land again?"

"It's my way of saying I have no idea at the moment what we are going to do with you."

Quimby saw the eyes widen at that and his color changed instantly, like a gray cloud passing overhead. The hard truth was that Quimby was being perfectly serious. He stood there against the bulkhead, arms crossed, peering intently at Duncan as if he were searching for a truth in his eyes,

"We have let very few people know the extent of our reach and our…abilities in over 100 years. I certainly never expected one of them to be a two-bit twit who…"

Duncan started to protest, "Hey, I'm a respected scientist…"

Quimby stopped him cold, "who sees money in everything he does and only does any good if he sees something of value in it for him." He pushed himself away from the side and went over to a very dejected and frightened human being who was trying mightily to show no fear, but his stink of sweat belied all his attempts.

Quimby glared at Duncan, "Mr. Duncan, I hardly think . . ."

"Oh please. Let's not stand on ceremony. I want to cut to the quick."

"Ok, here's the quick. I give you ten seconds to start talking and answering our questions or…you will leave on a boat that you might not ever be heard from again. Is that quick enough for you?"

Duncan examined his face to see how seriously he could take his threats. He leaned back in his chair and said, "I'll answer your questions, all of them, if you answer mine and tell me the truth. After all, once I know that, you can always get 'rid' of me whenever. Now, that would be a deal, wouldn't you say so?"

Quimby had to admit, the man had guts and determination, a little too snide for his taste but to each his own. He deliberately looked to the gray water slapping against the belly of the boat they were on and paused for a few seconds. He waited for Duncan to get the drift, which he did. Duncan's face paled and his voice had a quiver in it when he spoke, "Ok, I'll answer your questions, all of them."

"You are close to the truth, at least from our end of the research." Quimby surprised himself. Duncan stared at him and then slapped both knees, and let out a guffaw, "Damn! I never thought I would be witness to this. Holy shit, I can hardly believe…"

"Duncan, I wouldn't crow too soon if I were you. Since you have now made yourself a direct threat to all we hold dear, you might not like the outcome after all. We don't take bribes by the way, nor allow for blackmail. Just saying!"

'Hey, my lips are sealed, I wouldn't…'

"No, to cut to your quick, I have to let you know you have just given up your freedom for...a very long time."

"Hey, I get a phone call, right? I know the law...you must allow me to contact a lawyer."

"That might be true if you were on land or US Soil. You are on an island bought by a criminal, and this is property of our government. There is no escape from forfeiture and who knows what we do with an entire island to ourselves?"

Duncan was beginning to feel a cold chill down his spine and shivers breaking out in various places on his body, the hair on his arms standing up, "Hey, wait a minute...you can't..."

"Yes, we can and we most likely will...unless you decide talking is the better part of valor...Hmmm? I'm sure you want to get to the quick, right?"

Quimby stared him down and then made up his mind against his better judgement, "Let's continue this conversation below decks out of anyone else's hearing."

They went below deck and Quimby placed himself in front of the cabin door just in case Duncan tried something stupid. Duncan sat in the small corner of the berth at the metal table fastened to the wall under solar light, motion sensing lights from the darkening outside, and waited in the dull silence. Quimby sensed the man's tense frame and saw his pale face. He pulled a sheaf of papers and a pen out from his briefcase, "Sign these before we talk."

{*not as self-assured as he acts*}

"I need to read the...."

"You need to sign them, or we're done here and so are you." Both men looked long and hard at each other for leaden seconds that could be felt in the humid air and Duncan blinked first and broke into a sweat. He picked up the pen with shaking fingers. Duncan spent a few minutes signing papers, being fitted for a polygraph, having his hand imprinted for the Terminus machine and using the bathroom under watch before his bowels exploded all over him.

When he returned, Quimby asked immediately, "Based on the *Stellae* bathysphere, where did you get the plans?"

Without answering his question, Duncan looked hard at him, judging how far his defensive attitude might take him, "What is Iridite?"

Quimby didn't move or blink and didn't answer. He pointed to the chair and waited until Duncan has settled himself once again. He set out the electrodes for the polygraph and sat down across from him.

Duncan shifted in his seat and blurted out, "Voyager was an early Rover sent out over 300 years ago according to a movie that was made in my time, many years back. I think it was a Star Trek. It was sent to collect data from space and perhaps discover alien species. Am I getting close?"

"Duncan, the machine only answers to yes and no questions so I'll do the questions if you don't mind and you do the answers, shall we? But let me start with some observations of my own and a little history for you before we begin your 'interrogation'. Then Quimby began laying out some history for him that he would never get to share.

"Aurelius Rovers…" he began….

Duncan interrupted, "Are they from your planet?"

"Duncan…you won't have much time to get answers if you keep interrupting. Wait for my nod and then you can raise your hand for questions."

Duncan glared at him and Quimby tilted his head and

looked at Duncan until he shook his head in the affirmative, then he continued,

"As I was saying, Aurelius Rovers were also sent out to do the same as your 'Voyager' and well before humankind was walking upright." He ignored Duncan's astounded expression, but the man did remain silent.

"Each one was smarter and more advanced than the last and went farther into vast areas of space. They sent back research that would have been invaluable in any age with any alien race. More information was discovered of what was out there in space and then it gave our scientists years to develop plans for where to go and what to research and investigate further." He eyed Duncan.

"When was this?" Duncan couldn't help himself.

"It was an exceptionally long time ago and it took an even longer time to get through all those years of researching. We were constantly learning more and making evaluations, not to mention amassing the amounts of resources necessary to get actual trips off the ground. Some of those Rovers went through black holes, some burned out without ever sending back information, some made it to your galaxy, alerting us to the advancing technology that your planet was reaching. We made it our mission to send our own Rovers out to you over time and ascertain how advanced you really were… and are." He nodded again for what he knew was coming.

"But you never tried to contact us directly or communicate with us…why not?"

Quimby raised his eyebrows in surprise, "Duncan, I'd like to think you could answer that for yourself." he waited with a frown on his face and furrowed brow, questioning this man's actual mental abilities. After a very pregnant pause,

"You didn't like what you found? You realized it was far from the time you could trust us or alert us to your presence? We were… unacceptable?"

"In short...yes. Well, to make it clear, you were acceptable but only as ground zero subjects. We stayed home, collected all the data over 20,000 years…"

"What? How could you possibly have a research team for over twenty thousand years?" Duncan was flabbergasted, "Whole populations die off; new generations forget the events of the past. Money, tribute, trade goods for barter, all ebbs and flows while cultures fail. That seems very unreliable and unrealistic."

"Almost impossible to believe, right?" Quimby held up his hand and continued, "Records are often destroyed during wars, our planet being no exception. After all that was concluded, we established the foundation that was connected to our space program which was already so advanced compared to yours that we had contingency plans put into place that followed our scientific community generation after generation. Meanwhile we were examining the physical evidence still being sent back to us at times with luck and staying abreast of the rapid changes your planet was undergoing."

"But you said it was extremely difficult to get back information because of time and distance. How did you get evidence?"

"How do *you* get evidence from other countries when you have troubles, distance and time constraints?"

Quimby raised his eyebrows and then waited while Duncan thought about it,

"We have advanced computer systems, great transportation systems, new cyber technology that sends records and data... but then…so did you…okay, I get it but it still seems so impossible."

"Impossible…like the Golden Gate Bridge? The Chunnel…? DNA sent over a fax machine from thousands of miles, space stations exchanging crews at a moment's notice, like those impossibilities. Facetiming research results, data at a nanosecond and sharing information with many people at the same time in your Zoom sessions…?" he added for good measure. "That's not a possibility, that's reality!"

Duncan was lost in thought while Quimby hooked him up to the electrodes that would record his answers to all the questions Quimby had prepared ahead of time. Quimby started taking notes while watching the needle course all over the page. He started the polygraph and told Duncan it was being recorded and copies made to the various authorities, if necessary. They began a lengthy session of hide and seek.

When all the questioning Quimby cared to do at this time was over, it was beginning to show nightfall. Solar battery lights went on inside and on decks above them. Quimby was bone tired, and he knew Duncan had to be also. He had phoned to the men waiting in the office upstairs at the docks and they were on their way to pick up Duncan and take him to France. He moved toward Duncan with his knife and the man reared back and hit his head on an overhead pipe and yelled.

"Shut up Duncan, if I wanted you dead, you'd be dead already."

He slit the restraints on both Duncan's hands and feet and started up the ladder to the deck above. He looked back and Duncan was just staring up, looking extremely scared, almost terrified.

"What do you want with me?"

"I want you to get your ass up here and we'll see if there's any leverage in keeping you alive and well. How's that for restraint?"

When Duncan still sat there, Quimby finished with, "If you don't come, then you can keep your sorry ass on here and we'll just blow up the boat and be done with it or...I can have my men come down, put you back in restraints and haul your sorry ass up and out, your choice." He left and Duncan heaved out a small sigh of relief and he knew it wasn't over. "Sweet Jesus, I'm about to lose my shit and I can't do a thing about it...yet." He slowly climbed the ladder.

Chapter 3

Home Again, Home Again….

Rodane and Sabina arrived home to chaos, though they were not aware of that when they landed. They had heard nothing while they were on vacation in southern France. Before they had even secured their baggage, Francis showed up at the arrival terminal. They were only now made aware that the committee was assembling, with most having arrived at Amiens, already.

"We need to get your baggage and a car is waiting outside to take us to your assigned safe house." Sabina's eyes widened in alarm and asked,

"What's going on? Our car is in the park and ride lot, so…"

"No" he answered tersely then took a breath and repeated more calmly, "No it's been moved to another location."

They felt the tension in the air, like a storm gathering or lightning ready to strike. They both used the restroom while Francis waited outside, scanning the entire area. They exited and Rodane reached him first and felt the tension in the air, "What's up, what's happened?" Francis spoke softly,

"We can't talk here, and we can't stay out in the open. Let's get your baggage."

He started walking away and Rodane and Sabina followed him down the escalator to the baggage terminal. They were rushed through, sat quietly in the back of the car while Francis drove through congested streets. There were horns blaring like angry geese, curses flying like broken pieces of glass through the open windows, looking for something or someone to skewer. Rodane took Sabina's hand, leaned forward in his seat and spoke quietly, "Francis, you're not taking us to the cathedral. Where are you taking us?" Sabina felt his arms flex and the muscles were taut and hard.

"Francis looked in the rearview mirror and slowed down a bit while he fumbled on the seat next to him for a sheaf of papers. He handed them back to her.

"Sabina, you recognize the handwriting of each person on the committee, don't you?" He glanced back at her while she tried to process this strange conversation.

"Well, yes, I do but what has that got to do with…"

She showed the papers to Rodane as Francis turned the light on from the overhead, "Look over those please. You are perfectly safe here folks, I am no danger, I can assure you. Pay attention to the dates."

"These were signed in early morning, today." Sabina was peering intently at the signatures. "Everyone on the committee is here…no, wait, there are three names missing." She read them again, "Quimby's is missing as is…" she put her hand to her head and rubbed the beginning of a headache away for the moment, "Agatha isn't on here and…Raul. Where are they? What's happened

"Nothing's happened to them Sabina, I swear." Francis

glanced back to them for a second on a straightaway, "We needed to find a way to get you from the airport without any notice and get you out of the city if prying eyes might be looking. They're not, as far as we know" he hastened to add, "but if you can be patient, I'll explain everything when we get there."

"Where's there?" Rodane was still tense with his muscles still taut, ready for action.

"I'm not talking in the car. You know as well as I, how they can now track you from satellite, even while driving. Please settle back and we'll be there soon. There's water and snacks in the back console if you'd like." Francis continued the drive as the night lowered over central France.

New home, old furnishings

When an attack had occurred a little over two years ago, against the compound in Amiens, France, they never expected the continued assaults would be ongoing for this long. They had been secure for over six hundred years, or thought they were. It had failed, but the effects of the dead from the explosions and the knowledge that there was a mole among them, had spurred them on to make drastic changes in everything they did.

They found new methods to conceal their presence from their many positions of sensitive areas. They intended to use the newly redefined compound instead of the cathedral as before, to avoid foreign surveillance or prying eyes from their surrounding town. They started by reconfiguring the compound, using 'Skycap' overhead, to block any satellite signals from above when deployed.

It took weeks to redesign, test and set up a half-mile perimeter with electrified fences. There were more security cameras, implanted devices for detection and motion sensors around the entire area with a video surveillance system. The controls were set up behind leaded doors with volunteer service from various members of the 'families', both from town and from their own areas. Five people guarded them in rotation; people they trusted totally from their town, in six-hour shifts and stood guard 24/7.

Inside the compound, down in the depths of the seven underground levels, they had added two rooms restructured from large supply closets into a war room. It held the safer satellite system, monitors, state-of the art eavesdropping equipment in the committee room. They built another fire-proof, bomb-proof and lock-proof bunker as a safe room with a wall-to-wall steel safe to secure all their CDs, documents, and thumb drives. Those doors were also leaded and within, was a hidden access tunnel that required a thumb print of which only the committee was aware. It led to a cottage on the property with a mini, bullet-proofed, unmarked bus with tinted windows, parked in the garage.

All paper documents requested by the committee chair could be sent directly to the committee room through a pressurized pneumatic tube, sent concurrently through a fail-safe computer system to each station. A newly created virtual reality program was in place that acted as a sort of robotic librarian who accessed information requested and holographically appeared instantly. It provided for anyone's use with a security clearance, a thumb print and Iris recognition for biometric security. It allowed for a computer trail sent to the cloud with the name of each person who accessed it with date and time. Each person was supplied with a new, encrypted burner phone to be used only for the Committee members.

The main meeting room was upgraded with the latest, faster computer modules, each computer with encrypted software as viral or malware proof as humanly possible, with more efficient Whiteboards. Each sleeping room was now outfitted with the new computer system to allow for personal use if ill or disabled for any reason. There was a central control panel behind tempered glass, where one head supervisor oversaw all the passwords, IPO's and files for emergency connections and review of sensitive information.

They needed a secure place for their children to be educated and the compound in Amiens had the greatest ability to provide that. It was already being set up as a day care center for legal purposes and classrooms were being established in the main house on the ground level, where there was also a safe room connected. Their own 'family' members were certified and degreed in Early Childhood Education up to fifth grade when they would be assigned to the next center closest to their homes to continue their education under a few chosen members, who all had the ability to teach and impart 'family' history going back thousands of years.

The past months were extremely tense and the committee members could not avoid the feeling they were under constant scrutiny by… who knew? This was a long, overdue start. They recognized their complacency for so long and the feelings of vulnerability and possible exposure, had eaten at them. It had and made all of them wary and suspicious of each other until they all gathered and formed a plan of action for the future.

They discussed various ways to find the mole or moles, a constant threat to their very existence on planet Earth. They established new occupations for some who would begin exploration in locating family members still uncovered and those who were known but were never approached. There were so many details still not addressed and so many possibilities of things going sour. This was an extremely tender, stressful time when all hell could break loose.

They could be revealed and create worldwide panic. The upside could be the beginning of a more open, creative, extremely auspicious period of discovery. They had never felt both so excited and nervous at the same time.

While Rodane and Sabina were being driven to their secured, temporary location, trucks and vans loaded with supplies were driving through the countryside toward Amiens, to unload food, linens, tools, weapons, ammunition and medical equipment from the cathedral to the compound in Soleux France. It was five miles north of Paris and three miles from the airport. It had been closed while all the work was being completed and needed to be reopened, aired out and cleaned up from drywall dust, new paint and the smell of unused air that needed to be re-filtered. People from the town, already vetted and trusted as employees for years, had been alerted to their arrival and all hands-on deck had the place smelling fresher and the air a sweet, clean fragrance of earth and spring rain. The twelve committee members stood in the newly built Committee room and looked around at the walls and each other. Each one seemed to take a deep breath at the same time and Suri spoke first,

"Well, everyone, this is either the beginning of our battle preparations or the beginning of a new chapter of our life on Earth. Maybe if we are lucky, it might be a winning combination of both." Murmuring began from all corners of the room, some excited, some anxious and a few angry complaints that needed to be addressed from the start.

"No one here is required to stay. You knew the plans from the beginning. If you feel strongly that you do not agree with the majority, you are free to ride back to the airport with the vans and resume your life as usual." Silence descended.

"It's not like we don't want to be here" Evangela finally spoke, nodding with one or two others, "It's that we have jobs and responsibilities which might cause our absence to be noticed and talked about.

"We will certainly try to put your mind at ease with daily readouts and feel free to pin any one of us at any time. You may want a personal conversation or to air your questions and concerns as a group. We cannot rely on emails for security but we will be tied into a zoom meeting each night as a closed group to keep everyone up to date. What else would you have me do?" Suri waited.

"Suri" Nikos added, "we only want this to be over and I think some of what you're hearing is stress we relieve by griping. I know my nerves are on edge and I believe it's understandable."

Willow reached out and took Suri's hand and squeezed it gently, "It's just been so long since we have felt so threatened and exposed as well as our children. Can I let Phillip and Tegan know where we are or is that a secret also?"

"Of course! You can let them know and tell them that they are welcome here as well." Suri looked around the foyer, 'Is anyone returning to the airport in the vans? I think they're done unloading. If you need to return home to prepare your children for the change and to pack, please be back in four days if possible."

Everyone was silent, looking from one to the other. The very air seemed charged. Finally, each one shook their head and Suri breathed out a soft sigh of relief. "Ok, then, let's get to work" and turned to the elevator, "Five at a time and I'll see you at dinner upstairs at seven. Elsa will be here."

Right before the elevator doors closed on five of them, she heard someone waiting say, "Well at least we'll eat good. There is that little ray of sunshine." She smiled in gratitude for some humor. She was pretty sure there wouldn't be much of that in the coming days or weeks and hopefully, not months.

Danger Lurks in cramped quarters

"I only have a minute so listen carefully" the murmur on the other end of the phone was muted with a hand pressed over it. "**NO**, I'm not in the house, I'm 'taking a walk' to clear my head" … "No, you fool, there's nothing wrong and I just needed an excuse to get out so I could call you. Shut up and listen!"

Apparently, the person on the other end of the line must

have reacted badly to the comment with a few seconds of listening to grief.

"Do you want an update or don't you? There are twelve of us here. We are three short needed to vote… because Kiefer O'Brian is in the wind as is Egan Filbert…no, Rodane Arcos is on the roster, so he's part of the thirteen. I think two or three are talking about going home for a few days and returning by the weekend…because they have jobs that they can't be free of right now. After breakfast we'll have our first meeting… Who the hell do you think I am? I can't get you passwords for their computers.... Well, first off, they're all encrypted and secondly, they are under lock and key in a new safe built for an army to fail at opening. They… no…**NO**! I can't get the safe combination. I'm not the head of the group. Are you that dense that you can't understand how dangerous this is?" *(longer wait for another tirade)* … "Do you want my help or not? Make up your mind because I've got to go now. I'll call you as soon as… "Damn it, I don't know when Arcos will be here!! You should be grateful I even agreed to help you." **CLick**

The back door was unlocked so the re-entry would be quiet and away from most eyes. The people in the kitchen were busy getting breakfast together with pots and pans making clanks of metal and the clink of dishes and silverware. Footsteps would not be heard on the back steps to the lower level as the hall door was closed silently. The screens in the safe room blinked red behind a shield, while a camera recorded the open and closed door and recorded it with time noted.

Chapter 4

Committee Meeting in Amiens France

Part I-Compound in Soleux, France

Almost the entire committee was present for the first time since all the chaos had broken out. The starship *Mauritius* was safe again, at least for the moment. Coming close to bringing one of their starships up from the depths of the ocean had made them conscious of the need to prepare for more attempts to uncover their presence and form a plan to put a stop to it and protect themselves.

It was time for bringing Rodane Arcos up to speed, as well as trusting him to handle the very center of their world. They also had the task of replacing two of their committee with two others and inducting three others. Egan Filbert was never located after his attempt to cause more chaos and even assassinations. It was up to the security forces, now in training, to continue to search for him. Kiefer O'Brian was in Federal custody for fraud.

Later that morning, they had convened after breakfast; twelve members of the committee from the total of fifteen for the first time in fifty years and Quimby had been invited to attend but wouldn't make it back from the Pacific Island until later, nor would Agatha be there for the opening. Francis had brought Rodane and Sabina from their safe house a few miles out and they hadn't yet told him or Sabina about Terrence Gurlow. Agatha insisted she be the one to tell them of the presence of his mother and sister in France. Those were Agatha's first instructions, until she had a chance to talk to him and Sabina privately.

Suri took lead of the discussion and each person had their computers open in front of them and had the opportunity to add other questions. Their input would be ranked by an algorithm that pushed the most important historical points to the fore and all others after that in order of input. The first question was chosen by lottery and any person of the team could answer that or propose another question.

Sabina had entered the house first, while Rodane hung back and gazed around the awesome grandeur of the chateau. It was centuries old and showed wear but still retained a hint of its early, imposing airs. It was a combination of Gothic and Tudor style with battlements on each end of the rectangular shape and four floors tall of huge stone blocks, wooden walkways and narrow vented windows running the length of the building. The front porch was a long, angular stone deck with great double doors, centuries old and thick, with four wide stone steps leading up to them. It felt like entering a castle of old. A circular driveway could contain over a dozen cars without any problems passing, coming or going. The green lawns had a shimmer like emeralds in the lowering sun and the entire surroundings gave off an atmosphere of calm and splendor.

Now Rodane sat with his usual cup of steaming coffee,

sitting straight up in his chair, feeling a tingling in his fingers from excitement, as awake as he could ever remember in any class. He was finally going to learn more about the origins of his 'family' from over 200,000 years; either examining Earth from space and covert observations or settling on Earth and melding with its inhabitants. Suri began with some background on the materials that allowed them to explore space with diagrams and pictures of their subject on the Whiteboard above them,

"*Euphrenium*, a substance from trees on our planet, *Asturia*, gives off proton energy when entering Earth's atmosphere. On *Asturia* it has healing properties as well as on Earth. Also on Earth, it exhibits qualities that are used for weapons; properties which they do not have on *Asturia.* Euphrenium is not really a tree, more like a bush, a plant and a tree combined. It doesn't burn on entry, rather it reacts with the Iridite to create proton energy in huge amounts from little material and it replicates itself after use. There's very little of it found at this point on Earth but that could change with one auspicious find. We isolated two properties over the many years that allowed us to combine it with Iridite to power stellar engines capable of making it through Black Holes safely. It doesn't require rockets or boosters to put our ships into orbit. The engines act as swift elevators to take the ships to orbiting altitudes; Iridite provides the outer hull that withstands tremendous pressures to hold the ship together on entering other enormous pressures of a Black Hole and the atmosphere of any planet. The first attempts did not go well at all." They all looked askance at those last words.

"The warp engines are engaged and act like a slingshot to

take the passengers to *Triton* in a matter of months instead of years. The passengers and crew are placed in soma stasis from the time the ship approaches their designated Black Hole, of which there are many. They are assigned to travel specific ones and they remain in soma stasis until they are three months out from the orbit of *Triton* or whatever planet they are approaching. The crew awakens first, followed by the passengers that are given six weeks of exercise and physical therapy on the way to our landing base. It didn't always go that way."

A chime sounded and a comment appeared with the accompanying face of the questioner; Leander in this case, was on the Whiteboard immediately after; *Short history of the early stages?*

Suri complied, "We didn't recognize or expect the energy produced by combining *Euphrenium* and *Iridite* until many ships had gone ahead much before us. It was the beginning of our own space NASA program, if you will. There were...failures of outer hulls, ships that disappeared in some of the new-found Black Holes, never to be seen or heard from again. There was no evidence of what had happened to them. We had accidents of exploding elevators, ships that overshot their course and were spun out into space powerless, the collapse of some Black Holes with our ships in transit, sabotage from groups that revolted against the idea of revealing ourselves to primitives, some aggressive, ignorant species that could be our undoing with useless loss of life. We lost most records of their journeys and almost never heard back any responses to our transmissions"

Another chime sounded and Acacia's face replaced Leander's; *Share information concerning communication with our home planet with Rodane?*

Suri nodded and replied, "Could we share just some of that and return to the rest when we resume this afternoon? I'd like a chance to print out all the files from those journeys and can present them to him after reviewing them with Raul. We don't want to leave anything important out and it's been so long since…"

Acacia nodded assent and Suri continued, "Thank you Acacia, for reminding me of some of those early successes. Over many decades we slowly perfected our science, our measures of the right amount of the elements needed to fuel our engines **and** seal our hulls until one launch after another was successful. It gave us time to set up a system of communication that kept them connected to us and gave them a chance to create a solid base on *Triton*."

Rodane asked, "Did they have a way to keep in contact with you on your planet while they traveled?"

"Not at first. Their to-do list was extensive. They'd been out there for all those many years, going in for short periods of time to adjust to a prefabricated atmosphere, going underground, taking trips of observation to the planets in your solar system to study, take samples, experiment with the various microbes, soils and minerals. Then after an extended amount of time, with lessons, physical training and simulation training, they set out for Earth.

"Some of these 'tours' if you will, had been spotted over time, sometimes hundreds of years apart. There were occasions when it was necessary to remove certain people who found themselves face-to-face with us or who stumbled onto a landing. They were brought to the ship and to our base as necessary."

"Abductions, you're talking about abductions, kidnappings of Earth's people to prevent absolute knowledge of your presence here. Did you do studies and experiments on them or is that just conspiracy theories? Were they returned worse or better, or not at all?" Rodane was somewhat agitated.

"Earth went through many stages of development Rodane; construction, reconstruction...as did the people."

"Did you help it along?" he sounded frustrated and close to anger, glaring at her. "What am I thinking? Of course you did!"

The chime sounded and Sabina spoke without waiting "I think we've already shown you that we did, and I also think this is going to be one sticking point you will have in your craw for a long time." She searched Rodane's face, her own eyes narrowed and searching for... "Perhaps we made a mistake in bringing you into our sphere as quickly as we did."

"Perhaps Sabina's right, too much, too soon." Leander spoke out.

Rodane calmed himself as well as he could, "I actually think I've handled this pretty much with..." he waved around the rectangular table and included the unseen sky above as well "with as much patience and civility as I was able to muster considering the circumstances. Forgive me if the shock value still gets raised on occasion, like now."

Suri studied his face for a moment, made an on-the-spot decision and asked,

"Can you tell us what you are questioning right now in your mind? Don't try and spare our feelings or mask yours, just ask."

So Rodane turned to her and said, "Did you ever

experiment to the degree you terminated the poor souls who stumbled onto you?"

After a pause, reading a note from Suri, Nikos answered, "Only when our own safety was at risk. Neanderthals were a very aggressive species to calm and hardly able to reason with, as you can imagine."

There was a knock on the door and Suri nodded to Nikos who rose to answer it. Francis, Agatha and Raul all entered together and those already there let out an audible sigh of relief. After greetings for a moment, Rodane asked, "What about later; other people in more advanced, more developed times?"

Raul looked at Rodane, gauged his mood and spoke up, "You have enough experience in archaeology with other cultures and different ages to almost answer that for yourself."

Sabina looked at Rodane, took in his facial expression and added, "Studying humanity is never an easy task for any age. Our efforts to achieve acceptance on Earth were always stymied for various reasons but the most obvious was those who had suspicions about our presence here, who felt somewhat inferior. That led to jealousy and friction among the leaders at the time."

Agatha spoke for the first time out loud, "Humanity has spent thousands of years building religions, tribal authorities, and various cultures of very bloodthirsty peoples with sacrificial tendencies, much like your Indian tribes like the Aztec, Incan, Mayan or other Aborigines. All of Earth has a history of warring, human sacrifice, torture of enemies... some very inventive methods, I might add."

Rodane made a face, "You're right, I can admit that, but I can't seem to get past the resentment I feel for having so much...what we might have been... without your travels and colonization here."

Agatha snapped at him, "You know as well as I, how difficult it was to survive periods of beheadings, drawing and quartering, imprisonment, starvation, poisoning and…that's only from the people of Earth and there's so much to choose from." Agatha peered defiantly at Rodane, who now calmed, half nodded in agreement and added,

"Don't forget marauding hordes, mass executions and witch trials, mass frenzies of the victorious enemies as victors, Christian Crusades and a host of others" he turned to Agatha, "Please tell me what our visitors did with their subjects after they were done with them."

Agatha folded her arms and looked sternly at Rodane, little patience in her posture or her expression, "What do you think we did, with them? We ate them!"

She said it with such a straight face that Rodane startled, jerked in his seat, looked shocked for a second; heard muted laughter from those around the table and a guffaw from Suri. He then sheepishly realized her humor was macabre.

She continued, "If you think about it..." she waited as a few seconds went by and the humor in the group became a hushed pause as before the lightning strikes that accompanied a storm; loud, shocking, blinding and altogether scary to someone not prepared for them.

Raul spoke calmly, spreading his hands as if surrendering, "I have to say I think the passengers on the starships entering this world seemed for the most part to be concerned, civilized visitors on their best behavior. The drawings on Egyptian tombs indicate awe, respect, obeisance, not fear or terror. The Indian gods resembling helmeted aliens are also revered and worshiped as part of their history and legends. The middle Mediterranean area developed an entire regiment of gods and goddesses to portray their approval of other worldly beings that became their whole structure of ancient Greek and Roman mythology." Raul finished his thoughts and sat back waiting for all that to sink in.

"You mean that was truly based on your...*our* appearances on this earth over time?"

"Quite so. Where do you think they would have gotten those cryptographs, those drawings on tombs and rocks, hieroglyphics, those scripture scrolls and petroglyphs; all the carvings, just for instance...in the tombs of the Pharaohs in Egypt and elsewhere, all of them? It was their beginning of taking those that they accepted into their lives as more intelligent, more powerful and they made them part of their culture and religion."

"This is a lot to take in, you know?"

"Yes, it is. We've been doing this now for months and you still slip back into that untrusting attitude that makes us think that you still have not accepted the fact that everything we tell you is true.

"You won't do this alone Rodane" Nikos interjected, "Do you think we would let you conduct or make any decisions for our family' that we had determined not to be in our best interest? We haven't given you any reason to distrust us, have we?" Rodane shook his head slightly.

Raul added, glancing over to Nikos, "But we also haven't handed over the reins of our family fortunes or our permission to conduct any of our R&R's or our other means of protecting and furthering the interests of all of our 'family' including yours."

Rodane snorted a sound that was part snide acceptance with a sardonic take on that acceptance. "Which family are you referring to Raul…my human family, my American one or my Greek one, or are you referring to my alien 'family'? Which ones are Aldora, Cassie and I a part of... all three ...or …one or the other…or…which one?"

"Raul looked at him for a long, silent pause, then asked, "Is there something I can do to help you through this quandary you've found yourself in? You seem depressed, thinking dark thoughts, examining a conflicted conscience, and angry."

"I am most definitely in a quandary, but I think part of it is unconscious rebellion and I'm trying to deal with that."

"Rodane, I hate to put it so bluntly…" he paused to look him squarely in the eyes and continued, "but you need to settle this in your mind soon because the big guns are out, they're pointed directly at us and…"

"I know that!" Rodane was even more agitated. He moved from his seat and began his usual pacing when attempting to wrestle something out of his mind,

"Don't you think I know that? I, of all people, am very clear as to what the stakes are here and I'm still alive to grapple with them."

Raul allowed a look of compassion and pity cross his face for just a second or two and then answered him, "Yes, we know how close we came to losing you before we even knew we had you but…"

Rodane stopped pacing, looked back at Raul and attempted a grin before he said, "Yeah, shit or get off the pot, right?"

"Well, I wouldn't put it that way but…yes, that's about it.

Our enemies are closer to exposing all our 'families' around the globe and if that happens, then you and your own family are in greater danger than ever before."

Agatha stood up and they turned off their computers in sync. "I think perhaps it's time to take a break and get something to drink or eat or maybe stretch your bones as I will mine. Agreed? The murmurs were low but in concert. "Back in one hour?" They all agreed and she nodded to Nikos as he left.

To be continued

Chapter 5

Mother and son, Sister and Brother

As everyone else left the room, Agatha went over to Rodane and sat down across from him. She asked Sabina to please give them a few minutes together and Sabina, surprised, said "Of course." Once they were alone, she folded her hands, arms resting on the table and bent a little forward while looking up at him, "I have some news I would like to share, but I want to warn you it's not pleasant and it involves your own family. There is no danger, so put your mind at ease but I promised to wait until you got back from your vacation to tell you."

"Promised who? Tell me what?" He seemed calm enough.

"Your mother and sister are both here in the chateau and ...yes, I know it's a shock but wait."

"How...What for...? How did this happen when I wasn't even allowed to tell my mother...or sister for that matter about you or...this" he swept his hands around the chateau "or the 'family'..." and his voice petered out.

"Rodane, I have known your mother for years and I have

watched your sister grow from her infancy, so we really aren't strangers but…"

"Why didn't you tell me that from the beginning? More fucking secrets!" His voice had risen but he caught himself, "Sorry…"

"You're more upset than I thought. Maybe I was wrong to keep this from you, but I promised your mother and…" She looked at the watch on her wrist and at that moment a knock came on the door, "Right on time."

She watched the door as Nikos came in with Cassie in tow. Rodane rose and she rushed to him and threw her arms around him, surprising him by breaking into sobs. He held her tight, murmured in her ear and stroked her hair until she calmed down and her sobs became hiccups. Nikos went over to Agatha and asked her something quietly. Rodane watched her shaking her head '*no*' more than once but then Nikos said something else, and she took in a deep breath and nodded '*yes*' and Nikos left the room.

Rodane held Cassie away from him at arm's length, 'Ok now? Can we talk?" She nodded her head, hiccupped a time or two as he snickered. She then punched him lightly on the arm. They both went over to the table and Rodane pulled out a chair for her and sat himself down next to her. He looked over at Agatha as she handed Cassie some tissues but sat there with folded hands and motioned for him to talk to Cassie.

"What are you doing here…and Mom…What's wrong?"

"Tears began leaking out from her eyes again and he saw her hands shaking. It gave him an inner shock that made his stomach lurch. She reached out and took his hands in hers, "I'm ok, I can talk. Listen…Mom is sick..." he jerked his hands… "She's been sick for some time, but she wouldn't tell us and…"

"How did you find out? Why did you come **here?**" How did you know about this place?" He pulled his hands free and rubbed them over his face and through his hair, "I'm more confused by the minute."

The next twenty minutes were used up by Cassie's tale of her house being broken into, her dream of Rodane and Sabina in danger; her mother admitting to her recent illness that was getting progressively worse. She left out the part about her meltdown when she learned of her mother's failure to care for her after her dad was killed. She then told him of her call to Nikos, the plans they made after Nikos had made several phone calls.

"I have no idea who Uncle Nick called or what plans he had made for mom but…here we are. We've been waiting for you to get home and mom made Agatha promise not to tell you anything until you were back here."

She took his hands again, "Roddy, Mom is really sick and…" her voice hitched, and Roddy found a calm he did not expect. "I'm sorry I didn't' tell you before but she made me promise too, that…"

"It's ok Cassie, I knew…" She stared at him with wide eyes "Well… I didn't know how sick or why, but I knew something was wrong and I was determined when I got home to get it out of her and tend to it. You beat me to it…as usual." He squeezed her hands and got a small, ridiculously small grin out of her through her tears. She told him of the car following them from a doctor's appointment and Uncle Nick coming to the rescue. That got a reaction from him more than the news about Mom. "You shouldn't have come…it's far too dangerous. Tomorrow..."

Agatha interrupted at last, "No Rodane, this is the best place for them and they are safer here than home, away from you. Nikos and I are working on..."

"I can go home with her and get her to a doctor and..."

Cassie filled him in on the doctor's visit in Paris and then told him about her house. She cried again when she had to tell him about the skunk she had befriended, 'Flower' and his ending. "The bastards!" he exclaimed. Cassie blew her nose and wiped her red eyes.

Agatha stood up, "Rodane, they'll be coming soon to resume our conference and there's more that I need to discuss with you but maybe you would like to visit with your mother while I can resume our meeting? You can return whenever you feel ready. How does that sound?"

Rodane let Cassie lead him out toward the second floor and the room where their mother was resting while Agatha sat down and took in another deep breath "He hasn't even heard all of it yet" she said to herself aloud, "All the gods and goddesses better be on their best behavior and get us through this."

Sabina and Nikos were the first two through the door and Sabina looked at Agatha with a facial expression that told her Nikos had informed her of all that they had just talked about.

{Time to get back to work. What was left? Oh...ye gods... Terrance Gurlow, Quimby's wife and Eugenie. Oh, and the ship under the mountain and Asternem II! will this never end}

She steeled her shoulders and rose to greet the ones returning. It seemed their testing was not yet done. It was almost time to introduce some of them to the *Asternem II* crew. She needed a breather. She saw Francis coming in the door and signaled for him to join her.

Out of the Frying Pan into the Fire

Cassie tapped on her mom's door and then entered, stopped short and Rodane almost stepped on her heels, "Aldora! What are you doing here?" Rodane thought he detected a hint of resentment in her words and was sure when he saw her face. Cassie was never good at hiding her feelings and that was especially good for him so he would know what was coming when she got on one of her tears about something she thought he should have done or ought to have done. They were thick as thieves, but sometimes it had its disadvantages.

Cassie moved to her mother's bedside and took her hand, "Mom, Rodane and I have had a talk and we can explain later." She looked directly at Aldora who sat in the comfortable lounge chair and was silent.

Their mom had lost more weight just in the week she had been here and it showed in the tight lines around her mouth and the gaunt look of her jawline over tighter skin. Rodane was certain if she was up and about, she would look more emaciated than usual. She put out her arms to him and exclaimed, "You're back, safe. Thank heavens!" He hugged her just a little tighter than usual and held on for a few seconds, "We have a lot to talk about Mom and…" Iona sighed, "Maybe now Cassie will get a good night's sleep." She looked up to her and squeezed her hand and smiled with thin lips.

Cassie cut in, 'We can talk when we're alone and iron out..."

"Cassie don't be rude" her mom was stern now and forbidding, "There's no reason why you feel you must treat Aldora as a stranger. She's part of the family now and she has a right to know what's going on as much as you and Rodane." Cassie started to reply, as Iona cut her off, "uh uh...no...I insist! You're better than that. I taught you better."

Red roses formed on Cassie's cheeks. She had to struggle not to give Aldora a nasty look. Cassie pursed her lips and looked at Rodane, "I guess you two have a lot to talk about."

Aldora looked back and forth from one to the other and rose from her chair, "Iona, I'll be going. We can talk another..."

"No Aldora, please don't leave" She motioned to Rodane to close the door and he took the other chair in the corner next to the brand new, spacious bath that was attached. "I have no idea how long I will be here..." She looked at Cassie's expression, "that's not a cue for you to cry Cassie, it's the God's truth and we need to talk out whatever we need to because I don't have the time or energy to beat around the bush. Sit." She patted her bedside and Cassie sat down and was quiet and somber.

"Iona, I can understand the need for family so..."

"Aldora, you **are** family as far as I'm concerned. You're blood of my Addie and half-sister to my own two, so that's as family as I can think of." She coughed and Rodane got up and filled a tumbler with water from a pitcher and brought it to her then went back to his seat and waited.

"So, Roddy, tell me about your vacation and your girl, Sabina. She was nice enough to visit me right before you came up. She's a darling."

"Mom, I think we need to talk about your health and your stay here and then…" Iona shook her head back and forth and took a big breath in and let it out in a *Phhft!* "Neither of you get it, do you? I knew this would happen when I allowed Cassie to start to 'mother' me and I also knew what your reaction would be Roddy, as sure as I'm lying in this bed. Aldora, would you like to join in on the takeover of my life or what's left of it?" She threw her hands down on the sides of her bed and took another deep breath. There was total silence in the room. They could hear the chickens cackling out back in the coop and hear dishes rattling in the kitchen downstairs.

'Roddy' chuckled, then laughed louder as Cassie began to try and hold in a grin that became wider while Aldora stood there and looked back and forth between all the players here. Then she broke out in a wide smile and chuckled as well. The pall was lifted, and they all looked around at each other while Iona finally had a smile on her face of peace and a hint of mild humor. Even the air in the room felt lighter and fresh. Iona gave a hard look to Cassie, who got up and held out her hand to Aldora, "I'm sorry. Can we begin again? I'm Cassie, you already know my very stubborn brother, Roddy."

Aldora seemed more at ease and asked if they could talk about Rodane and Cassie growing up and they agreed if she would then share her early years with them and tell them about their dad in her family. It might be awkward at first, but it would at least be a start on opening some doors that had been closed for far too long. Iona began with each of their births and in a few minutes, they were chatting away like magpies sitting on telephone wires and alerting those around them to the presence of strange birds but all birds none the less. Rodane excused himself after he and Aldora made a tentative date to meet after his visit to Caroline and Sophia before he left for his next trip. He headed downstairs to the meeting and heard peals of laughter coming from his mom's room. He smiled, shaking his head gently and headed for the committee room and his 'other family'.

Meeting with Commanders of *Asternum II*

Commander Haller and his chief engineer, Devin Socrat, had gone over the plans for their exit from *Triton* in two days as well as their emergence from the Black Hole they would enter to slingshot them into Mars's orbit and take them to *Phobos*, one of Mars' two moons. They were reviewing all their charts and figures since this was all conjecture and theoretical at best, having never done something comparable to this before. They had a rapt audience.

It was another tutorial in a private room away from the committee room where mostly everyone was taking the time to eat or drink or just relax. Others had left to make phone calls to various people they knew would be wondering at the results of the meeting. Francis had invited Rodane, who was peering astonished at the screen in front of him, watching two people from another solar system in an unknown constellation; now millions of miles away from their home and on *Triton*, speak to them as if they were in the next room. Rodane was beginning to get the distinct feeling that

Francis was anything but a museum security guard.

"*Phobos* is the larger of the two moons of Mars with a diameter of 22.2 km or 16.8 mi with *Dimas* being the smaller with a diameter of 12.6 km or 7.8 miles with a heavier weight than *Phobos*. *Phobos* has a semi-major axis closer to Mars and takes 7.6 hours for one complete orbit around Mars" Commander Haller paused, and Francis chimed in, "You could make a trip from one city to another in the state of Kansas in hours."

"Yes, and the camouflage action of being on the dark side would be immensely helpful. In 1988 two probe failures from Russia attempted to jump- land on *Phobos,* though the second one stayed in Mars's orbit until 2011. It did manage to send back some great pictures. Another project was launched in 1997 and one in 1998 called *Aladdin*, also from NASA as part of its Discovery program. They scrapped Mars as their destination and sent them for a mission to Mercury instead. In 2007 the anxiety ratcheted up when they got even closer. The European Space Agency proposed a landing and sample-return for 2016. The Canadian space agency…"

"Hey, I didn't know they had one" Rodane look surprised.

"Well yes, and it has been considering landings as well as NASA. They've never really given up on landings that will send samples back while the lander itself continues to travel the moon and keeps collecting core samples."

Rodane was curious with all this knowledge coming from a ship so far away, "How do you know all this, Commander?"

"Our mission and repairs have kept us on *Triton* far longer than we had anticipated. We had lots of time to study your recent space exploration and eavesdrop on all your conversations and communications from one space program to another."

"So, have they gotten farther" Rodane hunched forward anxiously, "and why is that a concern?"

"Yeah, they're closer. Flybys are prepared for 2025 or later and this time, word is they'll be closer to a successful mission. That would disrupt our entire plan to use *Phobos* as our next waystation. Now Russia is making noises about repeating their own *Phobos*...the 'grunt mission'. They've made great strides as well. Don't you have your own people inserted into the space program to send word back to you?" Haller looked suspicious and incredulous.

Francis looked puzzled, "Yes, we do Commander but some of this is news to me and I'm sure others from our committee. That will have to be examined quickly."

"So, what are you doing now?" Devin Socrat frowned.

"We've been shoring up our private communications to avoid any spying activities or breaches of communication among us and we've been preparing to send our team to Utah in two days to begin looking for ways to short circuit the dig that is planned for this month." Francis hesitated, then continued,

"Can you let us know when you think you may be traveling?"

"There are a few solutions for the short-term but that's not our problem. We've done the math over and over and there is no other moon in the solar system that has a continuous dark side to Earth and could not be seen from any Rovers all over the lighted side of the moon where telescopes could be trained on it at any time of day or night. We need to plan our landing so there is no chance we can be seen from your array of telescopes or your satellites in space."

"And your problem with that would be?" Francis leaned forward; tense and anxious.

"Just that our people are not quite ready to go into soma stasis and there might be some real blowback if we tried to move it up."

Rodane asked, "Why is that, if you don't mind my asking?"

"Socrat answered him with a half scowl on his face, "You wouldn't have to ask that if you had ever been placed into stasis. It's a 'little death' as they say and not as pleasant as you might think. Then there are the children to worry about with their parents anxious as to how they will fare if something were to go wrong."

Francis looked surprised, "Has that happened recently as far as you know Mr. Socrat?"

Commander Haller quickly inserted himself into the conversation, "There are always possibilities of something going wrong on a space journey sir, correct? We try and account for any eventuality." Rodane stayed silent as he watched Socrat purse his lips and stay silent. He felt they had just been lied to very smoothly and were missing something important. Both commanders of the ship from the stars, *Asternum II,* nodded to them, then cut contact.

He glanced over to Francis who was a little tense, having watched both men from *Triton* and listening carefully. Rodane turned to Francis and spoke bluntly,

"Perhaps you'll tell me why you invited me to this session completely out of my scope or need to know?" Francis spoke after a few seconds of silence, "Can I show you something that you might find helpful?" Rodane looked at him, gauged his serious expression and agreed.

They left the room and headed down one of the long well-lit hallways to double doors that were solid mahogany and difficult to push open. Entering a large open classroom, he saw seated at two large, round tables, about 15 children around 10-12 years of age. Some were working together; some were wearing headphones and totally immersed in quiet, individualized work. Over in the far corner to his left, on mats of carpet squares, were another 5-10 little people somewhere between 4-6 years of age, ear buds in, busily writing on laptops in front of them each placed on a shortened music stand.

They all stopped what they were doing and looked up, curious who else was coming in their room where they were in the middle of a class. Tegan was seated on a stool with rollers and looked up from his pupil sitting next to him where they were both engrossed in reading a document on the screen open in front of them.

Francis looked around smiling at all of them and spoke, "Morning boys and girls. How are you this very cheery, school day?"

They answered in singsong fashion from familiar experience, "Good morning, Francis."

One little girl rose from her place on a carpet square and rushed to Francis where she threw her arms around his legs and gushed, "Francis, you came!" and looked up at him with unabashed affection. He lifted her to his arms and turned to Rodane, "I'd like to introduce you to one of my many, wonderful pupils who are very smart and sweet. Marjorie, I'd like you to meet an exceptionally good friend of mine. His name is Mr. Arcos..."

"No, please Francis, I'm just Rodane if it's ok to let them use that?"

Francis looked at Marjorie and smiled, "Is that ok with you Marjorie?"

She looked over to Rodane, tilted her head of luxurious Auburn curls and examined him for a puzzling moment then she asked, "Can I please call you Roddy instead?" and reached out for him to hold her. He was unaware he had stepped back a little at his astonishment when he saw the expression on her face, one of sweet confidence and close to an adult look of tolerance at his action. He reached to hold her as she wrapped her toddler arms around his neck, releasing Francis,

"You don't have to be afraid of me, I'm going to be one of your favorite people soon and Sophia and I are going to be great pals forever."

{whoa how do I manage this}

He tried not to show his surprise or consternation, but she felt his tenseness and spoke softly in his ear, a tiny breath, like the touch of a butterfly wing, "I can do what you do and I know more that I can teach you. You're much, much more talented than you think, Roddy." He was speechless as she wriggled down from his grasp and went back to Francis.

"Francis, am I going to help Roddy today?"

"Do you want to help *'Roddy'* boys and girls?" he grinned slightly. Rodane looked around the room and all of them were looking over to them in anticipation. He felt the hairs stand up on his arms and knew something very weird was happening, yet he felt excited, eager to hear their answer.

"Yes!" they all answered in unison.

Francis looked steadily at Rodane, "Would you be averse to having the children answer your questions about space travel and the continuum of time?"

"Would I be...the children can... wait.... Are you saying this is the instruction time for..." he stopped, unable to form a coherent sentence.

"Rodane, we've told you we would be prepared to tutor you with any information you wanted or needed to answer all your questions. Would you be offended if it were the children who answered any question you might still be needing an answer to? We would, of course, be here with you in case they weren't able to answer something or were about to make an error in their explanation. It would be like a testing session for them and an instruction period for you."

Francis looked to Marjorie, "I must say my dear, I wasn't counting on starting so soon but..."

Marjorie smiled at Francis, "The sooner the better, right Francis? You're always telling us that."

"Quite right Marjorie, quite right. How about it Rodane? Want to test our little scoundrels with their knowledge base?"

They all looked so eager and excited, "You won't mind if I have trouble getting it and won't make fun of me if I'm slow... and..."

"No sir, our mission is to learn and understand so we can live safely, secure in our knowledge and our understanding of our family." The boy answering was no more than 7.

"We can be capable and responsible for keeping our families alive and well and serve all the people of this earth, our home." The little boy had a crew cut and freckles over his nose and looked so proud to be able to recite their mission statement so easily.

Rodane turned to Francis, "I would be proud and grateful to learn as much as I possibly can. It would be a privilege for these youngsters to be the ones to educate me."

Francis went to the double doors and closed them quietly as he left while a young boy at the table directly in front of Rodane smilingly offered his seat and his computer and took another spot. Tegan came around to Rodane and shook his hand and said, "Welcome to Space Travel Seminar. Boys and girls, show Rodane what we are working on now." They settled in for a lengthy and enlightening tutorial while Tegan pulled drinks from under each table area and handed one to Rodane, "You'll need this if you want to keep up" and smiled knowingly at him.

Chapter 6

Committee Meeting Part II

Continued from Chap 3

Everyone was gathered again in the committee room, prepared to continue their question-and-answer period with Rodane. Francis had arranged to meet with him in two days to drive him to the meeting place arranged for Aldora and him with Sabina tagging along for company. They had yet to spend any real time away from the committee and Rodane was beginning to chafe inwardly at the monopoly on her time away from him. Looking out the one window set high in the wall of the lower level, it was mid-afternoon with the weather outside chilly and damp and the gloom permeated the room.

Rodane had returned from the classroom, overwhelmed but happy with his lesson. He knew and felt they were expecting more of his arguments, maybe what they considered as his debates. He felt inwardly edgy and unsettled as well as

wary but put it down to being tired and hungry and… tense, like a willing subject under unwilling circumstances. Agatha began as soon as everyone had turned on their computers and the white screen was up, "We've shown you with our information..."

"I understand that" Rodane snapped "but my mind is different than my feelings." She tilted her head a little surprised at the interruption and waited a few seconds before she spoke.

"We all know that too."

He sighed, weighed down by an enormous, unseen, internal pressure, "I'm sorry, it's very hard to take my feelings and put them aside so that I can simply think logically and accept everything that's presented to me."

"Then those feelings are going to be interjected constantly."

"To tell you the truth Agatha, I really have a struggle about it all the time, but I'm getting there. I understand that what you, well not you, but your people, did hundreds of thousands of years ago in your eyes, was necessary. The part of me that is human and a good part of me, also questions whether the lengths that you went to were justified or ethical or moral. That's a conundrum for me, a very big one."

Nikos looked squarely at Rodane, "Consider humans over all the centuries having been on the top of the pyramid. There have been great strides in cultivating culture, arts, inventions…there have been severe drawbacks and backslides with violence, greed in staking out territory, stealing it, enslaving those less powerful. Remind you of today?"

Leander spoke up for the first time and he sounded weary, "At times, humankind is little better than the animals they use for food or the lesser humans such as Neanderthals or Denisovans they replaced…with bloody massacres and the enslavement of those they had to torture to acquire their labor, their territory…to make their selves feel more powerful and more advanced. What they proved was they were little better than those they looked upon as lesser."

Rodane sensed his sadness and disgust, "You had the tools to step in and take over if you wished to maybe change all of that, didn't you?"

Agatha left out a short laugh, "Ah hah! So now maybe you're also thinking about that interference you're always claiming we used indiscriminately. Yes, we had tools and weapons if you wish to designate them as such. We could have taken over with our knowledge and those tools but Rodane...even we had rules of engagement and our laws to obey, to blend in with the world we found ourselves in when we landed here."

"You had no reason to adhere to those rules or laws once you were here, right? You could rule if you wished or continue 'tweaking' the inhabitants you lived among if you wanted to."

"Yes, we did" Raul stepped into the conversation, "and a few did just that. Rodane, you know as well as I do, the nature of man. You've studied it in school, seen it in person, felt it in your own life events. I don't have to tell you why we decided to obey those laws and the majority stuck to the rules. Theras Gallo was one who decided not to abide by those laws and rules..."

"Wait, you said *was*. Has something happened to Theras Gallo?"

Everyone around the table began to murmur to each other and he caught phrases from those near him, *'no accident', deader than a doornail' 'I'd be terrified to even think about ...'*

His voice rose, "What's happened? I can't leave you folks alone for a minute!"

That got most everyone's attention with a group laugh and Agatha clapped her hands to get the rest of them paying attention. She turned to Rodane and for the next ten minutes she, Suri, Cornelia and Francis gave everyone a detailed account of the island, the ships alerted, the attack on the *Neptune* by the *McCain*. Then came the telling of the journey of the bathysphere and the ignominious end of 'Terrence Gurlow' aka, Theras Gallo. She allowed Rodane a few minutes to process all that. Agatha got everyone quiet once more and Leander took over from where he left off.

"I could share with you an entire file of others of our 'family' who broke the same rules and set up their own laws for their own advancement. I'm pretty sure you could name some of them without my help. Society didn't fare well when they used our advanced tools and employed any of the weapons, they could get away with using."

Leander surprised Rodane by entering the discussion, He listened well and hardly ever voiced his own opinion, "It didn't go well for Earth's populations at any time during that era. Our 'family' sometimes took the perpetrators of cultural chaos into their own hands and dealt with them. They sometimes had the help of the people who believed in the goodness of man and hope for future generations. I might add, those generations of our own families as well as those not directly connected to us."

"How did 'family' members decide when to use those tools or weapons that you brought with you? What were your guidelines?"

"Believe it or not, they were strict." Agatha got up and went to the Whiteboard, and pointed to the graph placed on it, "If it benefited man and us, a determination was made by the committees formed at every age. If it only benefited us, we had instructions to bury the tools and weapons or destroy any evidence that could endanger our presence here. Our first and foremost rule was never to interfere with normal evolution or advancement of the cultures we were amalgamated into unless our entire existence was at risk. We had our guidelines and procedures to protect ourselves with as little damage to the indigenous populations as possible."

"But you did it anyway if some of the files I remember were factual. You sacrificed hundreds, thousands, probably tens of thousands of people for your secrecy and protection."

"And we helped millions more with our knowledge, our guidance with new inventions and farming methods, our science and medical advances...does any of that count in your mind?" Raul was distinctly frustrated.

"Raul, I have only just been appointed as the possible titular head of this family unit. I haven't come to terms with that yet."

"Why not?" he raised his hands to clarify his query, "You don't have to share with us if you don't want to. It's not like you would have the authority alone."

"I am conflicted after believing I was nothing but human for over thirty years. That sounds so...elitist but that's my history as I knew it and now..." Rodane scowled at his own inner thoughts.

"Now you're being asked to simply accept our explanation and our actions and accede to our wishes and our rules, based on our word and our facts that you may or may not accept. Is that about it?"

He finally found the deep inner need to smile at those around him, "Well yeah, but it's more than that. It's the knowledge that I can lead you the way I might go that could cause harm or be a danger to you. Or…I could push for change if I saw a benefit to it and cause a backlash of the family that could also cause chaos of a different kind. I'm not sure if I'm ready for this…" he rifled both hands through his hair and his shoulders slumped under the tension.

Raul saw the look on Rodane's face and forced his voice to lower and he spoke more calmly, "The bad guys are smart, well-armed, and extremely wealthy over the centuries and also determined to cause as much damage and destruction to our way of life as possible, even granting that it might harm them as well."

Leander interjected, still a surprise to hear him offer anything aloud,

"Because evil lives in darkness and they've been there in that dark; planning and gearing up and waiting for the moment to strike and take over in the ensuing chaos that they've created."

"So how am I prepared for that? I've had less than two years to learn what took most of you decades to learn."

"Actually Rodane, we're still learning." Leander smiled, a rare thing.

Rodane returned to his chair, plopped down in it with a huge sigh, "Now what do you mean by that? You've been the leaders of this last committee for longer than most. What more are you missing?"

Nikos got up and moved to the Whiteboard and put up two graphs on the screen, "This is the amount of money spent on weapons from unknown buyers in the last three years and most are military grade on the black market. But more importantly, these…" pointing to the other graph, "are the results of DNA tests done by all businesses that have a stake in identifying your present family and your ancestors, all non-profit businesses and medical facilities as well as For Profit sites."

Nikos looked around at all the astounded expressions on most faces. Rodane looked around and noticed that Suri, Agatha and Francis were not surprised.

{so there ***are*** *levels of leadership here}*

"We've been spending enormous amounts of resources keeping some of the results private and withholding others with the excuse of faulty results, bad specimens, and anything else we can do before we can withdraw those people from the sites where they are being investigated…again by unnamed buyers."

Evangela spoke to Nikos, "Are they targeting those they think may have our DNA? Do they have proof positive… and who is 'they'?"

Nikos walked over to the table and put his hands on the top, leaned in and spoke with a hitch in his voice, very unusual for such a taciturn man, "We think…no, we are sure that is exactly what they are after. When you ask who 'they' is, I can only say I think it is someone or maybe more than one who are our own survivors from *Mauritius*. I can't possibly imagine any others more than 50 years back who might still be active and able to absorb the cost of doing this after so long."

Rodane asked, "May I ask a question?"

Suri answered him, "Of course you may Rodane. You need to know all you can about this as much as we do. No time like the present."

"It's really two questions: One; has anyone taken blood samples of the two survivors that attacked you here in France, in the Chateau?" He looked around and saw everyone look around the table at each other while they shook their heads 'no', one after the other.

"Ok then. Two; have you tracked down any of those whose DNA was suspect and/or any that were possibly released before you were aware of what was going on?"

Agatha answered that one, "That is a definite *yes* Rodane, but no one else bothered to ask that. Why do you ask about the survivors?"

He looked up and pointed at the graphs on the Whiteboard, "You never have the whole picture, not until the final pieces of the puzzle are placed where the missing spots are. Sometimes, they're in the wrong place and very hard to discover. I learned that on digs and research projects."

"What empty spots do you think we're missing Rodane?"

He again felt the need to rise and pace while thinking, just to gather his thoughts, "Do you have any idea how many Earthly mysteries there are, still unsolved, with no definitive answers? Some of the answers that we have are being debunked in record numbers each month, maybe each day." They all thought about that and you could have heard a pin drop in the room.

A thought occurred to him at the same time as those around the table began murmuring among themselves and his face registered what his own mind had just revealed to him. He was shocked and just beginning to realize something, "You don't have all the facts about your own people who traveled here from before, do you?" He stood stock still and waited, looking at each one in turn.

"No" Agatha answered, her chin high in the air, "we don't, which is why we are continually reviewing our files, going on

R&R journeys to try and uncover those missing pieces that I've told you about."

"You still don't have your own stories sorted out after all these years?" Rodane was astonished, "How can that be? How do you expect me to learn all this if you…how could I ever…" he ran out of words.

"You don't need to know it all, any more than we need to know it all. Not right now, this minute. It's a process that we're going through, just like you are, one mystery at a time, one clue uncovered by many people all working toward the same goal, but separated from each other by years and miles and language"

"How about the bad guys, do they know what they're searching for?"

"Everything we have and anything we might miss. So, I guess what I'm saying Rodane is…the train is loaded, it's ready to leave the station and you need to get both feet on board if you don't want to stumble and fall off. We're going… no doubt about that, we have no choice. We'd like very much if you were to join us and headed for the same destination we are."

"So, you're saying you still don't trust me, is that it?" His voice held some frustration and disappointment.

"I wouldn't say 'distrust' Rodane; I'd say maybe some caution is called for, before we entrust you with our children and our secrets, all of them."

This time, Raul grinned back at him and the tenseness in the room was broken. Rodane began to speak, thought better of it, and finally let out a breath and said, "That's fair!" Rodane felt himself getting so tired his head was drooping in the middle of a conversation.

Chapter 7

To the Moon Alice!

They broke up for the night and Leander and Rodane set out on their travel back to the cabin by the lake. It was pretty much a silent ride until Rodane expressed surprise that it was Leander and not Raul who was his tutor for the night since Raul had been the primary teacher for these many months.

Leander smiled, looking ahead to the road, "Raul is heading for his home with his wife, Evangela. Both were called away for a meeting about some crisis with the University of Madrid and Raul thought it best to settle it before we had too many issues dancing around us at one time. Don't know when they will return. Maybe they just needed some alone time" He winked. "I was elected to fill the spot."

"No problem there. It's time we got to know each other better."

"Agreed" and the rest of the ride became a question-and-answer journey initiated by Rodane. Leander sure kept things close to the vest.

Once there, they had a quick dinner and were settling

down in their easy chairs. A knock on the door had both turning at the same time and Leander looked at him and raised a finger for a pause. Another set of rhythmic knocks had him smiling and rising to go and open the door. Suri entered, her shoulders covered with a light coating of snow, her cape stiff from the cold. She swiveled her head, saw Leander and seemed surprised as she moved directly to the roaring fire in the fireplace. She stood with her back to them as she placed her cape over the chair in front of the fire where the droplets snapped and sizzled from the direct heat, "Sorry to intrude on your session Rodane but I thought this was important."

"Uh oh, what's happened?" Rodane tensed immediately, waiting for more bad news.

Suri turned and smiled this time, "The news is not bad, but it is important." Both men waited patiently while she rubbed her hands to warm them up.

"Raul is heading for his home with his wife, Evangela. They both were called away for a meeting about some crisis with the University of Madrid."

"If caution is called for, I can only tell you it will remain with you and me, my solemn word." He grinned at Leander.

Suri sat down in the other empty chair and let out a deep sigh, "Okay. What I'm about to tell you isn't a done deal yet but if nothing happens to throw a monkey wrench into it, the ship that has been on *Triton f*or years is now about to move to another safe zone and they've agreed to help us."

Both men were equally surprised, as Leander blurted out, "What! How did this happen so fast? What are..."

"Hold up" Suri lifted her hand, "I'll fill you in on all the details when we meet in two days at the compound. I'm just here to let you know what you will be discussing."

"All of us?" Rodane was eager to see Sabina again after a week apart since they had returned from Spain. Absence from her was becoming more and more difficult. A space opened somewhere in his self, though he couldn't say how or where.

Suri smiled with her eyes sparking, "Yes Rodane, all of us. Now, here is some of the information I can give you right now, but I need your help. That's why I'm here instead of waiting until the next meeting."

Leander was eager to hear but Suri made Rodane aware of a few details to prepare him for what was necessarily going to be disclosed.

"Rodane, I'd like you to bone up on your knowledge about Black Holes, Star Fusion engines, now on the calendar at NASA for future missions and the moons of Mars."

She added, "Concentrate on *Phobos*, Rodane, and you'll hear a lot more about it at the meeting. I'd like you to fill me in now on your meeting with the governor of Utah and that executive from his office who gave you the **Stop** order."

"Something's wrong there?" Rodane asked. "I just figured it was more bureaucratic bullshit."

"No, not so much." Suri added her own thoughts to a confusing situation, "The governor knows nothing about that order and curiously, no one else in his office knows either."

Leander was agitated, "You think someone is aware of our plans to protect the avalanche site?" Suri shrugged and looked over to Rodane, "It looks that way. I may be sending Helene and Scully with you Rodane. They would be listed as hired help in case anything happens that requires immediate intervention. I think from here on in, we can't take anything for granted and certainly not believe in too much coincidence. Oh, I almost forgot, Leander, you're to come home tonight and someone will be by in the morning to pick up Rodane for his trip to Caroline's. Sorry it's so last minute but plans are constantly being changed now. My head is spinning trying to keep them all in order."

"Can't we stay here tonight? I was counting on some time to spend recounting all the information I might share with Rodane to prepare him for his meeting with…"

"No, I think there is something Agatha wants to discuss with you."

"Oh, ok then, I'll leave with you when you go. I may as well get there for a good night's sleep. Who's coming for Rodane tomorrow?"

"Not sure, Agatha didn't say."

They spent the next hour discussing the proposed dig in Utah, the successful trip they took to Spain, minus the end of the trip, and Eugenie's condition in the Nursing Care Facility where she had been relocated. There was also the hunt for any information they could get as to who were the culprits of the past energy crisis global in nature. Suri watched every word out of her mouth so she wouldn't slip and give away any information about his mother or his sister Cassie

Visiting the Sick

The air was filled with tension and aggravation. Nikos was livid "You can't go traipsing off on a drive of that length!"

"And why not?" Iona was just as irate.

"Because…you're ill, you've only gotten the results of your tests back and we haven't even had a chance to discuss what you're going to do about it and…" watching her face… "you haven't even told Rodane or Cassie yet, have you? She looked sheepish, "**Iona…?**"

"Don't you *Iona* me. I'll tell them when I'm damn good and ready and you don't have a thing to say about it and if you don't keep your mouth closed until I say so Nick. I'll…."

"You'll what Iona? Unfriend me?" He stood up, folded his arms and said, "I've never known you to spend money unnecessarily. You don't have a car so how do you suppose to get to northern France? Do you even know where you're going or how to get there?" He had a smug look on his face. At that moment Sabina appeared in the doorway and answered,

"With me of course. Oma, are you ready?" Iona was pleased to see Nikos looking nonplussed and at a loss for words. "Way past ready" as she slowly rose from her seat. Just then she heard footsteps hurrying down the hall, rapidly clicking like martinets marching in parade, "Uh oh" she murmured, "We almost made it out. Follow my lead folks" gave Nick a dirty look and snapped out, "especially you!"

A little tyrant appearing, a little black raincloud in the doorway, lashed out,

"Where do you think you're going" to her mother and glared at Nikos, "and you of all people Uncle Nick, should know…"

"Cassie, dear, we were just on our way to get you." Iona smiled sweetly at her.

"Me?" She stopped in her tracks, "Where are we going?" The air and the attitude had been plucked out of her as if from a soccer ball that got kicked so hard it popped. She looked around, somewhat mollified.

"Didn't I tell you Cassie?" Nikos was playing along.

{he had better if he knows what's good for him}

"I'm sorry dear, things have been so hectic here with moving in, I thought I had told you yesterday." Nick was good; she had to give him credit.

"No one tells me anything. I listen at doors to know what's happening." Then she blushed when she realized what she had said aloud.

Sabina put out her hand, "Hi Cassie, we haven't met before. I'm..."

"You're Sabina...must be. You're the only one I haven't met who might be of interest to my brother. You **ARE** a looker." The she looked at her eyes, "You've got my eyes!" She was astounded.

Sabina chortled "Well, no, I've got my own eyes, but I must admit yours are just like mine! I'm older!"

Cassie was flustered and Iona took the opportunity to seal the deal. "We're going to go and visit one of Rodane's and Sabina's friends in a nursing home for rehab. We thought you might like to meet the angel that saved Rodane's life in Naples. Sorry it's so quick but we just got permission to visit this morning." She smiled sweetly at Cassie once more.

{didn't know I could lie so easily, must be getting slow}

Cassie looked around the room at each one, her, lips pursed. They could see her mind racing and surprised them when she broke into a smile and said, "Of course, let me get my things." She left to go to her room. Iona looked around the room first at Nick, then Sabina, both standing, eyes glazed from the rapid trip to amazement, looked out the door and down the hall,

"Wow! That was easier than I expected. I'll have to remember that little ploy for the future."

Nikos parked his car in the outer parking lot, and they walked a short way to the front doors of a quaint but large building, built with gabled roofs, mullioned windows and lovely, manicured gardens around the whole building. The entire place reminded Sabina of the Tivoli gardens that she so loved walking through. They signed in at the front desk in a small foyer with easy chairs around a huge stone fireplace and a winding stair going to the second floor. Under the stairs was a double door, opened and leading to a corridor that went the length of the building, with an elevator off to the side and everywhere, potted plants giving off a mild fragrance of baby roses.

The soft lights filled the hallways so there was no dark atmosphere, with bright, yellow walls looking like sunshine or new daffodils. They moved down the hall to room 304, saw it was open and heard laughter from within. Nick and Sabina looked at each other in surprise. When they reached the doorway, the first thing they saw was Eugenie, propped up in bed but with eyes closed and no reaction to the laughter around her, attached to a monitor and a glucose drip and pale as a wraith. It was a rather large room, about 10x15 with a beautiful Persian rug on the hardwood floor and at least five chairs of various designs and fabrics spread around the room. Two of them were occupied by...

"Phillip! How good to see you" Sabina went over and gave him a hug and kissed him on the cheek. He responded with a tighter hug which got an '*oof*' out of her and then Nikos strode across the room and shook hands with him "Phillip my boy, how good to see you." Nikos and Sabina looked at the other two people in the room and Nikos was amazed to see Caroline, Rodane's ex-wife.

He looked long and hard at Caroline. He didn't know her as well because he didn't see her often since she and Rodane had been divorced. She was not one to be sociable around his family. But…he sensed a sea change in her that he couldn't quite put his finger on in this short encounter. She was thin, almost rail-thin, and, aged beyond how he remembered her. She was noticeably quiet, lost apparently in her own thoughts. He knew the heartache she had gone through in the last two years with the murder of her boyfriend…Adam. He remembered now, the attempted kidnapping of Sophia and their surreptitious removal to France for a very different life. Wait! {*something about the attack on Eugenia and her coma)*

Yes! Now he saw the connection. They had been attacked together and the culprit never found. His mind was putting two and two together. He saw her staring at him, face confused and puzzled, probably at his attention to her.

He looked to Rodane's daughter, Sophia, in the room and…a dog; the funniest looking dog he had seen in many years. "And who's the fluffy, lanky mutt?" Sophia spoke to the dog who was sitting perfectly still but there were vibrations you could feel in the room even through the floor. It was the strangest feeling when Sophia spoke,

"Beaker, say hello to Uncle Nick and Oma. You know

Oma, Beaker, don't jump." He had been sitting perfectly still and when she told him not to jump, he twisted his head, his tail went wagging like a metronome and he made noises like a puppy, huffing to get to his mama. He got down on his belly, wiggled his way across the floor and went to the chair as Oma sat down. He rose on his hind paws, placed his front paws gently in her lap, lowered his head, and let out the biggest sigh you could imagine like he had finally found her. Nikos just stood there and stared at this fluffy, russet-brown, furry friend with a long snout. Love exuded out of him like a strong perfume or the strains of a beautiful piece of music.

Cassie was in love. Her eyes shone and her breath was one sigh after another." Where did you get this wonderful animal?" He looked at her, twisted his head back and forth making a noise like Scooby Doo as if it were a compliment but an unexpected one.

Sophia laughed, down deep in her belly, with a tinkling of bells, "He doesn't see himself as a dog but just one more family member." He lifted his head from Oma's lap, walked over to Cassie and put out his paw to shake. Cassie broke into peals of laughter. "He's precious!" Cassie took his paw, blurted out, 'I'm in love" and he shook his head *yes*. "What? Where did you get this dog? I want one!"

"Sorry" Sophia said, coming to Cassie and putting her hand out to shake. "He's one of a kind and not for sale. I'm..." Sabina moved farther into the room, "Sabina!" She totally forgot about Cassie and ran to Sabina and threw herself into her arms, "You've come!"

"Cassie laughed and said, "Well, it looks like I'm the third wheel here."

"Sorry" Sophia said, chagrined and blushing, "it's been

so long since I've seen her." Sophia took Sabina's hand and led her to the bedside where Eugenie, (now Genie to all) lay pale and still. She took Genie's flaccid hand and put it into Sabina's. "Let her know you're here. Talk to her." Sophia moved away.

This entire time, Phillip had been watching, scrutinizing all the people in the room and looking back and forth from each one to Genie, lying like Snow White in her golden bed. His forehead wrinkled. "Cassie, is it?"

She shook hands with him and jumped when she got a shock as he did. They stepped back at the same time and stunned, sniffed the faint odor in the air and looked at each other in wordless amazement. Caroline stared at them both and a look of surprise and more confusion spread across her face. She tilted her head to Nikos and raised her eyebrows. Just then Sabina said, "Phillip, she tightened her hand in mine!"

The room stilled immediately, as if time stood still and the air felt heavier but gentled, like a warm blanket spread over you while you slept when you felt cold. Beaker whined and Iona sat like a statue, afraid to move or breathe. Sabina turned her head and said, "Cassie, would you please come here?"

Cassie looked at her mother, hesitated and fear spread across her skin while shivers made her body shake. She moved to walk and could not take a step. It was as if she was underwater, and the buoyancy kept pushing her back. She was holding her breath without realizing it and beginning to be dizzy. She made one more attempt to walk to the bed and couldn't do it. She reached out her hand but there was nothing to hold onto.

Then Phillip was at her side, and he took her hand. Suddenly she was free and taking three steps to Genie's side. Sabina took her outstretched hand and placed Genie's hand in hers. Then Cassie took her other hand from Phillip and placed it over their two clasped ones. No one could move, not the humans in the room nor the unusual dog that seemed to know what was going on even though they were just witnesses of what was occurring. Beaker whined softly and pushed his head against Sophia. She wrapped her arm around him and stroked his fur, murmuring in his ear.

It was a very strange tableau that made it feel like there was moving electricity swarming through the air, touching every piece of furniture and every person in the room. It might have been minutes, seconds, but then Genie made a noise, a sob, and tears drifted down both sides of her face. She remained still and silent. Cassie swooned and Philip caught her before she hit the floor. She recovered instantly while Sabina's shoulders slumped. She shook all over for a few seconds. He led Cassie from the bedside to a chair and she sat, slumped over and crying softly.

They all took a few minutes to calm down and get their racing hearts slowing down, trying to make sense of what had just occurred. Sophia said something that no one in the room remembered until much later. She looked long and hard at Beaker and said very softly, almost out of hearing "Good boy, Beaker, thank you" and he shook his head *yes* and smiled at her!

Chapter 8

The Little Engine that could

"We now have the technological capacity
to test gravitational theories in ways
we've never been able to before.
"Einstein's theory of gravity is
definitely in our crosshairs."
study co-author Jessica Lu, an astrophysicist
at the University of California, Berkeley 2016.

A knock on the door the next morning had Francis coming into the cabin. Rodane had just woken up and saw it was 5 o'clock…

{lord, even the birds haven't started the day yet}

When he looked out the door, there was a thin layer of snow on all the trees and the driveway covered, making everything look like a fairyland. It was a wet snow that stuck to the branches and made them reach to the ground and coated the porch railings where it could, with wonder for those who could still wonder at snowfall.

Bright red cardinals with their rust-colored mates were

in one tree blasting through the white with swift rustles of feathers and sharp whistles to alert all the others with the air floating into the cabin, crisp and cold.

"Want some coffee, Francis? Won't take a minute to make it."

"I brought **you** some" and handed him a large Styrofoam cup of very aromatic coffee that instantly had Rodane's nose bombarded, sniffing with his eyes closed in satisfaction. They moved to the sitting room and Rodane started a fire in the fireplace.

"Have you had breakfast?" I can whip up toast or cereal but that's about it. Are we in a hurry?"

Francis shook his head, "Not at all. Take your time. I understand Suri was here last night and let you in on our latest plans. Ready to go over your knowledge about black holes?"

"Sure, but..." he hesitated, trying to ask his question without seeming critical, "Is Leander always so quiet and introspective?"

He saw Francis' face take on a thoughtful look and just for a second, a curtain came down, "I'm sorry, I guess that's not in my purview or my business. Forget I asked. I'm just getting to know all of you."

"No, it's fine but can I ask you why you got that impression? Anything he said or did to make you wonder?"

"No, just that all of you that I've met so far have been so vocal and helpful imparting information and Leander seems ...so circumspect...and forgive the term that comes to mind, surreptitious."

"Well, Rodane, Leander is a high-powered attorney dealing with some heavy stuff in the courts and maybe he's just of the mind 'never ask a question you don't already know the answer to' kind of guy. Anything else?" Francis was relaxed and enjoying his tea and a glazed doughnut which Rodane had passed on.

"I don't think so and...well, no, one more question... how to phrase it..."

Francis chuckled, "When someone says that it makes me think they're afraid of being too critical or finding a way to be critical and nice at the same time. Out with it Rodane, I think you know me well enough by now that you can say anything, and I will take it seriously and with good nature."

"Ok...I get the feeling Leander doesn't think too much of me or...humans in general. Am I wrong? OR... am I missing something?"

Now it was Francis' turn to hesitate and think about his answer, "It's not that he doesn't care for you, but he deals with the worst of the worst; white collar crime and those who try and bend the wheels of justice to suit themselves, the businesses who thrive on greed and all those who are in it for their own power as well as all the crime and injustice he sees on a daily basis. It's made him somewhat jaded over the years about humans in general. He thinks some of us are not strict enough or stern enough in protecting our own people while still protecting man's interest as well. That's simply put but I think that's the gist of Leander's 'suspicions' where you are concerned. Does that help?"

"Yes, it helps a lot.' Thanks for the insight. I don't want to rush to judgement."

"Good man, keep an open mind. Now let's get down to business before you go to see your wife and daughter."

Rodane smiled, "My ex-wife and daughter and I really didn't have much time to bone up on anything last night."

"You have an eidetic memory if memory serves me, yes?"

Rodane laughed out loud, "Good one Francis. Raul is good with quips too. By the way, do you know when he'll be here again?"

Francis sat back in his chair, chin in hand and thought, "We really don't know what's happening in Spain that needed his instant attention. We're waiting to hear from him or Evangela as to what the problem is and how long to fix it. But I'm hoping it won't be long. They're both good problem solvers and better together."

"Now that, I've noticed. Great couple together."

"Well, with your eidetic memory, tell me what you already know about Einstein's theory of gravity."

"Gravity?" I thought we were talking about Black Holes."

"We are, but the first thing to know is Einstein had his model of gravity expounded on and explained to a tee until black holes became a known thing. Most accepted his explanation of gravity but not of black holes."

"Well, I do remember from my physics classes that these phenomena make known laws about gravity show that they fold in on themselves. Since no one has ever been in one that we know of, then Einstein's general theory of gravity and the theory of relativity break down and defy rational explanation. When his theory of gravity held all the way to the edge of a black hole. There was a cohesive joint effort to discover where Einstein's theory fell apart and a new theory was presented."

"We have the answer..." Francis looked hard at Rodane as he said this, "but it's not for sale and certainly man is not ready for it. We don't even have it down to an exact science, but we do know how it works and each trip here is a roll of the dice. Some have gone badly, you're a part of one of those trips and some have failed spectacularly and tragically."

"Think we'll be ready in the near future, like a hundred years?"

"Truthfully, no." He saw Rodane's look of disappointment "It was hard enough for us for over five hundred years to see our planet's space program always playing catch up and fail in the process, year after year, decade after decade."

"What changed it all?"

Rodane's cell phone buzzed. He excused himself and took it in the kitchen. Caroline was online and crying, attempting but failing to talk through her tears and sounding panicked.

"Caroline, take a breath hon, take two." Through his own fear, he remained calm because he was expecting anything at this point from anyone. "Take a minute so I can understand you." He heard her inhale and saw her let it out slowly, "That's it, one more deep breath."

She hesitated with her first words, "Eugenie is…" and his heart stuttered, he could feel it in his chest and his bile rose in his throat, "Genie? What's happened, just tell me Caro… tell me, please."

One of his most loved people who he only knew from the worst of his travels. For such a short time, she became one of his main concerns in leaving for Utah. He was scared to death now that he might be staying for a funeral.

{I didn't even get to visit her before I leave}

He found himself almost in tears as well as Caroline, "She's waking up Rodane, it's almost like a miracle, it **is** a miracle, I saw it happen!" Then she started to laugh through her remaining tears "She's not awake entirely but the doctors are saying it's only a matter of a day or two, maybe even hours." We were all there, it was ...amazing!"

"Who are 'we'?"

"I took Sophia because she begged me after all this time, and she wanted Beaker to go with us..."

"They let a dog in a room with a coma patient?" He was flabbergasted.

"Rodane, if they hadn't, I don't think she would be waking up."

"What are you saying?"

"Well...Phillip was already there. Your mom came in with Cassie and your Uncle Nick and..."

"All those people in one room with Genie still in a coma?"

"Yes Rodane..." He could hear her frustration because he kept interrupting her, "I'm sorry, go on."

She told him rapidly what had happened in the room and how Genie had responded when the nurse and doctor had rushed in expecting to see her in distress with quite the opposite unfolding. They tested responses and they were faint but there. Her eyelids were fluttering with tears leaking from her eyes which Beaker tried to lick from her face. The doctor sent them home but promised he would call at any hour if anything else happened. They left elated and hopeful for the first time in months. Sophia and she had both slept soundly that night.

When he had ended his call from Caroline with a promise to get there mid- morning, he walked into the sitting room; partly in a dazed condition trying to wrap his head around what Caroline had told him. He was relieved that Genie might live after all, and Francis was overjoyed at his good news. When Rodane was mostly calmed down, they decided to continue their conversation on the road immediately after breakfast, because mid-morning was now closer than ever. Caroline had asked if he could come earlier so they could visit Genie together in Rehab center and of course he agreed.

"Ok, my friend, where were we?" Francis settled back into the chair with his feet up in front of the fire and his wool socks hissing from drying out in the flame's welcoming heat. "What were we talking about?"

"We were discussing the five hundred years of your trial and error in handling Black Holes. I can't believe I'm talking seriously about this. What changed it all?"

"Well, first thing that was an eye opener to our space scientists was that Black holes move."

"What, they move?"

"They move, just as all space objects move."

"Well yes, I know space objects move as does the universe. It's constantly expanding and that requires movement through the universe as well as within the galaxy where they are located. But you're telling me Black Holes do the same thing?"

"Even scientists on Earth now recognize that. Not surprisingly, they are beginning to get a glimpse of what we found so long ago. What we discovered had our space program ballooning in one or two years to where we sent out the first stellar engines as soon as they were developed. Black Holes pass through interstellar matter and draw it all inward. It's called accretion. It can tear the star apart as it pulls inward on itself. Moving black holes emit x-rays..."

"Yep, gamma rays, anti-magnetism pulls that stall the growth of new stars and..."

"spit out matter," Francis continued, "like our starships that might be drawn into them, with more ships going out, and some returning. Yes, that's established. However, small, dense neutron stars can't trap light and conversely, they can't trap our ships. When Event Horizon is reached, time stands still, and the collapsing star becomes frozen in place and time. When the black hole and a star collide, it produces a new, bigger Black Hole. Two of our ships that got sucked into a Black Hole were luckily able to return to let us know how the trip went. It gave us information for our research and our own space travel in the future. One of very few successes at that time."

"When was that?"

"Oh, about seven hundred of earth years ago, more or less"

"I thought you told me you were using Black Holes five hundred years ago."

"Yes, we were. They were the successes we were building on. We had sent out hundreds of ships over the years that never returned. They didn't use Black Holes any more than you might today. No, the problem was not how Black Holes worked, but what kind of engine we could build that would withstand the pressure and the density imposed on matter pulled into the Black Hole. Then… how to extricate ourselves from it once we had reached our destination. How would we know when we had even reached the destination? No GPS at work. See our quandaries?"

Rodane breathed deeply once or twice and looked over at Francis and noted,

"Yet here you are, and here I am, talking about Science Fiction."

"Science Fiction can be science in the process of becoming reality. There is no timetable for that to happen or not happen."

"Tell me about the new engines you developed and the fuel you used to move them such huge distances and …"

"Hang on Rodane, all will be answered, either here or at Amiens but we'll do our best to answer all your questions before you or I die of old age." He laughed heartily and Rodane grimaced at him.

They set out for town for a committee meeting that meant he would not get time to see Sabina. Then on to Caroline's cabin about an hour away from there. They first had to scrape windshields and brush snow off all the windows. Neither one remarked on the car down the road left in a drift of white that most likely had been there all night. They left… it left.

Chapter 9

Tomorrow is Today

The labs found on the second underground level below the previous dungeons of the chateau were still works in progress. They were slowly beginning to resemble what they were familiar with before they had left *Asturia* for their flight here to Earth. It would be some time before they could count on performing tests and research to go beyond what was found on Earth now. They knew they had the knowledge to perform those same procedures as their home planet afforded them. Without the resources, especially the materials or the secrecy involved in finding people to research them, time was always the truth teller but not a kind master. Quimby packed a duffel bag with what he needed and started up the two flights of stairs to the one occupied cell of the dungeon.

The other three cells now consisted of three separate rooms with bathrooms, not luxurious but meeting all needed requirements. A sitting area and a nook with a double bed in it for sleeping took up the rest of the 15 x 20 sized space. The furniture was of the foam, summer porch kind with no screws or bolts holding it together but tongue- in- groove for the frames. One chair was welded together with no need for screws. There was a metal mirror plate above the sink, built into the walls so no one could use even a sharp tool to loosen it.

There was only one person in the room who was lounging on the bed, flipping cards and watching the door when he heard a noise in the hallway.

The door opened and Quimby walked in carrying a rather unwieldy duffel bag. He put it down on the bed and motioned for Duncan to open it. Duncan looked hard at him with squinted eyes, wondering what could possibly be in there for his benefit or maybe not. He untied the strings and reached gingerly inside.

As soon as his hand touched the object on top, he knew what it was. He tried very hard not to let his expression give him away. Quimby was no dope and he brought it to him like this for a reason. He wanted a reaction from Duncan. Damn if he didn't get one!

"I found this too, under your 'toaster oven' and handed Duncan the small remote that he had not had time to hide before the Coast Guard ship had invaded their space. Quimby took it to the table, looked at Duncan with a puzzled look on his face, "Strange, because there was no TV or musical piece of equipment that would have required a remote. Care to help me out here Duncan?"

Duncan lifted his hand and waved it toward the little 'oven' that was not an oven. "My little invention to see what was going on, that I was not privileged to know about." He used the remote to turn on the camera imbedded in the wall of the oven and the tray lifted and moved to the front of the glass and turned opaque. A hum started up, very low frequency that only those two could have heard it.

Quimby checked anyway. "Where's the tape for this or the thumb drive or...whatever?" He folded his arms and stood with chin in hand. Duncan went over to his sneakers, pressed on the inside and a flap opened in the heel. He extracted a very tiny, circular tab and handed it to Quimby.

"No wonder we missed that in your check in...your own design?"

"Yep, my design" Quimby couldn't help but be impressed.

Quimby sat down on the one chair in the room and Duncan sat up on the bed while his body said, 'on alert'. Quimby watched him for a second,

"Why so affable about this?"

"I aim to please and maybe get out of here soon." There was no humor in the remark.

"What is it?" Quimby waited for his answer. Duncan decided truth was the better part of valor. He filled him in on his need to know just what Gurlow was going down so far to recover or discover. He had to admit he was just curious as to what cost so much money and danger that the bully, Gurlow, would need to do this alone, "I didn't think he was a courageous person by any means. He was adamant he would be the only one to reach his goal, whatever that turned out to be."

"Ok, show me."

They sat while Duncan fitted the disc into a tiny slot where the temperature control was located. It took almost a half hour to watch Gurlow arrive at the edge of the rift he was following in his bathyscape.

'Man, look how smooth that baby is, diving faster than anything in the seas today and going down with no thought for the pressure." His voice was praise, stroking him, looking with an avid stare at the opaque screen, clear and concise as could be, like a 3-d movie.

Quimby sucked in his breath and leaned over until his face was almost touching the screen, "What was that? Roll that back."

"What was what? It was just..."

"Roll it back, now!"

"Ok, ok, just a second."

They both watched it again, more carefully this time, 'Can you slow it down?" Quimby was still sitting tense in his chair, staring at it.

"Is the Pope Catholic?" Duncan quipped. "Of course," and he did.

He used his remote and tapped it once. The lights mounted on the top came on and made it ten times brighter. He began to move the remote from one end down the side of the bathyscape as the camera showed murky water. Then a tiny ribbon of light began to emerge. They followed it from one end to the other. Suddenly a small porthole developed, like film being processed from a polaroid camera and they were looking at a huge, gray hulk of a ship on the bottom; the size of at least three aircraft carriers if it were on the surface

"Holy mother of God and all her handmaidens, bless their souls." Then Duncan was speechless while Quimby felt the sweat beneath his armpits and a buzzing in his ears.

'You ok dude? You look like you're about to faint." He rose from the bed, went to the sink and got a glass, filled it with cold water and brought it over to put into the shaking hands of one Quimby Papadakis. Duncan had never seen anything less than utter reserve from him in stressful situations.

Quimby cleared his throat a time or two. "Give me a minute…This is…"

"Yeah, it sure is."

{I'm a witness sweet Jesus almighty, I got me a spaceship here in front of me.}

"Duncan, under pain of instant death, you cannot say one word about this…ever, if you value what may be your final hours."

Duncan looked at him and saw he was perfectly serious. "Now…can you make a copy of this?"

"Yes, if I have access to a computer."

"You'll get it but under guard. This has earned you a walk out in the sunlight." Duncan felt himself feeling excited at that prospect.

Time to Wake Up

Phillip had stayed all night and kept watch with every noise or movement from the bed next to him. He thought long and hard of the best way would be to stir the pot and make something happen, anything. Each day in a coma left the person more debilitated and physically weaker. They were at risk of infection or system failure as well as the possibility of brain degeneration. *He had to…*and he drifted off in thought…then he sat up straight and looked over at Genie; still, hands at her side against the snow-white sheets of her bed.

{Maybe if I poked a little…or a lot…)

"Genie, time to greet the morning. I'm sorry there is no morning run for you now, but the therapist will be here soon for your morning exercises and..."

It's morning, I sense it. The room is colder than I remember it if I can remember anything. Well, Phillip is here. He's bothering me again. I can hear him droning on and feel his impatience with me. Why can't they all just leave me alone and let this end? I'm so sick and tired of fighting and feeling so lost and isolated. This is not life, this is torture. If it were them in this hell, they might feel differently in trying to coax me back to the living. There is no light, no warmth and no connection with anything. This is not living. This is a slow death, my worst nightmare, to be stuck here and never have even a touch I can remember. Never to watch a sunrise or sunset. What the hell is he babbling about now?

"...so, we all thought you might like the idea and work with us to make it happen. It would take some doing but I know you could do this. We have great hope it will work. Well, I won't lie to you, but we think..."

What is he talking about? What plan? She listened harder and more attentively, hearing scant phrases and words...deep... long trip...machines and tubes...

"... but nothing we can't work out. We've got the resources now to do it. There will be four of us and you but there's room... Agatha has high hopes it will work. What do you think?"

He looked over at her still, silent form and watched to see any sign that she was hearing him. When he said Agatha's name, her hand twitched on the side of her bed then... nothing.

What machines, what deep...tubes! NO! No, you can't! I won't let you. Phillip, Nooooo! Damn you, let me GO!

Her body spasmed and her head and neck went rigid as the machines began to beep rapidly. The nurse rushed in and headed for her bed.

"Wait, give her a minute. Please. She's fine; just letting out some anger." The nurse halted, "Please…just a moment?"

She looked at him as she would a crazed person. But she had her orders, "I'll give you ten seconds, no more."

The nurse stood stiff and stressed, ready to hit the code red button, her finger hovering just above the surface watching the blood pressure monitor on screen. Genie's hands were fisted so tightly, they had turned white to match the sheet. Her face had a grimace to it that surprised them both when she spat out one word, "*No!*" Her voice cracked even on that one word and sounded more like a grunt.

The look on Phillip's face was pure exaltation. "Genie"! He took her hand and bent close to her, "You **are** there, no matter how you try to fight it, you **can** hear and I bet if you opened your eyes, you could see. Open them Genie, I'm here."

"I need to call the doctor to…"

'Five more seconds, nurse, please, look for yourself, you can see she's relaxing, the rigidness is gone, and her pressure is going down. Five more…"

"I'm going out to the nurse's station. I'll be watching the monitor for no more than ten seconds, then I'm calling the doctor." She looked like she would like to throttle him. He returned to his seat and readied himself for a nap.

In another part of the rehabilitation center, Quimby was in a closed off section of the wards and therapy rooms, standing in the doorway of a single room with one patient, hooked up to various beeping machines and an IV drip. There was a feeding tube inserted in her stomach that could be seen snaking its way past her hospital gown . Her head was heavily bandaged from past surgery to relieve a brain bleed.

{jumping off a boat from a high distance will do that to you}

She was the size of a smaller child, with stick-thin legs slightly outlined through the cover sheet over her, face skeletal, white as the sheet. What little hair he could see under the bandages was grey.

{she'd hate not having her all-year tan and rinse}

Five more minutes, five more lousy minutes and she would have known she was being rescued. Would it have made any difference? He could not see his wife in there anymore, not the one he remembered. The Marian he knew was a distant thought and it came with shame; for cheating on her though she did it more times than he could count, for allowing their marital problems to affect the boys and their relationship with their mother. He was ashamed he gave her things to make her happy when he knew what she wanted was more time and more attention and that he refused her. He was ashamed he thought the worst of her when she went missing. He made little effort to find her.

From the looks of her, she was close to starvation and from the reports they had given him, she was determined to make it to the rail and jump. That meant she was determined to end her life. He felt you had to be at a very desperate point to attempt that.

{Christ, I hate Terrence Gurlow and he's dead and I wish I

could kill him over and over. It was too easy for him, too simple}

He watched her for another minute or so, then turned and headed for the doctor's office where he was to meet up with Agatha.

Dr. Ardsby sat in a dark brown, leather office chair and swiveled it from one side to the other in a rhythmic movement that bothered him for some reason.

{maybe I just want peace and stillness for a moment or two}

Agatha sat on a single chair covered in a cloth fabric that looked like it came from a Victorian townhouse with a floral pattern of flowers in bloom of various colors on both overstuffed arms. It looked too busy for his tastes.

{what's wrong with me today}

He shook himself inwardly and sat on the other leather chair across from the desk. Dr. Ardsby couldn't waste any time in chit chat and spoke with his pen in his mouth and his glasses perched on the tip of his nose. That annoyed him as well.

"I highly advise you to rethink your decision to take her home now. She's far from awake and we don't know how much damage she has sustained until we take her out of the induced coma. She's not ready for that… in my opinion" he added.

Agatha peered over her own glasses and tilted her head downward so he had to look into her eyes, "I've found in many instances of this type you really can't know when they are ready until you try. You said yourself, she's healed from the surgery, she has normal responses to her reflexes and there are no more underlying possibilities of stroke or heart issues that all the tests have ruled out."

"Well, if you're adamant" Agatha and Quimby both

nodded their heads… "I see no reason why we can't do it as early as this weekend with short staff. No one will be in this wing to witness your coming or her going." He had a look of frustration on his face but kept his remarks to himself.

Quimby stood up and Agatha followed, "I want to thank you for the excellent care you've given her. We have nothing to complain about, do we Agatha?" He looked over to her as she shook her head slightly, "We're hiring nurses round the clock. They are certified to handle all the equipment and change IV's and feeding tubes. Best of all, her boys will be able to see her regularly without it being a four hour drive each way. Your new wing will be given a substantial donation to help you along." Dr. Ardsby smiled broadly and turned back to his desk.

Leaving the office, Quimby was headed to his car for the ride back to his hotel, "Call me Agatha or pin me and let me know how she is and if there's any change. Are you taking her back to Amiens when they come to get Marian? Everything already set?"

"Not quite but we have to get hold of *Asternum II* and iron out some details. We're close and that makes me nervous. What if we…"

"Let's cross that bridge when we come to it, shall we?"

She laughed a little, "You mean when we make that dive."

Agatha went down the hall to Eugenie's room to speak to Phillip before she left to return to Amiens. She wasn't sure what she would find there.

Dr. Ardsby answered his phone with trepidation. He knew who was calling before he tapped the screen. "Where is she being taken?"

"I have no idea. Quimby is quite the secretive…" The voice interrupted, "No, you moron…the one in a coma!"

"They're both in a coma although Quimby's wife is in a…"

"Where is the one going that came to you months ago?"

"I was given no address or location, just told to have her ready by the week-end."

"You've been paid handsomely to get us information and you've just given me a load of bullshit! Get me something before they leave or…"

"I **can** tell you that Quimby's hiring private nurses. You might want to check out the companies that deal with coma patients" He was sweating profusely. Oh… it's at least four hours away but I don't know in which direction…"

"You seem to know shit! Look through her files and get me anything you think might help us or you can expect a significant decrease in your 'funds' **Click!**

Chapter 10

Cassie and Duncan Earn Points

The very loud argument had turned into a disagreement which had turned into a discussion of sorts, making its way with trembling, spindly legs to a compromise. "It was my dream, not yours, so don't try and tell me what it meant. I'm pretty sure after all these years and my track record, I can decode my dreams for themselves and be spot on."

They sat in Cassie's room and looked at her; Rodane with frustration and Sabina with curiosity, the kind that leads to your own conclusions which could be 'spot on' or terribly off base. Sabina had that gut feeling and Rodane was aching for a fight. She could see it in his expression and his posture.

"Look, I need to go back home, and you need to …do whatever you're doing. It's time I set this mother fucker straight and I can't do it from here. He's like a ghost, a miserable, cowardly ghost but still able to shift in and out and he needs to be stopped."

Rodane blurted it out like a knife stabbing at a mist "How do you even know it's a 'he'? What if it's some deranged, vindictive female for a slight from years ago you never even guessed you caused?"

Cassie smirked at him, "Rodane, are you serious, after all these years?" He started to answer, paused and looked crest-fallen, "Yeah, I know" and his face had taken on a flush as close to embarrassment as Sabina could ever remember.

"But think of Mom and how she needs…"

She interrupted with a stab of her own, "Don't use that guilt trip on me, I'm too used to dealing with it from her. I won't put up with it from you too." She took a deep breath, "Look, I know it seems crazy and impulsive, but Mom is doing better. The medicine and treatments Dr. Depenier has her on have made a significant difference for the better and this is the only shot I might have to do something for you to help in your little crusade."

Rodane was shocked, "Help us? What are you talking…" Sabina stepped in which she usually tried to avoid, "Let her talk Rodane, she's trying to explain."

{there's that gut feeling again}

Cassie went to the window where the curtains were gently fluttering with a soft breeze on a very warm day, "You are all a part of this…whatever you want to call it…spying, casing…reconnoitering…of my house and my life. He tried to burn my house down; he trapped my buddy and cooked him alive in a microwave!" She was breathing hard with tears flowing like a rivulet of grief held in for days! "He peed and defecated all over my house and used Flower's blood to write filth on my walls. If anyone needs to take care of this shitty scumbag, it's going to be me." She stood silent and limp, exhausted by the flood of anger and grief she had held in for so long.

Sabina went to her and held her while her shoulders

shook from pent up emotion; her mother, her buddy, her dreams, her knowledge she kept to herself in that deep, secret space of foreknowledge and premonitions. For now, this was necessary and the rest of what was coming could be shared well in advance of its onslaught. She **had** to get back, to keep the other things from being as deadly and destructive as they might be, without her actions now.

Rodane walked to her, turned her around and folded her into his arms and whispered in her ear, "You're not telling us everything, are you? Truth, Cassie."

"I'm telling you everything I remember from my dream and sharing the reason why I need to go. Please don't argue with me on this. It's hard enough leaving mom at this point."

She scrubbed at her wet, red eyes; left his arms to turn to the window, put her hands on the windowsill and stared out to the lush, green lawn in the front of the chateau and looked out, "It's going to get much harder in the weeks to come and…no, I didn't see it" looking at Rodane's facial expression, "but I can put two and two together and come up with four as well as any person who knows what has been happening during these past two years."

She then paced around the room and Sabina watched her with a half-smile on her face, seeing Rodane in her every move, "I wish…I'm sorry you didn't see fit to tell me when you were hurt in Naples and almost killed…" Sabina was taken aback, "Yes Sabina, I know all about that and the rest of the trip as well. I might have made a positive difference …" She looked behind her and smiled at Sabina "but then that would have changed events and you might not be with him now." Sabina smiled back at her, "or maybe…no, I've tried to change things before. It never works and usually, things get worse, so I won't try that again."

Rodane was resigned, "When will you leave?"

"Uncle Nick is taking me to the airport Wednesday morning. I'll see mom tonight and explain but I know she'll understand. I should be back here...no, I won't say that because I don't know. I'll keep in touch." she saw his face, "I promise!" He nodded his head reluctantly "Besides, you'll have your own troubles to take care of...oops!" Her hand flew to her mouth.

Both Sabina and Rodane, said at the same time, "What troubles? Did you see...?"

"Forget I said that. You'll be..."

"Cassie! How can we just forget what you said when we need to know anything to keep us safe, and mom, and all the others and **damn it**, we need to know....!" She paused in thought, looked at the door ajar, went over and closed it tightly and motioned for them to gather with her on the sofa and began to describe her dream, the parts she left out when arguing for her travel home. The vent above her bathroom was open and the door was open next to the sofa. The sounds of their conversation were clear except for murmurs and surprise at something she said.

I think I can, I think I can

Later that morning, Quimby and Emmanuel Duncan were strolling around the lawn that sloped down to the stream running past the chateau to the river about a mile away. Duncan was very glad to be out in the fresh air, even if it was for the purpose of being a stooge and a thief.

"So, you still have your contacts? They don't know anything about your latest invention?"

"I've told you they don't. You'll have to trust me if you want this to work Quimby. Otherwise, take me back inside, though it pains me to ask."

Quimby looked long and hard at him and seemed to come to a decision he was not about to share with the man who had built the very thing he was asking him to redesign. "Show me the renderings."

Duncan pulled out a sheaf of papers he had retrieved from the captain's watch before all hell broke loose. He had been in his cabin when he heard the shouting and the klaxon of the Coast Guard cutter coming in for attack. He had cowered in the dark, hoping anyone who boarded the ship would not check single cabins while rounding up all the men above. He heard them coming down the narrow walkway and decided giving up was better than being shot resisting arrest. The papers he had in his cabin were confiscated by a sailor and now here he was, holding them again, seeing the fruits of his labor; spoiled, rotten and decayed. He was confined to a cell in a dungeon in a foreign place he didn't even know where. Talk about a fantastical graphic novel!

Quimby pointed to a bench to one side where they sat, while Quimby looked at the drawings in front of him and took out his phone to punch in some numbers. When Duncan began to rise, Quimby reached out a hand and grabbed his arm with a grip that hurt even one who was in excellent shape. Duncan reseated himself grudgingly "I was only going to stroll to the edge of the stream."

"Don't make me regret giving you this time outside when

you should be confined to your quarters." They both heard steps on the path and looked up together to see Rodane coming toward them at a leisurely pace.

"Rodane…glad you're here. I was going to come see you next. This is…"

Rodane looked at Duncan askance and gave him a curious tilt of the head like a cat canvassing the joint and getting the lay of the land as cats do. "I know you; I saw your file the other afternoon. You're quite the…I'm not sure what term to use for you."

Duncan gave him a dirty look and scowled at Quimby, "Your comedic friend here either lacks manners or is trying to get a rise out of me. He's succeeding."

"Rodane had a vested interest in taking down your boss. He's eager to get some payback, even from those who worked for him."

"Well, I for one am not sorry he doesn't get his pound of flesh off me but happy to remind both of you that now I am a necessary part of your organization."

Quimby retorted, "Don't think for a damn second, we need you as much as you need us. You're never a part of our organization as you put it. We have scientists that could take over from where you left off and do a better job in less time."

"Ah, that's the rub, you don't have the time and I've got the fixes already in my head." He went silent, not wanting to stir up anything that could curtail his newfound freedom, even if only short lived.

Rodane looked at Quimby, pointed to the drawings and said, "They're the real thing. No alterations either."

"Thanks, Rodane. Good to know."

Duncan was surprised for once with no smart remark

to snap at them. 'What? What are you talking about?" He looked down at the blueprints, "Of course they're the real thing, what do you think..."

"We had to be sure before we used them in case you might make changes and perhaps try and scuttle our dive."

"Well, are you satisfied and how in the hell does he know if they're the real thing if he's never seen them before?" He stared from one to the other, searching each face for... "Holy Shit! You can read them for proof? How..." he broke into a sweat, "You're one of them, you're..." He stopped talking and wiped the sweat out of his eyes.

Doesn't' matter what he is or isn't. At least we can now get started on making a change to fix the *Stellae*. Let's go in."

"Wait a goddamned minute" he was practically livid with anger, "Where does that leave me?" I've kept my part of the bargain and I deserve..."

Quimby stood and got right up in his face, "It leaves you anywhere we want you to be and any way we see fit to leave you however and wherever we decide to send you." He practically spit in Duncan's face.

"My wife was held captive for months by that monster and you knew she was there. Don't shake your head no, you **KNEW**! You didn't lift a finger to save her or help her or contact anyone to let them know she was there or..." With each word following, he jabbed his finger into Duncan's chest harder and harder as Rodane stepped forward and laid his hand gently on Quimby's shoulder. He shrugged it off with a violent twitch of his arm. "**You... don't... even... deserve... to... live!** Don't you even dare tell me what you deserve or don't" and he stood up and walked away while Duncan breathed hard and bent over ready to vomit from the churning guts in his belly.

Quimby threw the next words behind him, like throwing stones, "Now get the hell up. We have some work to do. You will be watched every second. Every day we allow you to live or breathe or eat or even take a shit, will be with us watching you. When we're done, depending on our largeness of heart and any sympathy we can muster for anyone who worked for that monster, we'll decide what happens to you. Now **MOVE,** damn you!"

Duncan got up very quickly, all bravado gone and the realization of where he found himself, finally sinking in. The bright sunny day just got very cloudy in his eyes. He looked up at the chateau that he thought might be his final resting place.

Chapter 11

Power Corrupts-Usually

Cornelia and Cloe were waiting in the anteroom for President McAndrew. The appointment had been for 9 and it was almost 10 but they knew from experience that would never happen. He was enjoying his second term in office a little less than his first and that had been a doozie. He had a little less than three years left before he would have to find a different path for himself and his wife, Lori. For some reason, they had found themselves a part of what that decision might be. It certainly wasn't because of anything they did or said, or was it?

Both found themselves in a quandary of how much to tell him now that he was no longer in the dark as to their 'family' ties and Cloe's unique talents that were growing stronger every day. They were not single-handed in stopping the attacks on their country or others as well. It was almost certainly their handiwork that caught them in time to avoid the revelations of their origins, their aptitudes and their secrets to keep them safe. Their fear was of being exposed to the public. That would have created chaos throughout the entire globe.

"How much do we tell him?" Cloe was the first to air her thoughts.

"Well, how much does he really need to know and what would be giving away some of our secrets that no one has ever heard before?" Cornelia turned toward her and lowered her voice so Cloe had to bend nearer, "It would put him in a very precarious position Cloe, and not safe for him or his advisors if he had to tell them."

"But if this attempt by *Asternum II* is successful, won't we be required to let him know and then what about the survivors from *Mauritius*? What do we do with them and where do we put them and …" Cloe's voice was taking on an edge and it wouldn't do to cause unwanted attention, "*Shh*, we can work all that out when it's a go. Until then, it's just a maybe, and we must consider all these things with the committee. They're a little tied up right now" and she smiled a little.

Margo, his Chief of Staff, came out and motioned them into his office where the oval rug matched the room for size and the pattern stood out brilliantly of the eagle in the center, fronting a globe and the dark blues and golds that were his favorite colors. He was on the phone sitting on a comfortable sofa and waved for them to come in and sit on the opposite sofa across from him. He lowered the phone and said, "I'll be with you in a jiffy, ladies" smiled and went back to his call.

"It's been over a month now and you're telling me we still have no idea who else was involved? How can that be? Sure, I know they weren't the masterminds, so we need to get this right, damn it! I can't have homegrown terrorists trying to wipe out all we've built over the last 300 years. Or the goddamned entire globe for that matter!" He grimaced at whatever was said on the other end.

"Send me what you've got. I have some people..." he looked over at Cornelia and Cloe, winked and continued, "who have some very special skills and I think we need them now.... Yes, straight to me, bypassing anything and anyone, too important for any other eyes to see."

Margo came in and sat in the one straight chair in the room except for the desk chair. She came right to the point, "We've got a shitstorm on the way if we don't get a handle on this fucking group trying to take down our communications and god knows what all." The President looked surprised at her, "Margo, in all the years I've worked with you, I don't think I've heard you use that kind of language more than...well, maybe twice now."

She just made a face at him, "Strong feelings call for strong language and we couldn't be in a more tenuous position than we are now sir, sorry for the language."

"Please, don't apologize, you've heard a lot worse from me over the years."

"Yes sir"

He grinned, "You don't have to agree so fast Margo." She grinned back at him.

They talked for an hour concerning the ship based on *Triton* and the previous attacks on their internet and broadband attacks. Cornelia laid out the plans they had for Utah and President McAndrew pledged to reach out to the Governor of Utah personally with a plausible excuse for what they were about to attempt. They kept the most urgent information from him and watched what they revealed about the people involved for a future meeting if this entire plan went the way they were hoping. The less said the better, for now.

After they had left his office and Margo was walking them down the hall, she stopped at the elevator and said, "Lori wants to see you if you have a few moments." She looked…concerned.

"Does she know why we had a meeting with the president?"

"She's the one who asked him to contact you and arranged the time so no one else would know."

Cloe smirked, "Of course she did."

In the upper level of the White House where Lori met them, she had put out tarts and tea in the solarium and sat with them while they chatted about her boys and Cornelia's daughter, Hallie, and Cloe's parents, Isabel and Nikos Kostas. When the conversation reached a lull, Lori dived in,

"My dreams are becoming the bane of my existence, so I thought I needed to share them with you in case anything occurs, so it doesn't hit you out of the blue." She sat back and sighed into her mug of now lukewarm tea.

"I'm so sorry you're going through this with us. It's not fair, you're in no way involved." Cornelia reached out her hand and grasped Lori's for a squeeze.

"I beg to differ. When I signed up for President McAndrew, I got the title First Lady for a reason. He needed someone on his side that was totally invested in him and what his tenure would produce. I took that on willingly Cloe…" when she saw her face, "not just because I took an oath for the country but because I took marriage vows and I stuck with them no matter what and there have been some pretty, hair-raising 'no matter whats" She exhaled.

Cloe looked shamed, "I wasn't trying to belittle your efforts or…"

"I know that dear and I wasn't directing that at you two. All those who somehow see our roles here as divided; he in his place and me in mine, don't realize or don't care to, there is no 'place' except at each other's side when things get tough and when things are praiseworthy. Let me tell you about my latest dreams and we can discuss what to do about them."

The afternoon wore on into midday and Margo called Lori's cell and told her President McAndrew could see her now.

"Well, you've been great listeners and I think I know how to present this to Sheamus without him having a stroke or going ballistic, either of which is still an option, knowing him. Thank you both for being here when I need you."

"Always" said Cornelia and Cloe hugged her saying "You call us when you need us, no matter what time of day or night, you hear?"

Cornelia added, "When you tell him about the man on the *Asternum II*, be sure to let him know we're really not sure of his intentions but we needed to take precautions…just in case…one of those 'no matter the whats' we discussed." They went down on the elevator together and the President's wife went toward her office. They went out into the sunshine and fresh air. How lucky were they?

'How do you think he'll take it?" Cloe wondered.

"If I were him and I knew what was about to happen and no one else did, well… maybe a trusted few, how do you think you might react if you had all the control and power he has?"

Cloe thought for a minute while they reached the parking

garage for her car,

"If I were a praying person, I'd be on my knees. If not, I'd be heading for the toilet to vomit or lose my bowels or a combination of both."

Cornelia chuckled with a snort at the end, "No, seriously, with what we know of Sheamus McAndrew, what do you think he'll do?"

"Sheamus McAndrew is the most honest and brightest person I have ever had the privilege of knowing or working for. Being a president of a pack of wolves at the best of times and a pack of cannibal werewolves at the worst, who attack each other, he's also the worst enemy you could have when you threaten his family, his country or his friends. I think if all goes as planned and we get out of this with few scratches or bites, we've hit the jackpot and can call ourselves the luckiest 'family' on earth, literally." They drove off down Pennsylvania Avenue toward home. "Well," said Cloe, "I wholeheartedly agree."

Chapter 12

Pack your bags, We're Moving

Commander Haller, Captain Devon Socrat and Piri Cassel were in the small communications room behind the Botanical Gardens, away from all other prying eyes and ears. It was the safest and most secure room on the ship and available only to those of rank or in the company of Haller. No one was at ease and tempers were on edge but not yet out of control.

"Captain Socrat, please explain to Mr. Cassel why we cannot take the route he has advised us to travel since apparently I cannot make him understand with my limited abilities.' He stood ramrod straight and his cheeks were flushed in anger and impatience.

"Sir" Cassel squared his shoulders but was not cowed in the least.

"Commander, I did not infer, nor do I think you have… limited abilities. I was merely pointing out that with my abilities, there is little chance of a negative outcome and more possibilities of getting through this trip faster if you align yourself with my proposed routes. Isn't that why you requested my presence on this journey in the first place?" He folded his arms and waited for a response.

Socrat responded instead of Haller, "We know from all our experience with Black Holes as travel conduits, that we can detect their effect on other matter nearby. Is that not true Mr. Cassel?"

"Yes, of course it's true" he was irritated at being treated like a common being with lesser brains, "What's your point?"

"Well, if we passed through a cloud of interstellar matter, for example, any Black Hole we encountered would draw us in as it would any other matter in its path in a process known as accretion. Is that also not true?"

"Get to the point and don't treat me as if I am a dullard." His anger was increasing as was his voice.

Haller stepped closer, "A similar process can occur if a normal star passes close to a Black Hole or, for instance, ***us***, as a rather large mass of moving material through its space. In this case, the Black Hole can tear the star apart, or in this case, ***us***, as it pulls it toward itself. As the attracted matter accelerates and heats up, it emits x-rays that radiate into space. It can be seen by any satellites that are roving in space and any telescopes trained on this area from a vast distance, ***like Earth***." He looked to see if Cassel was following and saw that he was.

"Also, and more to the point, recent discoveries by our own scientists have offered some tantalizing evidence that Black Holes have a dramatic influence on the neighborhoods around them - emitting powerful gamma ray bursts, devouring nearby stars, in our case, ***our ship***. Do you want to take that chance with all our passengers?"

Cassel opened his mouth to respond, hesitated, looked

squarely at Commander Haller and spoke, "If I can show you that it is almost impossible for that to happen, would you consider it?"

Captain Socrat blinked, and his eyes widened as Commander Haller stood there and seemed to be considering it.

{what bullshit is this, how can he even consider…}

"Mr. Cassel. How many souls are we considering here?" Devon Socrat couldn't believe he was even thinking about this impossible scheme.

Cassel stood in thought for a few seconds, "About 530 or so?"

Haller said, "548 plus two on the way. That makes 550 lives you are playing with to get what you want. What is that Mr. Cassel? What do you want that you would imperil 550 souls about to go on a very perilous journey, instead of using the best coordinates we have at our disposal? What's worth 550 souls to you?"

Cassel realized he was being chastised and he never took accusations well.

"I merely asked if…"

Haller was done with patience. Socrat could see it in his face, even if Cassel was oblivious to it, "What you were doing was asking me to ignore all regulations, all proven travel routes, the lives of 550 beings as well as endanger the very mission we are preparing to take for millions on Earth because of your faith in your 'ability'. I'll ask again, what for? Are you so pompous and sure of yourself that lives mean nothing to you so long as your unproven theories make you look good and bolster your ego?"

There's no need to be insulting Commander…"

"Now there's the first thing you've said that makes sense... Commander. Yes, I am that Mr. Cassel."

Socrat interrupted, "Sir, I think you..."

"Captain Socrat, this in no way lessens your position in this..."

"Sir, I think you should..."

"Honestly, can you not just back me up where I..."

"Sir, look!" The last was said in frustration, "Look at the screen!"

"Both men playing schoolyard opponents heard the insistence in his voice and turned at the same time to view the screen.

Below the dark, almost opaque waters of an ocean on Earth where the *Mauritius* lay in a deep trench, there were dozens of sea creatures gathering outside the one porthole. They could just about make them out from the foggy light that managed to penetrate the depths. Then they all realized that many of the creatures swimming in various patterns through the water were giving off their own light, some from the tops of their heads; some from within their bodies and some from tentacles and antennae that floated back and forth in a kind of rhythm. Suddenly, light sprang from within the vessel, bright and in motion like a strobe light. A figure appeared at the porthole and began signaling with his fingers in code as if he knew he was being seen, repeating the same thing over and over.

"Socrat, what is he saying? Quick man, he may leave at any second!"

Devon Socrat watched as close to the screen as he could get without his mouth on it and said out loud, "*Seven... alive...one... dead...low... supplies... air... is... bad...engine*

...failing...come...soon. That's all sir, the rest is repetition."

The Commander was all business. The rest of what they had been discussing was out the window for now. "Contact both Agatha and Francis immediately. Send them the message and ask for a consult, ASAP."

"Aye sir, right away!"

"Mr. Cassel, we'll continue this discussion soon and we can sort this all out without being disagreeable about it. I apologize for losing my temper, very unprofessional of me."

"I look forward to finalizing our plans for your mission." Cassel almost spit it out.

{I'll be damned if I apologize for being right}

He knew Haller wasn't being sincere and Haller was perfectly aware he knew it is as well. The ability to read someone's thoughts even on a level one, though shrouded and muddled on purpose, came in very handy at times like this. He realized he had already lost this one battle, but he would win in the end.

{pompous my ass, ego shit! you haven't heard the last from me}

Commander Haller had a few of his own secrets that would best be hidden for some time yet. He watched Cassel's back as he left and felt the heat of his anger; shook his head and returned to watching the now dark screen.

Timetables Are Meant to Be Kept

Agatha got on the com system installed throughout the entire chateau and called for an emergency meeting immediately. Francis went to check the grounds on the CCTV and see if anyone was out on the grounds to alert them. When everyone had assembled and they had shared the message sent by the *Asternum II*, they were struck silent until Suri stood up,

"Is there any possible way we can rescue them now? Do we have to wait for…"? Agatha held up her hand and cut her off. "I've already contacted Quimby and Rodane and they will be here in two hours' time. The trains are late…as usual

at this time of the day. Any other questions?" She looked directly at Suri.

Suri grimaced as she *harrumphed* from her seat but asked "Are they sure he said seven?"

"Quite sure; seven alive, one dead. Very encouraging after all this time, wouldn't you say?" The murmurs in the room were clear and the faces were finally smiling. She needed to keep that going "The most important thing, the engine is apparently still somewhat viable. They have a lot of time left even if the air is bad but at least it can be flushed." The murmuring got more pronounced, and she sensed hostility from… someone.

"I know this has put a strain on our resources and our people, but it comes at a good time. We have the bathysphere up and running and the architect is working on alterations that will enable us to …" She looked around the room, taking in all who were there, "use it in the near future for some exploration and possibly we will be ready in a month's time or at least we're hopeful."

"Will the scrubbers hold out that long?" Leander sat back with folded arms and looked directly at Francis.

"They've held for almost one hundred and fifty years. I think another month won't be too much to ask."

Acacia talked over all the mutters and whispered conversations, "Do we have our plans in place for where to take them and what to do about them?"

"Good question Acacia, we need to meet with you and see who's in the safe houses now, both here and around the globe…who is scheduled to use hotels and rental cabins so we can work on immediate housing and future homes to repatriate them when they are ready. Can you meet with me after this?"

Acacia nodded, the committee broke up and everyone went about their previous tasks. There were so many files to go through since their last attack and some of their members had been sent out from all over the globe to track down a list of people identified by all the various ancestral sites that identified ancestry and geographical locations. Others were tabulating finances, resources and organizations that supplied them with the funds they needed to stay afloat (no chance of becoming poor any time soon) and pay those who worked for them.

One group was perusing files to find connections to the communications debacle that the last attack had inflicted on them. They had managed to identify those already found or at least the main culprits. Another group was examining archeological finds from the last 50 years to continue planning their next move to find any evidence of other, unknown 'family' inhabitants, plus do their R&R's if necessary to keep them safe from prying and expert eyes. The last group was still researching the latest viral and bacterial disease rates and numbers of fatalities and those now immunocompromised.

That group was unable to do their jobs so long as Quimby and Rodane were still out. They were the contacts for pharmacies and research labs all over the world. When they got back, no telling what they would want to do about the new developments.

Chapter 13

A Greek Island Getaway

It wasn't the best flight she could get for time allowed, but it was the best one for being circumspect and able to keep anyone from following her or knowing where she was heading. It was a clandestine meeting, after all. She needed to at least cover her tracks, even if she couldn't hide the fact that she was traveling. Her little ruse would work if Agatha and Suri did their jobs and Nikos could uncover and identify anyone who showed interest online.

Aldora had spent hours the night before examining all the flights out to the different islands of Greece and attempting to figure out which one she should pick for where she might find her. The message by itself was cryptic and she had to be the smart one to decode it.

{just like her to demand anything with no hint as to where or how to get there.}

She poured over all the information she could find until her eyes were closing against her will and her fingers were slipping to the desk, while trying to copy notes; the pen dropping with a small *clink*, rousing her from her drowsiness.

She narrowed down the eight islands surrounding Greece with the islands most populated. She dismissed four of them because they didn't offer enough anonymity once she landed. Her fifth one researched, Koufinisia, offered more space and a smaller population of tourists but was taking her down the entire coast of Greece to get to her destination. She doubted even Melodia would make it that hard to figure out.

The final three offered remote access (could only be reached by water taxi), fewer tourists and all three offered quiet, as well as privacy. A few real roads and two of them had rugged trails to the mountains; not for the faint-hearted. She eliminated Meganissi, the last one on her list because it was a deserted landscape which would allow for easy spotting for curious eyes or those searching for someone specific. It would be at the bottom of her list if the other two were failures.

She was left with Koufinisia and Alonissos, each one fitting the parameters of what and who she was looking for; seclusion, tavernas for food, few people that weren't natives, peace and quiet. The best reason for Alonissis was it fit her personality and her innermost qualities and likes; rife with wildlife, surrounding waters filled with dolphins, monk seals and various species of unusual birds.

Koufinisia came in second because it was a place that escaped the hustle and bustle of the touristy islands; it was off the mainstream routes, and it was a two-and-a-half-hour ferry ride to Thessalonika which she intended to visit while she was there...and it had Greek donuts!

"Addie, remember when we decided to come here and your μαμά (mama) wouldn't hear of it because of all the tourists and especially all those 'bad European boys?" Aldora had laughed

with her aunt, turning in circles and spreading her arms to all the streets and alleys they were walking through, "Well, Aunt Melodia, here we are but where are the boys?" She turned around in circles and laughed at the sun and the air and the wonder of being in such a large city with so much going on.

"I think for today, it's you and me, we can forget the boys. There's plenty of time for that" seeing Aldora's expression and rifling her dark brown curls, "and we have to catch the ferry in a half hour if we don't want to go home with our tails between our legs."

"Nothing else Melodia? Must we go home from Thessalonika with our tails between our legs and nothing more?" Her smile was mischievous to say the least.

Melodia hugged her close and whispered, "You naughty little girl. We are tucking this away with all the other memories we share with no one until we meet again, no one."

'I still don't understand why you must go and not tell us when you are coming back or where you are going."

"I can't little Addie and I wish I could but someday, you will understand and forgive me for leaving you in the lurch for the summer."

" Will you bring me something home from your travel, please?" her eyes begging.

Melodia tugged on her curls and kissed the top of her head, "I promise I will bring you some delightful gift that you can keep for your whole life and remember me..."

She shook herself from her daydreaming at that point and realized her eyes were wet from tears and remembering. They had reached the ferry that day just in the nick of time. She now pulled on the chain of the cameo necklace she wore everywhere and got back to work planning her journey; Soleux to Munich by air. Stay the night in a safe house; ride by taxi to a different airport and travel Munich to Thessalonica on a Condor flight arranged by Quimby for a four hour and twenty-minute flight. She was going to visit the museum there on the way back, but this was one direct way, no stops except transportation transfers. Finally, she'd sit on a ferry for a little over two hours the next day to Alonissis. Maybe she'd get lucky the first time. If not, on to Koufinisia. She was totally done and eager to get a few hours of sleep. Her neck hurt from the beginnings of a headache.

Aldora took the first flight out of Soleux airport to Munich and the flight was uneventful. When they landed at the airport, she took an Uber to the train station and zipped into the one tunnel open for bathrooms and hid in a stall until the train left and the next one was heard coming on the track. Then a different person left wearing a different hairdo, swept up into a Parisian beret, different jacket and sunglasses, searched the small crowd and then went back up the stairs and hailed a taxi from the five or six waiting. She ignored the first one pulling up and got a dirty look from the driver for picking the third one in line.

She left the driver a normal tip and assured him she would be fine; that she knew where she was going. Looking around the part of town reserved for shops, all closed, run-down houses and some local groups hanging out on street corners smoking and laughing, she smiled and told him in German she was very used to this part of town. He looked leery but tipped his hat and told her to have a nice day. She walked away from the corner, went down the block and slipped into an ally and then through the open door on her right, left ajar with a picture in the back window of a For Rent sign. She locked it behind her and went up a flight of stairs to the first stop she would be making to sleep, shower and change clothes the next day. As soon as she got into bed, she was asleep and dreaming of boys on the streets of Thessalonika so long ago.

She arrived in Thessalonika on time, even a few minutes early the next morning. She looked around the airport, trying not to be obvious or attract attention and walked toward the Ferry docks a few blocks away, then stopped in her tracks. She felt the eyes on her neck and the hair on her arms stood up and made her body shiver slightly. She turned immediately to the shop on her right and looked in the window at whatever was there. She used the glass to peer out to those behind her and didn't see anyone paying any undue attention to her.

{but if they are, I can't continue with my planned trip}

"Shit!" she said loudly as people passed her and a short, stout woman looked at her as she swerved and bumped into her. She clicked her tongue accompanied by a dirty look.

"Me synchoreíte – sta elliniká kai syngnómi!" (Excuse me, my apologies). The little old lady squared her shoulders and walked on.

She had to change her plans, quickly. She thought for a few seconds, turned off her phone, turned around and hailed a taxi going in the opposite direction, gave him instructions and told him to hurry. He dropped her off at the Archaeological Museum of Thessaloniki and she hurried in a side door, using her passkey that hadn't seen use for at least sixteen years.

{thank the gods it hasn't been changed}

The basement halls were cool and empty. She was sure if anyone was following her, they might have lost her on the way. Her stomach was still in knots and she needed a few minutes to collect herself.

The short, stout woman ducked into the nearest clothing store, grabbed something off the racks, went into a dressing room and pulled out her phone. She punched in a number with jabs, to take the place of that bitch who had given her the slip.

"She's gone. I lost her in the crowd."

"No, you didn't. We had both phones tracking and you were about 12 feet back of her; you moved on and..."

"She must have known I was following..."

"Please, don't be any more foolish than you are now."

Her hands were shaking, "She must have gone into a building or gotten in a car or taxi because she disappeared off my screen in the opposite direction."

"Don't lie! You'll only make it worse for yourself. Do you have any idea of the trouble I went through to get you that information?"

She gulped, wiped the sweat off her forehead, "What do you want me to do now?"

"Fuck off. You'll only screw it up again!" **Click**

The Archaeological Museum of Thessaloniki was huge. The rooms were large, dim-lit for preservation and heat control and quiet, with few patrons visiting. There were three central rooms that held exhibits from the archaeological excavations conducted in Thessaloniki and the broader area of Macedonia. Two new wings hosted two exhibitions: the Gold of Macedon, with artefacts from the cemeteries of eight different ages of history and The Thessaloniki area in Prehistory, with material from prehistoric settlements dating from the Neolithic to the Early and Late Bronze Age.

She looked around and wondered at the changes that she had missed over the years. In the run-up to the 2004 Athens Olympics, the museum was extensively renovated with its permanent exhibits reorganized. There was an expansive new lobby where a large showcase displayed some finds from the excavation of the Neolithic settlement at *Makrygialos* in Pieria, accompanied by information about the progress of the excavation. The PA system announced the showing of a new film on the hour. She had thirty-five minutes to check out what she knew was there.

{guess I wasn't meant to stop here on the way back}

She was a firm believer in the fates stepping in when something needed to be done to change direction and usually for good reason. She'd go with the flow and get a good look at something she had been promising herself to see for years.

Walking around the glass cases, she stopped short and sucked in her breath. There on the ledge, lay an etching of a large bronze key. It was mixed in among sculptures of all periods from *Macedonia* with exhibits from the excavations in the palace complex built by Galerius in the Thessaloniki city center. It was turned sideways, pointing at a scale model of an Ionic temple of the 6th century BC and a reconstruction of the façade of the Macedonian tomb in *Agia Paraskevi*. On the key, if you knew where to look, was an etched drawing of the gold pin she wore on her shirt.

She turned so quickly, she felt and heard her neck crack like a bullet careening out of a pistol. She looked around, walked slowly out the door and down the stairs to the side entrance with butterflies dancing in her stomach. She knew exactly where she was going and headed to the docks for the ferry even if she was not alone. It was daylight, so she'd have to take the chance. **Now** she knew she was expected.

Fond Memories

The ferry was on time. She watched it dock from her vantage point in an alcove of a small cafe that gave her a good view on all three sides. Waiting until she saw people begin to board, she got up quickly, threw more than enough on the table and walked right up to the steward and presented her ticket. Done! The ride was uneventful and boring, five and a half hours to get somewhere she could drive to in half the time the way she drove. This was more secure with no trail.

Sitting on the lower deck for easy debarking, she leaned against the cabin with her back to it. She watched each person through her darkened sunglasses as they came on, moved around the ferry, ordered drinks and relaxed, with some working on their computers and others reading papers or magazines. Inside were people eating their dinner or dozing from a long workday. She pulled out her itinerary and checked all the facts she had printed out for her final part of the journey. She used her phone to make encrypted calls to Agatha and Nikos. Both were happy to hear from her but dismayed by the knowledge that she had been followed, even if Aldora had managed to evade at least one possible spy out there.

"How sure are you that you've found her?" Nikos asked.

"Perhaps ninety-five percent but if not, I always have the other island to check out. But this feels good. It seems to be the better shot."

At the end of the journey, she was not the first one to debark but also not the last. She walked up the sloping dockside and turned left to the road that led up into the hills. The pain that she felt was not like a headache so much as a dull ache from too much sun and it caused her eyes to water. She turned around and headed to the right where the shops were lined up against the side of the hill.

She had not gone farther than three shops down when a figure in a light blue dress with sandals on her feet came out of the shop and walked behind her and said, "Follow the road to the first turn and take that to the end."

Startled, she managed not to turn around, followed instructions and found herself at a dead end in front of a masterpiece of stone, glass and weathered wood siding. It sat at the top of the rise and had a view of the entire town below, with all the docks laid out in rows. There were various glass hands jutting out as scattered transparent fins of the dolphins that swam in the harbor at various times during the day and often at night. From behind her, the loved voice she remembered so well spoke kindly,

"Addie, it seems you are still as naughty as ever but much cleverer with time. Let's go in to escape prying eyes if there are any."

The voice moved ahead of her as hands tapped in the code on the keypad. The door swung open to the cool air trapped inside, waiting for a chance to escape its cage.

Once inside, Melodia turned to Aldora and smiled fleetingly but with no hint of anger or annoyance, "I've been waiting four days. What took you so long?"

Aldora reached out to her, smiling sardonically and they hugged tightly for a few seconds. It was as if it was yesterday, but so long ago that Melodia's curls had gone from a deep russet-red to a soft brown with many strands of silver. There were no facial lines and she looked exactly the way Aldora remembered her at their last meeting.

"It's good to see you. I hope I'm not imposing but this is…"

"Yes, I know…important or you wouldn't be here."

"It's not just important for me but the entire 'family' and …some of those you love as well."

At that, Melodia tilted her head and mused for a pregnant pause. "If that's true, why didn't you reach out sooner?"

"I…we…the family wasn't sure you wanted to see any of us, and we didn't want…"

"To impose…yes, I know." Melodia motioned and led her to the back of the open, vaulted glass cage that reached at least 40 feet with a welded, railed, open deck on three levels with rooms across the entire length to the South. They passed a wall of artwork in very impressive frames and Aldora stopped short, "Mellie, is this …the original?" Her face was stunned, with open mouth.

"Gracious gods, I haven't heard that name in…ages" and she turned her head and smiled at her again. "Of course, it's original. Why would I hang copies of those beautiful works?" She continued back to the glass doors that spanned the whole width of the room and looked over a cliffside down to the rocks below. There were three levels outside with doors to openings on this side, with stone carved into stairs on each level and more spread across the bottom where the waves were washing in. About fifty feet out in the water, dolphins were swimming back and forth in front of the house, lazily making figure eights in the deep green-blue waters. They both stood watching.

Aldora took a deep breath for the first time that day, "You've chosen a life of peace and tranquility. I truly envy you."

Melodia stepped closer to her and took both her hands, "You too, could live here and it would be just as serene and peaceful for you. Isn't it about time, Addie? There's room for both of us, more than enough. I promise you would be as free as you chose and no pressure of any kind."

Aldora closed her eyes, dove into the past, breathed deeply once again and quickly relived the days they spent of her being 'little Addie' and Melodia being her beloved 'Aunt Mellie'. She removed her hands, turned to look out the glass wall and spoke from pain," You don't know how much I would like that…"

"Then it can be arranged and…"

" But that's not possible now. Maybe when…"

"…when the 'family' is safe once again?" Melodia's voice sounded defeated and sad, as she turned to her, "That will never happen, and you know it. An edge of anger had replaced the smile, "You could live to be a thousand, ten thousand and the 'family' will never be safe. **We'll** never be safe" the last words spit out like sharp knives. She turned again to the glass wall and she and Aldora stood there quietly, watching the waves and the dolphins. "Tell me what's happening and why it had to be me you sought for help." Her voice had a tone of regret and resignation.

"Mellie, there are three people whose lives will change drastically, not for good or ill necessarily, but change their lives and we aren't sure if it will harm us or hurt us more." She waited.

"Who?" Short and sweet, Mellie was nothing if not brief.

She would be just as forthright even if she was now quaking inside, "Nikos' daughter Cloe, Rodane Arcos and Cassie Arcos and I guess I could add a fourth to that equation, Iona Arcos."

From her peripheral view, she saw Mellie's shoulders slump and her left hand clenched into a fist, then opened as she flexed her fingers. Silence deepened as the afternoon did also.

"Let's prepare a meal as we did so often when you were younger, and we can talk over some good food and wine."

They did just that, avoiding anything serious, chatting about everyday things and reliving fond memories. They sat for an hour or more at rest, eating pasta and salad and drinking some excellent red wine. Melodia looked at Aldora and spoke with fearful determination, "Ok, let's face the elephant in the room and get it over with. Why now Addie, why you?"

Aldora took a big swallow of blood red courage, laid her plate aside and spoke hesitantly, "I'm all grown up now Mellie and I had the same instruction and education you did. I know I've been left out of some of the information I'm bringing to you, but I know enough to realize it's a deep wound and I absolutely hate being the one tasked with bringing the message to you. Forgive me?"

By now the night was closing in, and Melodia rose and went to the wall of glass to look out, a life lived with some events best forgotten, buried so deep they would never be unearthed …until now?

{what does she see now in her mind's eye}

"I've dreaded this part but almost certain it was coming."

Aldora was perplexed, "You anticipated this? We had no idea…"

"Oh, I'm pretty sure Agatha anticipated this as well as Nikos. They are both crafty devils, with too many secrets for my taste or my own good, and… Francis. But…I have my own secrets." She continued watching the dark night and searching for…

"We're starting an investigation into all the members we haven't notified yet and those not even identified but with tests in the workings to identify their lineage and originations. At this point there are hundreds, maybe more and some are most definitely 80-90% direct ancestry." Aldora showed her the graph on her phone.

"That's going to let the cat out of the bag, isn't it? Whose brilliant idea was that?"

"Rodane's". Melodia laughed with a shake of her head and snorted, "Of course it was!"

"To be honest, it was the best idea they've gotten in quite a while. They've been going on the assumption all those of the 'family' would try and get in touch with us and this allows us to get in touch with them before someone else with worse intentions attempts to do the same thing."

"What if they already have?"

Aldora looked skeptical, "How could they? They have no way of..."

"Yes, they do." Melodia walked the room back and forth; wringing her hands for the first time, showing anxiety or stress, "I've known one of them for years and he most definitely knew exactly what you were going to do, and he got there first. I didn't know until right before I escaped when I ransacked his files before I got out of there." She slumped onto the floor.

Melodia folded her arms around herself as if in pain and bent over slightly. Aldora stared out in thought at the black darkness, crawling all over the glass and attempting to enter their hidden sanctuary. Her brow was furrowed in thought and then a stunned look grabbed at her face and roiled her stomach at the same time as she heard a low moaning from Melodia; an animal in pain, stifling its cries from predators with sharp hearing.

"Who...Gallo! You worked for Gallo! Oh, good Christ and the saints that died for us, how...when..." She was struck dumb at the thought.

Melodia came to the soft cushions on the floor; sat on one and took Aldora's hands in hers, "I didn't work for him. I...lived with him and...after I couldn't take any more, I ran away to some place where he couldn't find me." She wrapped her arms around herself once more and swayed back and forth with her head bowed and tears sliding down both cheeks without stop. "I moved around in panic for... years, to every spot I could think of...every person who would hide me; put up with my maniacal obsession and paranoia of being hunted, where he would not think to look, and it lasted for a time with me in hell. I had no choice."

"But...Gallo was...you were..." she stuttered to a stop, reaching out and then withdrawing her hand, shaking like a leaf dropping from a tree.

"He was my **BROTHER!** The last words screamed out in agony. She broke into violent sobs as Aldora rushed to her and folded her against her even as she struggled to be free. Melodia thought she would never stop crying, ever again. One secret out that was known not to be a secret after all. Aldora tried to stop the memories of her time with Gallo, but they pushed and shoved their way into her brain, eating at her soul as she too, sobbed of times past where a devil ruled her every thought and dream and nightmare. She also had much to sob out in the silence of this glass tomb where memories were dead things, resurrecting in front of them.

The night grew blacker still and the sharks patrolled the shoals looking for their dinner no matter what it was. A half-moon shone enough light to show the two behind the glass doors, huddled over, almost making one person; four arms intertwined, two bodies shaking and holding each other for comfort, to avoid screaming into the night.

Chapter 14

Home Where the Heart Is

Aldora's flight was landing in Greece while Cassie's flight home landed in Philadelphia early. Jacob was there waiting for her when she came through security. International flights were under much more scrutiny after all the attacks on global communications of every kind in the last six months, so the line was long and it took almost an hour to get through, packed in with dozens from other flights.

She felt awkward when he hugged her, so she angled away from him and moved directly to the baggage claim section. They hurried to get her luggage and get out of there before traffic became worse. Under most circumstances with Philly airport, workdays were the worst, with factories, businesses and the port letting out from the day shift.

They managed to avoid I95 taking side routes and made it home in good time when he pulled up in front of an unfamiliar house. She really hadn't been paying close attention.

"Jacob, where are we? What are you do…"

"Now Cassie, don't be mad but…"

Someone came out the front door and Cassie looked over at him and tightened her lips, tilted her head to him, "Your sister, seriously? You decided to stop at your sister's? What were you thinking? With **me** in the car?" She sat back, folded her arms and seethed.

"Cassie, hear me out, please?" He was pleading but also firm. "You are a target. You've been a target for a…long time. If you had been home that night…"

"But I wasn't. I…" He put his hand up and stopped her.

"IF you **had** been home that night, it would not have gone well. You wouldn't be sitting here with me now. No one was caught; no one was even seen or identified. You live out in nowhere…"

"Huh! Nowhere? Isn't that just a slight exaggeration Jacob?"

"Not much of one. Who would hear you if you screamed while an intruder might be breaking into your house? Or… attacking you? You won't even have a dog for cryin' out loud."

There was a knock on the closed window and they both looked up at once and both snapped out, "Just a minute!" She turned, went back to the porch, went in the door and slammed it.

"Well, now we've done it!" Jacob was flustered.

She turned toward him and the look on her face could have curled his hair, "We've done it? Really Jacob? **WE'VE** done it. Jacob I'll…"

He reached over, grabbed both her shoulders, yanked her head back with his right hand, grabbing her hair and kissed her soundly. She felt a hole open in the pit of her belly and reached all the way down to her very private parts as well. The heat built by the second and it was quite a few more before he let her go and looked at her, waiting for that slap he deserved. She was too stunned to react for a minute. Her cheeks felt on flame, her mouth was wet from the kiss and that excited all his impulses, private sections too, even more than those that first led him to act on those impulses.

He was still waiting for that slap. She grabbed his left arm, pulled him over and slapped her lips on his once again with even more feeling than the first time.

When they both finally broke at the same time, they were breathing like they had just run up the 'Rocky steps' back in Philly.

They looked into each other's eyes and broke into full on laughter until tears were rolling from their eyes as they both turned and looked through the windshield and out to the empty street.

Jacob ran his hands through his hair, rubbed his face and said softly, "You don't know how long I've been wanting to do that Cassie…and how hard it was to not do it for fear of driving you away."

"I'm not sure how to respond to that." More precious seconds went by.

"Maybe tell me you don't hate me for that or…you liked it too? I'll take either one and still be respectful of distance and our professional relationship." He sounded discouraged.

Cassie reached over and touched his face, "Jacob, you're a dear friend and I trust you with my life but…"

"Uh oh, here comes the *'but'*…"

Her voice softened and she looked square into his eyes, "I can't promise anything now, maybe not for a while but that doesn't mean I didn't enjoy that kiss or …" here she grinned at him, "want more…"

His face lit up like a Christmas candle in the window, outshining the dark all around it. He held his breath without realizing it while she sat back in her seat, sighing out loud.

"I'm in the middle of a mess…Jacob…breathe for Christ's sake… and I'm not involving you in it or…"

"Now hold on a minute, I am involved, have been since I first laid eyes on you and…"

"No" her voice was firm, "You have a job here, you have family and friends and I…no, don't try and interrupt me here, it needs to be said" as she plowed on despite his look of annoyance, "I have so many people looking out for me I'm suffocating from it all. That doesn't mean I don't need you. It means I may not be able to be here for a time and I won't be able to tell you when I might come back."

"What have you gotten yourself into Cassie? Why won't you tell me what it is so I can help you? **Who the hell is after you?** Why won't you let me help you?" He sighed deeply and his shoulders slumped as his head bowed and his voice choked off.

"Because…" she spoke almost in a whisper, "I care too much for you to get hurt and you will get hurt or worse if you're around me." She was crying softly with a look of abject sorrow on her face that cut him to the quick.

She reached over and took his hand, "How about this?" She rubbed the tears off her face "I'll definitely be here for the next couple of weeks; taking care of the house and managing to settle all my bills and buy what I need to set up housekeeping." She wiped her eyes as she saw him shake his head, "I'm not letting this house go or moving somewhere else. I'll put in a very expensive security system and maybe even get a dog…for rent."

"He laughed, broke the tension, "You can't rent a dog Cassie, and they're yours for life, like a kid."

"Well, I'll get a squawking parrot; set traps all around the house, inside as well…" She saw him shaking his head but smiling at her as he did, "but I'm not selling and I'm not running."

'You are the most stubborn, pig-headed, determined female I have ever met in my life and…"

"…you love that about me and wouldn't change a thing." and she giggled. "Let's continue this at another time. Tell me why we're here?"

"Miranda has graciously offered to let you stay here while your house is still under tarps. Besides that, you have no air or water yet. They're still running the ducts and wires for electricity to put 'your house' up to code without changing the structure since it's on the Historic Register. You owe me for that!"

"Why do I owe you for that? I left plenty of funds at the bank for…"

"For bypassing the board on a number of issues that allowed the inspector to do his own final inspection without their second guessing him for all your changes that 'might' have meant less changes and more money."

"Well, thank you for that but that doesn't answer…"

"You can't have occupancy without the electric and the air completed, and all the plumbing must pass inspection as well. All of it must be up to code before you get electric… Don't look at me like that, I don't make up the codes, they're statewide, some Federal."

"Miranda thinks I'm a…"

"Miranda's playing big sister who thinks her baby brother

is not to be trusted around a conniving, man- hunting…"

"What? For the love of Mike, I'm no more a …"

He looked sideways at her, took her hand again and grinned, "Mike, not me? Now that hurts."

"It's just a phrase…it doesn't mean…"

"Just kidding, I didn't think you would want to tarnish your sterling reputation by moving in with me so I thought Miranda would…"

"Well, you thought wrong. I think we can keep our hands off each other for a short time while I take care of all the details. If she can keep her mouth from wagging, no one even needs to know I've returned or when I leave again."

"What about buying furniture and household items? You'll have to shop. Even if you buy online, packages will have to be delivered here."

"Now you're just thinking like a cop!"

"Thanks for the compliment"

She stared him down "One night, just one night. If she tries to pick my brain or get me to bare my soul…I'll…"

"We're talking Miranda here, Cassie. You've got nothing to be worried about unless she wants you to watch reruns of Baywatch half the night and gush over Jamie for the rest of the night."

She lifted her head, "*Arrrgggggghhh*!"

He got her suitcase out of the car and they walked up to the porch. She opened the door, waiting for them with a smug smile on her face. The next morning Jacob arrived right on time and Cassie came out the door, ready to go. "Let's get out of here while the getting's good" and plopped into the car.

"Shouldn't I at least say hi to Mir…"

"Nope, all good! She's still asleep." He looked at his watch "We stayed up late last night and I guess she's not ready to get up yet."

"Huh! Miranda's not one to sleep in late. I bet she's got a list on her kitchen counter, and she usually gets going as soon as the light comes in her window to start checking things off one by one. She's nothing if not organized."

"Nope, no list, she just gave up and went to bed."

She saw his look, "No, I didn't drug her!" The look got intense, "Well...I might have suggested that she was tired and needed her sleep. She was perfectly fine with that. **What?**"

"Suggested...or done one of your 'little magic tricks of the mind?"

"Jacob, why would you even suggest such a thing?" A look meant to be coy looked entirely too mischievous in the extreme, "We're here" he said as they turned into the lane that led to her cottage.

Cassie's hands flew to her face and her eyes widened in shock, "St. Patrick on a stick and saints be praised!" She turned to Jacob; mouth hanging open and eyes leaking tears, she couldn't speak another word.

She opened the car door and stepped out like she was trying to avoid a pathway of eggs. She stood silent; hands folded against her mouth.

Jacob hurried around the hood and took her by the shoulders, "I can fix anything you don't like. We can take it down and start again or..."

"Shut up! Don't say another word." She stared at him for a few seconds and then she wrapped her arms around him and thoroughly kissed him for the third time with enough passion to have them both breathless when their lips finally broke apart.

She whispered in his ear, "I didn't know you had the gift of reading minds."

He was still recovering from their last lip lock, "What? Read… I can't read mi…" She kissed him again and this time he put a lot more of himself into that one. She broke off and stepped back, "Now don't be getting any other thoughts because there's a lot I want to see and I'm so excited I'm about to pee myself. The plumbing works, doesn't it?"

He looked sideways at her and smiled, "It surely does."

She shook her head, grinning, moved to the front porch and stood there looking at the fairy cottage she had always dreamed of creating even if she had to draw the blueprints for it herself. The slanted roof had a lovely little overhang that gave shade to the wrap-around porch on two sides and columns on both ends with hanging baskets of flowers: red and purple with white alyssum spilling over the edges. There were two more with filigree gingerbread on the corners that gave it a fairytale look and the front porch had a glider at one end and big, fluffy pillows spread across the large foam cushion for the seat. Next were two upholstered chairs and a small deck table between it and a hammock stretched from the column to a rafter on the front of the house. The cedar shingles were a pale blue with stark white trim and flower boxes under each one with Mexican roses blooming in multi-colors and vines trailing down the front. Even the tarps on the roof looked good.

They entered through a locked front door and Jacob handed the keys over to her. She checked the door, "It's a steel door."

Jacob grinned, "It's a composite and stronger than anyone

who wants to be hanging around trying to get in. The frame is re-enforced, and you'd break a leg trying to kick it in."

She looked at him and opened the door. The inside was quite a different sight than the outside with some walls already completed and others with wires hanging and ducts exposed. It was far different than what Jacob had described to her of the night it had been trashed and almost burned to the ground.

To the left through pocket doors was the front room, open all the way to the kitchen with a breakfast nook against the left side of the house. On the right, off the kitchen was a small guest room, which served more as a reading space for her and all her books with another door leading to the hallway and the new powder room.

The ceiling had been raised to at least 9 feet and gave it a look of a much wider, open interior but left the huge fireplace as it was in the back of the room against a solid brick wall. They added a wide, solid wood mantle the whole length of the brick surround. There were hooks for ladles and spoons and a pot hook that swiveled, attached to the sides with a cast iron pot hanging, waiting for vegetables and simmering meat to fill its empty belly. An island with bar stools sat in the middle as a separation. There was not one bit of evidence of blood splattered walls or charred fire from the attempted arson.

Boxes of all sizes were against the finished walls stacked at least halfway up and larger boxes waited patiently to be opened in the breakfast nook with a window seat looking out to a side garden. The kitchen was modern but gave the impression of being rustic with rafters on the tall ceiling and a chef's dream of a stove and refrigerator not yet hooked up.

The cabinets were rough-hewn with hand carved handles and the sink was a farmer's kitchen sink, deep enough to probably bathe that big dog she didn't have.

Pendant lights were above the island and holes were cut in the ceiling to implant pot lights for a bright interior with firewood stacked in the left corner in a wood box adjoined to the fireplace and a single French door leading to the back yard. A black fire screen closed off the interior where a grate sat quietly waiting for the cozy flame to hold off the cold when it arrived.

"Jacob, it's perfect, you've outdone yourself. Whoever helped you was..."

"You can thank Miranda for that. She's a shopper so it thrilled her to pick and choose...like Christmas for weeks."

"I've got a whole new perspective on Miranda."

"She picked my brain for hours...what color is her favorite...what kind of fabric was on the sofa in here before...does she collect anything... what style does she like for lamps... honestly, you'd think she thought we were an old married coup..." he stopped and blushed and stammered, "I just told her what I could remember and..."

"It's ok Jacob, you did good. Let's check out the rest."

They moved through the new powder room in the hallway, checked under the stairs to make sure the door closed easily, leaving it looking like a solid piece of wood. She *oohed* and *ahhed* over the new guest room and was totally taken with the higher ceilings and wider windows. They gave so much light to the rooms without erasing the charm and character. There was history locked in the very walls and nooks of a two- century old house. On the right side of the sitting area in the hall was a staircase leading up to the loft area that held her enclosed bedroom and a new larger bath, a smaller one bedroom with a bath, with half of the remaining space empty for storage shelves and a huge, walk-in closet.

"How did you get so much more space than what it was? The guest room is…wonderful. I have a reading nook!"

"They had to replace the center beam for structural soundness and that gave us the time to take down walls and move them in enough to make it four feet larger all the way down the length. You needed a new roof so that gave us more height. That makes a huge difference in the end. Take a little here, add a little there, and reconfigure the bathroom pieces…it turned out to be fun!"

"Minus the headaches of plumbing and electricity, right?"

'He grinned at her and said, "Want to see the back yard?"

They went out the back door to a patio that was open with a pergola at the end protecting outdoor furniture. She stopped and gawked before she exclaimed, "You made me a vegetable garden in raised beds!" and she skipped to them by the back fence.

"Stop!" She froze in place looking behind her to see what had caused him to yell so loudly." He moved quickly to her side, "Look at the back fence, carefully. What do you see?"

She looked around and didn't notice anything. She shook her head and he said, "Look toward the bottom."

Then she spied it, a thin green wire that blended with the grass, disappearing for the whole length of the fence. She looked over at him "You put in an electric fence?"

"We put in an underground one in case you get that dog you might rent" and he grinned. He took a small hand controller out of his pocket, "This is the controller for the fence. "You can dial it down for times when you are here working in the garden and just relaxing and dial it up for nighttime when you go to bed. Don't want Fido coming out at night to pee and electrocute himself."

"Fido huh? Who says it will be a boy?" She looked at him and it heated up his face and his innards,

She took him by the hand and said, "Let's see the rest of the house."

"There's only the upstairs and it's empty. No furniture coming for a couple of weeks. "She took his hand and smiled, "I want to check out all the plumbing" and he followed without really thinking; his brain had just shut down.

Chapter 15

Secrets, Sharp Knives That Cut

Two in the morning came and went and still the two women talked as if it was their last chance to ever do so. Two lives, shattered by the same evil person, were being discussed in the quiet of the night while wine was poured. Food was bypassed after a few minutes, both feeling nausea at this baring of ignominy, shame, embarrassment and guilt. Exchanging their tales would not take away the guilt for all the time they had debased themselves for the same man who was evil to the core.

Theras Gallo was as bad as, or worse than any predator in history that used charm, blackmail, self-loathing, fear, guilt, wealth or manipulation to get what he wanted. They saw that he used the same tactics on so many women they could remember from growing up; watching him use those tactics to get what he wanted no matter the lasting damage it caused. Finally, he was banished from their village and became what he had died being. They could find no solace in his dying but then they could find no sympathy for his death.

Aldora was the first to form a theory, "He was so greedy for acclaim and power that he was willing to endanger his own life thinking he always knew best. He believed he would never suffer what 'lesser' men suffered. He was a bastard from start to finish. I put up with that for years and it…nearly destroyed me." She gulped, drew more wine from her glass and leaned back against all the pillows they were propped against.

Melodia whispered, "Each time he came to my bed, I shuddered, and he thought it was desire for him or acceptance and even during sex… I will never call it lovemaking; he thought I wanted him and tried to please him and he always wanted more. I cried cups of tears after each encounter and…believe me they were many."

"How did it come to be that he…"

"Raped me?" Aldora nodded her head slowly and her cheeks were red with anger still, after all the tears spilled tonight.

"He was always fawning over me when he came to our dinners and parties and Mama thought he cared for me so much that she encouraged him to visit more often. I never felt that care and he made me feel…"

"Uncomfortable… itchy… squirmy inside when he laid his hands on your shoulders or on your bare back, caressing it?"

"Yes! He would stand at the pool in our back gardens and watch me swim.

When I would leave the pool, he was standing there with a towel, and he would wrap me in it with his arms around me and lean his lips to my neck and kiss the wet from my skin. I was wrapped so tight in the towel, I couldn't get away from his arms and if I did wiggle out of the towel, he would laugh and run his fingers down my arms and along my side. I felt…"

"Ashamed…guilty for nothing you could put your finger on?"

"I thought I was being difficult. Mama said so when I told her about it. She made me promise to be kind to him, the 'sweet little sister' who he loved so much.

I remember that like yesterday." Her hands were clenched in fists.

"One week Mama and Papa were away on a business trip. It was just me, Nikos and Theras alone in the house. Nikos had gone to play ball in the court at the end of the street and Theras had come up to my room where I was on the computer and he sat on the end of my bed, telling me stories of mama and papa when we were just babies and he made me laugh."

"He was a good storyteller and he made them so funny, you had to laugh."

"Well, I was laughing. He came around the bed and sat next to me and placed his hand on my thigh as I tried to wiggle away. He said, "I am showing you affection dear one. I mean nothing by it. All brothers and sisters should be able to show affection. It is human and kind, to be expected."

'He had a way of making you think it was something natural and accepted. We were too young to see we were being manipulated and our feelings didn't matter. He walked around my room and picked up my trinkets and asked me to tell him where they had come from. We had many conversations that week and I really did like when he was kind and generous with his gifts. He seemed to be what everyone said was the perfect son who cared for his parents and his family. So much so that they wished their sons could be as affectionate and kind."

Aldora sat quietly then, "You don't have to tell me the rest if you don't want to. I can see how painful it is to you to rehash this now after so long."

"Did he do the same to you when you were young? Did he ever…I think I would have tried to kill him if I thought…"

"No, he was gone by the time I was in my late teens and when he came home to visit, I would not go over there because…I felt the same as you, but I knew a little more about boys and sex by then. I…knew what I was feeling was right and I knew he was a very 'difficult man' where women were concerned. Everyone in the village whispered about him when he was around. You had gone by then."

Melodia got up and paced the floor, "The next time my parents were away, Nikos had gone to summer camp for a job and only came home on weekends. I was home alone, and Mama said if I needed anything to call on our neighbors. Theras came to my home that night and came straight to my room. He had been drinking, I could smell it on his breath and his clothes were stained with ouzo."

Aldora came to her side, and she realized tears were running down her cheeks and she was shaking, "Enough Mellie, you remember too well."

She continued talking as if she hadn't heard her, "We talked for a little and he asked me to try on my new swimsuit Mama had bought two days before. I told him he would see me wearing it to the pool. He begged me just to pull it out and show him what it looked like. With a lot of teasing, I finally went and took it from my drawer. It…" She looked ahead of her as if the memory rose in front of her like a screen, "even had the tags still on it.' It was blue and green like the sea. He ran it through his hands like he was caressing a woman's skin. I felt fear…I couldn't feel my own hands shaking as he took them and placed the suit in them and said, "Agapité mou (dear one) put it on for me. Show me how beautiful you look in it." Melodia was still crying but waving her hands around, "I was so young, I was so pleased he thought me beautiful and wanted to compliment me. I was a fool who took his words and was vain enough to believe him."

"Mellie, you can't blame yourself; He knew what he was doing, he had it baked into his brain that he ruled, that he was in charge. He could do what he wanted to anyone he saw, anyone he wanted. He was always like that. You couldn't be expected to know that as young as you were. Please, you must forgive yourself."

"He raped me that afternoon; pushed me down on the bed, whispered he would help me undress and then he … held me down and I lay there afterward, wondering what had just happened and why I felt so numb inside and mindless; I couldn't think, couldn't cry, just… nothing."

"I'm so sorry Mellie. It hurts now just as much, doesn't it?"

"He forced me every night that week and then showed up during the days when he knew Nikos was not there. He said we needed to make use of every room in the house to 'christen them' as he put it, with our 'love'. If I held back, he dragged me to another room. I threw up and he blamed it on lunch. I was terrified to scream or alert the neighbors. I lay like a stuffed doll and didn't even move while he was grunting and thrusting his disgusting self in me. What hurts the most was when I had the courage to tell Mama. She didn't believe me and when she faced him with it, he told her I was making up stories because I didn't want to admit that I had taken him to my bed while they were away. He said I made him promise not to tell them, because it would disappoint them so much and shame my father to have a slut in the family. Mama made me vow never to say anything to my father and from then on, I had no respect or care for her."

"He has done these things many times, to so many women." Aldora held her hands in hers, "I know because he boasted to me, he thought he was a kingmaker and a grand Casanova. I never let on how many settlements were made in secret for women from all walks of life that had similar experiences with him. So many were willingly bedded but then demeaned and degraded until they went after him. They never won."

"He left me alone after the meeting with my mother and I thought it was the end of it. But…"

"Once he has you in his sights and wants you, it's very difficult to find a way to get away from him."

"I found that out the hard way. He came to me when he saw me in a shop and told me he expected to see me whenever he sent for me or else, he would not only tell my father, but the town had a way of finding out whatever he wanted them to know. He had that much power over them. It was unbelievable. I became his 'call girl' in every sense of the word. It went on for years. What shames me is… over time I got to the point where I enjoyed some of his lovemaking and even found it satisfying. I knew nothing before. He taught me everything and rewarded me richly."

"That was his way. He trapped you and then made you think it was love. How did you manage to get out of it? It's terrifying how he can make you think he can hunt you down to the ends of the earth and I'm not sure he was kidding. Did anyone else know?"

"We went to Addy's wedding and Agatha was there and somehow, she knew. Theras stood close to me and whispered horrid things about Addy's new wife and other women he saw there; vile, ignorant, disgusting words. I had to move away before I was sick. Agatha took me outside when she saw me about to vomit."

"Did you tell her about him?"

"She told me. She laid it out like a story and told me of a man who was so evil that…and proceeded to describe him to a tee, even the tattoo on his shoulder."

"I remember you drawing away from me one summer and that was before you went away. I remember being very hurt that you would not want me to even visit you when I had summer break. Was that when…"

"I loved you so much and when I saw Theras eying you from the poolside and asking about whether you were dating yet, I knew…I had to protect you at all costs. I would take all the attention away from you… I kept him close by my side and my bed that entire summer."

Aldora got up and moved to her side and they clung to each other in the night and cried more bitter tears where the salt stung their eyes and they rocked back and forth in pain. That kind of pain cannot be cured by medicine or doctors but rather by an inner strength that is bitter in the making.

"I'm ashamed to say it went on for years when I had my own place. I think Nikos suspected something. He offered to have me come to the states and live with him and Isabel, but I refused from some dysfunctional, displaced feeling of protecting myself and you. In fact, I was protecting Theras as well, so crazy and so insanely destructive."

"What changed?"

"I found I was pregnant. I was stupid enough to tell Theras and he went berserk; I thought he was going to kill me. I finally reached Agatha in despair and told her of my predicament. She contacted me in the next week to tell me she had a plan. I went to Italy that month and she took me in, and I stayed with her through the whole pregnancy."

"Did Theras try to track you down?"

"Agatha told him where I was and told him she knew what he had done and if he tried to take me away or do anything to me, ever, she would make sure all his businesses knew exactly what he was and what he had done for all those years."

"Extortion…hmmm… I'm liking her more and more. No wonder Theras always kept his distance from her. What about the …baby?"

"She arranged for a very private clinic to deliver the baby and the adoptive parents were there to pick her up when she was born. I never even got to hold her once." Tears were again coursing down her face, dampening her robe.

"Did you ever try and find… your little girl?"

Melodia looked long and hard at Aldora; wanting to be sure she was being honest and there for the right reason.

"No, I didn't need to track her down. I knew where she was going and who would be raising her." Aldora was startled for the first time in the long night.

"You must have an idea of why you are here and why you

were sent and no other?" Melodia watched carefully for her reaction.

"I can't think...I just thought because I knew you so long...you're part of the 'family' Mellie, we were close.... what other reason could there be?"

"Agatha 'pinned' me a few weeks ago, and told me to leave a clue to my whereabouts, somewhere you might look; that you would be arriving, and I was to give you all the files I had from those years. She knew I kept journals and documents I could use in the future if I decided to go after him. Some I had even stolen from him when he took me out to lunch from his offices as a 'treat' for sex that previous night. He was in a business meeting, and I used a thumb drive to copy all his files before he returned. It was difficult to even swallow the food without retching."

Aldora was stunned into silence for a few seconds while her brain kicked in and then she sputtered, "I can't believe I didn't question that or realize ..."

"You're not the first one to be manipulated by Agatha and you won't be the last. Sometimes I think she and Theras were two of a kind, but Agatha has a conscience and Theras lacked that and a soul. She saved me that year and she kept me there until I had regained some balance because I almost went insane, I'm sure of it."

"How did she even know I would agree to do her bidding or try to find you?" Aldora's face slowly showed astonishment, "So...that's why she insisted it had to be me. She said I needed to help you face all your issues."

"and because it was Agatha." Silence filled the air, and it stirred the space around it with recriminations. Melodia peered at her beloved niece's face and thought it was time.

"Why did you go to work for Theras, Aldora? Aldora noted the loss of her nickname for her aunt, "You said you knew what he was even before you were grown." Aldora took a deep breath and let it out slowly.

"Agatha knew what he had done to you. She said she needed someone who knew him well to find out what he was up to. That we needed to protect the 'family' from anything Theras did to harm us. It seemed so right at the beginning, so when I started work there, she gave me instructions whenever I could get away to a meeting place, to pick up her messages."

"So, Agatha always knew what you had to do to avoid discovery? She convinced me to give up the baby for the sake of the 'family' and to avoid unnecessary legal challenges from Theras. I told you she was savvy and canny. I just didn't realize what depths she would sink to for the sake of 'family'. Melodia became quiet, gazing at nothing but remembered sacrifices and griefs she had carried for all these years.

"My baby was given to 'family' and I was never bitter about that. She promised she would keep me aware of how she was being raised and how she was growing or learning, and she did. Her parents have given her a life she never would have been able to have if I had kept her. She has been loved, well-educated, molded into a sweet, smart, caring girl. That couldn't have occurred under my circumstances. She has a wonderful life and has never known that monster that used his seed to create her. I'll never allow that to happen if I can help it at all. He's dead now but she won't hear about him from me, ever."

The light was beginning to peep around the edges of the glass wall and bring another beautiful day to fruition while two wounded, scarred women shared their lives and shared their misery, that had never been truly addressed or healed.

They went to bed to try and get some sleep to help them function during the day. Aldora woke to the smell of sausages sizzling and fresh biscuits baking in the oven. Then the aroma of coffee brewing had her smiling under the covers and pillows on the floor where they had spent the night. Melodia walked over to her and bent down to brush her hair out of her eyes,

"You look very comfortable there and I hate to disturb you but…do you want to take a shower?"

"Do I need a shower?"

"You most certainly do, and I will not ever lie to you about anything."

Melodia led her upstairs and showed her the room she would be staying in and the bathroom with all the supplies she might need in a reed basket on the marble countertops and fresh towels on the racks. She stood under the shower and cried as she remembered all they had talked about last night and the torture it must have caused Melodia to unload it all at once. She was pretty sure she had heard details Melodia had never allowed herself to reveal, ever before.

{revelations can help one heal; as well I know}

If she hadn't had Agatha and Suri to reveal the dark secrets that still ate at her heart and visited her nightmares, she would be in worse shape than her Mellie. How did she survive it all? Giving up her baby, being treated so ignominiously by Theras…used the way she was so callously…frightened for most of her young years, leaving all she knew and loved behind for so long just to escape his claws.

{the bastard, nothing was too good for him to destroy}

That took strength and she could do no less. It gave her searing anger and hate but it also gave her resolve and determination.

They ate a good breakfast and Melodia took her up to the second level and opened a door to the outside. It faced the leeward side of the house where there was a small cove that faced another hillside. There were three dolphins swimming and making all the little clicks and sharp whistles that was their language. When they saw Melodia on the landing, they dove and came up as one, inches away from her. She reached out and stroked one and they did it again and again until she had said good morning to all of them.

"This is our daily ritual and sometimes they will bring a friend. They are my friends, and we share all our secrets together."

Aldora looked over at her and realized she was being perfectly serious. She didn't say anything and Melodia laughed, a tinkling, bell-sound that made Aldora laugh as well, and the dolphins chittered and squealed. She studied them for a moment and then turned with astonishment in her eyes, "You really do talk to them, don't you?"

"I do and I am not crazy." She breathed deeply, "Addie, I have found my gift and it has graciously been passed down and helped me to heal over these many years. Sometimes, when I am sure there is no one around, I swim with them. My world is the sea and all the creatures in it. Maybe when you stay a while…I am sure you also have your own special abilities and Addie, you deserve whatever you have been blessed to receive. Guard it well. I have run away from them for so long. It's a wonder they were not snatched from my mind to admonish me for ignoring my 'family' when they surely needed me."

Inside, they sat at the glass windows and resumed their conversations as Aldora laid out what was needed to bring her here and invade her privacy. "We have spread out to search and find anyone who has been identified as direct descendants and the teams are tasked with informing them if they didn't know before or instruct them if they did. We need a directory, and we know you have the brains, the time and the space to maybe help us out there. No one needs to know because it can all be done from here or an office in any building that Quimby owns or anywhere you feel safe, your call."

"Sounds like you're building an army...with weapons?"

"Not the kind of weapons anyone not of the 'family' would dream of, not to kill or maim, just to keep our family safe. We have a goal to do the best for what we were sent here to do in the first place."

Melodia got up and paced slowly, hand covering her mouth in deep thought. Aldora kept silent and still.

{never disturb great thought at work}

'I'm certainly not the only one doing this, am I? There are others?"

"Of course, we will have at least one team on each continent, and other teams will be scouring the islands and we'll all be connected to any ancestry site that exists to get the information that will help us locate them."

"You could use native American tribes to test for ancestry when local vaccinations are given. That would also work for all jungle tribes not in touch with civilization...and those on islands who do not welcome tourists and..." She broke off when she saw Aldora grinning like a cat with a plate of rich cream. What?" What are you grinning at girl?"

"See, this is exactly why Agatha and Nikos thought you would be the perfect one to lead this mission. It's broad, it invites its own drawbacks that you can help solve. You'll do it?"

"I have lots of questions and a very healthy dose of fear plus some dark thoughts of working with Agatha and Nikos."

She came and sat down on the pillows again, "I know what you're going to say but the fear is not for me, it's the danger that some findings could possibly destroy some families with hidden secrets of their own, starting with Nikos."

"Like what? I don't understand."

"My baby…" she hesitated "my baby might not know she is adopted or even if she did, she would not know me as the mother or have my information. What if…"

When she couldn't go on, Aldora looked at her, remembered her words from last night. *'My baby was given to 'family' and I was never bitter about that.'*

"She might find out if you work with us. But what if she already knows?"

"I can assure you she does not"

"How can you be sure? Who did you …It's someone in our direct 'family' isn't it?"

"You were always too smart to allow a problem to go unsolved." Aldora's face finally gaped; she had figured it out. "Nikos Kostas, your other brother!"

"Yes, but…they don't know it was me who gave them Cloe… my...baby. It was all arranged by Agatha. I don't think she would expose me after all this time but…that's not all."

"There's more?" Aldora was trying so hard not to react.

Melodia let out a laugh that was nothing but strained, "There's always more with secrets, isn't there? Well, before that; this one is a doozy. Addison's wife couldn't get pregnant so he asked me after several years if I would donate an egg for her to use in vitro to try and have a baby. Instant success!" her tone was grim.

"So Rodane is not only my brother but my nephew as well, in a manner of speaking, but he's not the only one. I am generous with my gifts. A few years later, Addy wanted another child or Iona did, not sure who pushed for it so…"

"Cassie too?"

"Bingo! To be serious…I am fearful of them not knowing and finding out with the task we would be taking on. The information uncovered would be shared by the entire 'family'. That could cause untold damage to so many!"

"Does anyone else know? Does Agatha know about Rodane and Cassie?"

"I haven't a clue but… it looks like I will be going back with you to sort all this out." She stood straighter and sighed, "It's about time." She looked at Aldora, teasing her, "Let's go swimming!"

Chapter 16

Into the Wild Blue Yonder

Three men were sitting at a long metal table looking at them from over 2.696 billion miles from our moon. Commander Haller was pointing from the screen behind him but facing their direction, looking at his tablet.

"You can easily see the difference between that possibility from *Triton* and that of *Phobos.*" The screen put up the distance; 48.34 million miles. "Quite a difference you see, almost two thirds less risk and better odds of striking our target more accurately."

Three members were sitting in the committee room, paying close attention to what was in front of them. Nikos had stepped in for Francis while he was traveling with Rodane. President McAndrew had sent Vice President Harper, who had just been elected President from the previous election and had been flown to France by Quimby. He would be sworn into office in two months and Agatha was there as usual.

"Have you left yet?" Dwayne Harper, Vice President for now, was keeping his wits about him by doing some very deep breathing when he got the chance to remember to do it.

Commander Haller turned to the man on his right, "Mister Socrat, this is your department."

Socrat almost saluted and then turned to Harper, "Forgive me, I've forgotten your name... Mr. Vice President..."

"Harper will do nicely. Don't stand on ceremony. I'm just a fill in for the president and he couldn't be here due to..." he looked around the room and caught the nod of Agatha... "unforeseen circumstances. But I'm sure our notes will bring him up to speed, right Nikos?"

Nikos nodded and Socrat said, 'Not yet sir, but we are keeping to the timetable we sent you some time ago. Everyone is eager to get started."

Harper felt a little better knowing they still had some wiggle room before this scary scenario might play out or be a global disaster. Otherwise, he was in a half state of a mixture of surprise, stupefaction, fear and wonder, all rolled up in a ball that resided in his stomach, aching to get out. It wouldn't do for all his lunch to be spilled over the floor in their committee room. His next office would be a humdinger!

Harper was trained as an Aerospace Engineer and a Communication's Specialist among other skills before being a politician and was very eager to learn as much as he could by listening. It had been months since they (he) had learned about who was on *Triton*, why they were here in our galaxy and who 'they' were. His entire belief system was in turmoil as a result, but he was determined to muddle through it. Great changes might be in the making for the entire world. It wouldn't do for him to be a blithering idiot when it happened.

The third man on screen made a *harrumph* sound and peered at them with disdain, "My guess is you don't come close to understanding what we are about to do, or your question is rather…naive to say the least. We are about to put all the lives of our people…" Haller cut him off, "Mr. Cassel, I think it would be wise and save time if we stuck to the facts and let our personal concerns be left to us to deal with, don't you think so Mr. Socrat?" Devin Socrat peered around at Cassel…

{he's a cheeky fellow for not having a job}

…and responded, "Yes sir" to Haller.

Cassel seethed very openly, and with a sneer at Socrat. Harper sat and thought about what Cassel had said.

{it's as if the arrogant little twit read my mi….no not possible}

"We're almost at the point where we can begin fueling and loading all the supplies on board for the next four or five months. If nothing goes wrong…"

"*Humpf*" Cassel cleared his throat loudly and leaned back in his chair as arrogant as any moronic commanders Socrat had ever served under but never Haller. "Mr. Cassel, it does you no good to sit here with us, if all you have to offer are negative comments, snide remarks and lack of respect for those in front of us from Earth. I'm sure they do not need your sarcasm, your disrespect or your shameful behavior…" He turned to Haller, "Apologies Commander" to him.

"Neatly said, Cpt. Socrat, and timely as ever. Mr. Cassel, if this continues, I will ask you to leave the meeting and we will fill you in later…in your quarters…is that understood?"

Cassel was shocked at both men willing to berate him in public and shame him as well. Was he a child? He was about to get up and leave but…then he wouldn't know what had really been spoken here and what if…his job was in jeopardy as well as his reputation and his own plans?

{can't afford to be left out of these meetings and go in blind}

He cleared his throat, spit out an apology of some sort and sat back, quiet for a time. Socrat took a breath and continued, "The people are aware of our timetable and that gives them a little peace of mind. The children are being prepped in the methods and their symptoms if they need to let us know they are experiencing any negative effects…" Cassel grimaced and sat back, still sullen.

"Such as…" Harper blurted out without thinking. "Sorry, it's just that I understand what space travel here on Earth may cause but for children…it's daunting to think of little ones being put under…"

"It's quite different sir and I can explain it after we've concluded here if that might put your mind at ease? We have an excellent cryogenic engineer preparing them for soma stasis."

"Thank you, I'll hold you to that son." Harper had butterflies where there was lunch.

Cmdr. Haller knew what he had to let them know and what he had to keep close to the vest or jeopardize the entire space program, thousands of years at that. It was one thing to help the people they may be living among even sooner than thought. It was quite another to let them in on their own program or their plans if all went well here.

Nikos looked at Cassel and saw him wince and then rub his forehead as if he was getting a headache. He didn't care for the guy. He turned a wry face to Haller,

{pretty flimsy excuse to get out of a meeting}

"Commander, may we ask what engines you now use?

I'm almost certain in the time we have been here on Earth there have been major changes in our own science to make travel safer and healthier than it did on our journey. Is that not so?"

"Remember that we have been on *Triton* for some years so they're probably even further ahead at home than we are, but I can let you understand how we got here. It hasn't been easy Nikos, even more so than you might think."

"How does it work?" Harper was entranced at this conversation. Almost his entire life, he was thinking of finding a way to go farther, faster, be in space to explore, to learn, to...

"Well, the chemistry of your star, the Sun, is largely a result of a hydrogen proton-proton cycle. I'll let you do research for yourself since you can remember very easily what you learned at home before traveling in space. In stars larger than the Sun, central regions can have temperatures well over 20 million degrees Fahrenheit. Our planet gets the benefit of a star that has reactions in the carbon cycle that include that and are catalysts as a result. We can use this positronic engine to our advantage since we use the charged particles to convert the positrons involved into radiation that annihilates the electrons."

"You've gotten that far in just...wait. You've said a Positronic engine?"

Agatha interrupted, "What do you use for fuel, if I may ask?"

"That's where the *Euphrenium* I told you about comes into play. It can be formed and combined with other elements into a sort of Collider that traps the exploding electrons in a safe environment. They produce the energy we need to power our positronic engines and draw more energy as well as reproduce it from our own star. Even more impossible but true, the resulting fuel recombinants then continue to reproduce while traveling and give us unlimited fuel no matter how far we must travel. One of the secondary finds was *Iridite* to use as a shield to the ultra-radiation and the enormous heat exchange from the chemical reactions to everything involved. It was a fantastic breakthrough."

"How could people withstand that enormous energy around them every second? Wouldn't there be untold consequences from heat and radiation and…"

"We learned how to capture and contain it and found you could corral small amounts of antimatter to avoid outward explosions. As I said, it's done in a safe environment. The real fun starts when many positron scientists think as soon as five years from now, *Asturian* time, we'll have the technology to safely transport positrons the same way we transport tanks of liquid nitrogen or other industrial chemicals. Those advances could then be used to power a new generation of technology, from molecular scanners to rocket engines to the aptly named "annihilation laser,"

"What's that?" Harper was in his element and excited almost beyond control.

"It's a tightly concentrated energy beam fueled by annihilating positrons that act as an accelerator to movement in space where there is no friction."

'How do you control the explosions and the anti-matter?" Nikos had been silent until this.

"All of this is shielded behind a vat coated with *Iridite* and doubly insulated behind walls of tempered metal you've never seen the likes of there on your planet. So far, it seems almost foolproof."

"Almost? That's a scary word. Any accidents in this 'fool-proof' method you've developed?" Harper smiled sardonically and his lips tightened.

{too good to be true means…maybe not so good}

Cassel spoke up again, "Have you ever had any accidents in your space program?"

Harper looked up at him and smirked, "Point taken."

Socrat added his own thoughts, "Before we left *Asturia*, they were beginning work on an engine that would require no liquid fuel and we were just sorry we couldn't be around to use it."

Agatha sat forward with both hands on the table and leaned in, "How in the world would they do that?

"It's possible on our world Agatha, not yours. Earth is far behind in space travel though you have managed to help them come in leaps and bounds. No, this would be something your scientists are just beginning to question and research; flight by Particle Accelerator."

Harper blurted out, "Not possible, totally impossible!"

"Imagine a world where we didn't need fuel to propel rockets through space. Fuel is expensive, it's dangerous and it needs to be refilled and replaced. In other words, it seems impossible but so is Science Fiction on your world."

"Mr. Socrat, my parents were two of the scientists on the *Mauritius* when we left our world and even our scientists would tell you it isn't possible." Agatha was adamant but curious as well "There's too much risk with organic matter being pushed by force at incredible speeds." "Think of Isaac Newton's third law of motion: every action has an equal and opposite reaction. A weight that moves along a straight rod will only cause the tube it is in to move back and forth along a frictionless surface. There's no forward acceleration. *But…* our designers proposed pushing a particle accelerator instead of a weight, back and forth along a helix, with the mass increasing as it moves in the forward direction and decreasing as it bounces backward.

"This way, when the rotating ion ring hits the front of the compartment, it produces forward acceleration. Being flung through a Black Hole would lessen the danger of bouncing along like a bullet from a gun barrel. We believe that if the helical engine were given enough time and power, it could reach potentially relativistic speeds with the help of the particle accelerator; quick as warp speed on the 'Starship Enterprise." He grinned at their expressions,

"Let's just say that without the sun giving us these chemical reactions, we couldn't build an engine to travel through space or time."

"What? You can travel through time?" as Harper looked stupefied.

"Only in so far as going through some wormholes has apparently speeded up some of the earth's time cycles as has been reported in our histories and the opposite is also true, in slowing some down."

"How can both be true if you are going in the same direction?"

Nikos started to answer him and then thought better of it.

"We had to have something to pass the time on *Triton.* The kids were quite taken with this scenario as a comic book might be." Without another word, Cassel got up and left the room abruptly

{I need to get messages out ***now…get out of my head****}*

"Must have been something we thought" Socrat quipped. All eyes turned quickly to him, and he blushed when he realized he had said what he was thinking.

"How long Commander?" Nikos asked, knowing Haller would be completely aware of what he was asking,

"Weeks sir…instead of months."

"Let's leave off the 'sir' and get down to business. When do you think you can leave?"

"If all goes well with soma stasis and our supplies are not too much weight, we can leave in two of your weeks and be there in four. We're taking the Black Hole that propels us out close to *Despina* and cuts off half the time."

Agatha asked Haller, "Are you certain it has no great risk?"

"Everything in space travel has risks, Agatha. This, maybe a little more than usual but to do what you need...?" He let the answer hang in the thickened atmosphere. They disconnected and Cassel did not appear until hours later and avoided both Haller and Socrat. Nikos asked Agatha, "Did you get anything?"

"Oh yes, quite a bit. Cassel is a disaster waiting to happen and soon." They talked on for over an hour and then went to see the committee.

Chapter 17

Plans Delayed, New Plans Made

Agatha and Francis were sitting at the table talking quietly when Rodane walked into the committee room. He looked around him, obviously expecting others to be there, "Uh ok, what's up?"

Agatha motioned to the chairs, "Please, have a seat. Want some coffee first?"

Rodane knew both well enough by now to know it wasn't some earth-shaking issue or there would be more people here, "No thanks, I'm good."

Francis had lost some weight within the last few weeks. He had circles under his eyes and a haggard look about him.

{please, no more illness}

Rodane decided to hit it dead on, "Are you ok Francis? You look like shit."

{Jesus, did I just say that out loud}

Francis snickered, "Well, good morning to you too. Sleep well?"

"Did you?"

Francis pointed to Agatha, "We both got about two

hours of sleep last night and I guess it shows huh?" Then he yawned.

"Let's get right down to it Rodane, because we don't have a lot of time and the rest will be here shortly to hear our news."

"Why just me? Couldn't it wait until all of us…"

"No, it couldn't because they will not be hearing what you are about to hear. We can't afford to let this leak until it is a done deal as they say." She took a breath and faced him square on, "You know of course that your mother is ill and getting treatment here?"

"Yes, and I'm very grateful you are taking care of her. If you want me to pay for the medi…"

She shooed his thoughts away with a flick of her hands, "Not at all. That's not what I'm getting at. You also know we have in our possession, a bathyscape of ultimate design and capabilities just waiting for us to examine?"

"Yes" he looked askance at them both. He wasn't sure where this was going.

"You know about the journey here and the loss of certain people on that journey as well as some waiting to be rescued after all this time?"

Francis looked over to Agatha and said gently, "Agatha, we don't have time for a lesson here, we need to give him the details and he will surely have lots of questions for us. Rodane, do you want the long or short version?"

No hesitation, "Bottom line please."

Agatha looked annoyed but shook her head, "Yes, you're right. No time to lose. Rodane, we're asking your permission to use that bathyscape to go down and rescue those survivors in the next week, weather permitting, and it looks good."

He looked at her for a few seconds, perplexed and somewhat confused, "I don't understand why you need my permission."

"Because we want to take your mother down with us and treat her cancer there. It's where all the tools and treatment rooms are and there are none here to accomplish the same things. It's our one chance to treat her and…Eugenia."

That floored him and he sat back in shock, "Genie? What can you do at the bottom of a… how is that even possible to get them there and back? What if…"

He stopped and swallowed, breathed deeply and then tried to pull himself together.

Agatha said, "We're not even sure about Genie but we're working on it."

Francis held up a silver tube with four buttons along each side with two tines sticking out from the center meeting in the middle and a hook at the bottom. "I know that!" Rodane blurted out. Francis grinned, "Yes, I know, the 'silver thingy'. This is the key that opens the hatch and the engineer inside has an identical one to use at the same time. Otherwise, it won't open with its failsafe." He held up a metal box, "This is the module to control everything from up here on the surface. It connects to a computer program. Any questions so far?"

"Only about a dozen right now. How can you be sure they're alive? Do they have a way to contact you? What if we try and open it and something goes wrong? Does the bathyscape…what if it doesn't make it safely and…what happens to those on board if something doesn't work right?"

Agatha said soothingly, "Relax Rodane, here's what we know" and she told them of their contact with the survivors and the plans they had to use Duncan's design and have him adjust it to hold two more people "It's really a simple fix and it's foolproof and that has already been determined."

Francis added, "We don't anticipate any glitches, but we are prepared to take up the passengers if anything should occur that seems dangerous. We would scratch the mission if something happened on the way down."

"That...doesn't sound too comforting if you'll excuse my ignorance where these things are concerned...this is my mother. It sounds like a one-shot deal and "Via con Dios' if it doesn't pan out the way you expect."

"We understand that and it's why we are asking you for your permission to allow us..."

"Does my mother know about this? Have you talked to her and explained all..."

"Yes of course. She was the first one we talked to after we were sure it could be done, also your sister, Cassie. It was your sister that gave us the idea."

He got up from the table and paced the room and even Agatha and Francis were waiting for this signature method of forming a decision. He looked up, "I have a trip scheduled in three days to Utah and we're supposed to make sure that mountain never gets uncovered or even a dig started."

"You're not going to be surprised if we tell you that's where the glitch comes in? Or we wouldn't be having this conversation."

He returned to his seat, "What's the glitch? We've been planning this for months."

"Someone is attempting to put the monkey wrench into this particular project." Agatha was now very annoyed.

"What we have here is a failure to communicate." Francis

chuckled at his license to steal movie lines, "We think there is a mole in the Governor's office or in the two universities that are making use of their grant money to do this dig along with the teams we've organized."

Rodane thought a few seconds, "Sure it's not in our own team? After all…"

"No Rodane, we've searched every nook and cranny of any evidence of our own people putting obstacles in our way to prevent the dig at all. No, all the trail that we have uncovered leads back to the Governor's office or someone who has his ear or hears his phone conversations."

"Any chance he's being bugged or his office?"

"We don't know but we're sending two people you know out there to try and find out. They are not known by anyone in the 'family' that might recognize them, and they are both aware of the stakes."

"Huh? Who would that be?"

"Your two buddies from back home, Renata and Zoe."

"What the hell! You can't send them on a trip to insert themselves into a group that is this dangerous with no experience and…"

Francis rose and went over to Rodane still standing up, "Rodane, listen. Where do you think they've been all this time since you came back to France?"

"I have no idea. I haven't heard from them since they were on that plane ride back from Spain."

"Quimby has gotten to know them quite well and he thinks…"

"Renata is 'family' I know, or we think she's 'family' but Zoe isn't. I thought…"

"We're not sure. She was hired by Gallo. He has used her

talents and strengths for a long time but there's something we're still waiting to find out. Anyway, even if she isn't, she's as much like Eugenia and Helena as we could hope to find for two dedicated professional members who have skills and training…"

"Training?" he scoffed, "You should have seen the mess that was left behind those two and the danger they put themselves in while I was there. One almost died and one was not to be trusted with my little pinky much less …"

"Though she did save your life in Italy, right?"

'I'm still not sure about that one. Or the attack in Santorini."

"Well, Quimby feels certain they are two excellent choices for future R&R's and has had them at the farm doing training exercises for combat and stealth since you all came back from Spain. They are two amazing women if I do say so myself." Rodane looked at Francis to see if he was serious. He was.

"About that trip to the ship…"

'Ah yes, got a little off track there," Francis continued, "Agatha, tell him about *Mauritius.*"

Rodane came back to his seat and Agatha started by telling him about the ship *Asternem II* on Neptune's moon *Triton* that was scheduled to take off in the next week and make a journey to *Phobos*, a closer moon of Mars for a shot at taking down the mountain from space. He laughed, "I still can't get used to hearing you tell me about a space trip that is not part of some Star traveler TV series and its reality."

"This one is as real as it gets. If it makes it through the Black Hole toward *Despina* and…"

"Wait! Did you say Black Hole? They're really going

through a Black Hole?"

"This is as real a trip as those satellites and rovers combing the heavens as we speak. You know how we've talked to you about Black Holes?"

"Talking is one thing, doing is another. This is radical!"

"They should be here in a matter of weeks."

"How does that fit in with my mother and Genie going down in the bathyscape? I'm confused, not like I haven't been for months now."

"Not much but if we can show the passengers and the crew of the *Asternum II* that we can do this and recover our own people, it will make them trust us more than they do now. We need to show them we have a plan for when they finally come to Earth and deliver their passengers for a new life. At least we're hopeful that will be evident from our trip to rescue our own."

Francis added, "If we can heal your mother and Genie and use the tools and lab from the ship, it's possible the next step is bringing up those tools and our research lab on board and use them soon. We will just have to find a way to introduce them into this world as a scientific break-through that works and then the grants will start flowing in and…"

"Then there's a chance we can be safe and maybe even reveal ourselves to the world at large…"

"Hold on there Rodane, one miracle at a time…" Agatha smiled at the man in front of her like a kid overjoyed at being in the candy shop with unlimited funds.

"You need to contact the Governor of Utah and make up an explanation of why you can't be there next week with your team, without reneging on the contract you have with him and the state."

"What about the students from the Universities? Will they go there even without us?"

"That's the next glitch. You must try to find a way to have them put on hold while we figure out who is trying to sabotage the entire dig. They respect you and your credentials so I don't think it will be too hard to convince them..."

"That's a lot of faith to put in one man Agatha. What if I can't get them to agree?"

"We'll just have to cross that bridge when we get to it. Right now, I'm leaving it to you to tell your mother the trip is a go."

"Why me, isn't Cassie..."

"Cassie has gone home for a few weeks to take care of things at home. She feels her mother is in safe hands. I hope you do too."

Rodane looked totally surprised that Cassie had left without even trying to see him or connect before she left. The door to the room opened and others from the committee began to enter for their next meeting. Rodane greeted each of them, spent a few moments to talk with them and then left to enter the lion's den and face the mama lion. He was sure to figure out how to address that elephant squeezed into the den before he got there.

Chapter 18

Sophia, Growing Up

When Francis reached the latest safe place where Caroline and Sophia had been secreted, Rodane looked over and saw the curtains move. Well, someone was either on the lookout for them or eager to see when they arrived. He hoped it was the latter. After the attack on Caroline and Genie, when Caroline left the hospital, she was taken to another site with Sophia where it could be guarded much easier. It would give her protection she would need for herself and Sophia. Beaker was still with another caretaker but mending well and soon would be joining them. Sophia had begged for him to be with them in the hospital to visit Genie which turned out to be a very good thing indeed.

Rodane had only been here twice before, once at night after Caroline had come here after the attack; once when he was meeting with Caroline to explain Iona's illness and what had happened with Cassie. Caroline had made him swear to not keep anything from them that might be important for their own safety and security. She made good points so here he was again, getting ready to go on another journey with the edge of danger and the possibility of failure. Not an auspicious way to begin a visit with his ex-wife and his daughter. He felt guilty for leaving them to others to protect and stressed to be leaving them in those capable hands but not his.

The door opened and a fuzzy, furry bundle of muscle and energy bounded out the door and ran down the path. It stopped short in front of Rodane who was getting out of the passenger seat. Beaker sat at the car, watching Rodane with that tilted head as he seemed to feel the need to examine each person before he decided if they were safe or not. "Well, look who we have here. Hello Beaker, how's your day going? I'm very glad to see you looking so good."

Rodane put out his hand and Beaker gladly raised his paw and placed it in Rodane's hand and made a noise somewhere between *'woof'* and *'arf'* and his tail was wagging like a metronome on 3/4 time. Sophia came rushing out the door and came straight to Rodane's arms and held tightly as he picked her up and twirled her around in a circle, "Goodness Sophia, you must be growing faster than a tiny seed of a pumpkin and getting just as heavy!" He grinned widely as she kissed him on both cheeks.

"Bonjour Papa! Je t'aime, aussi!"

"Merci ma petite graine de citrouille" She laughed and said, "I am not a pumpkin seed, I am a growing girl, and my goal is to be as tall as you."

"And she's eating me out of home and hearth to try and reach that goal. Hello Rodane, how are you?" Caroline reached him, kissed him lightly on the lips and bent down to ruffle Beaker's coat. "He looks good, doesn't he? You can't even tell we…" and caught herself in front of Sophia.

"It's ok mama, I know he almost died and we're just happy he's still here, aren't we?" Rodane watched her, entranced at the change he saw.

{my little girl is not so little anymore and that makes me sad}

Rodane introduced Francis to them and Caroline took stock of him in seconds. Beaker smelled him and accepted him instantly. He saw her tilt her head to him and smiled. They moved to the house and Rodane watched Beaker move to Sophia's side and stay glued through the door then looked behind her to see Caroline lock it behind them. Beaker looked back at Rodane and nodded his head for confirmation.

{he doesn't miss a trick or the routine of the house}

He was feeling better about leaving them soon and he knew security was tight and extremely professional, especially at night. He recalled her anger and frustration when she came home from the hospital and found them around the house.

"We will not live like prisoners Rodane. They're not going to make me afraid to step out the door or go into town or…do my job…" even while she was fighting back tears.

"No one wants to make you a prisoner. We also want to make sure you both are protected and safe. It's only until…"

"Rodane, pardon me but you have no idea of when this will be over and what 'they' whoever 'they' are, will try something else again.

"That's why we want you guarded and Sophia…"

"Damn it Rodane, I have no life, Sophia has no life…" she broke into sobs, "Genie is hanging onto life by a thread and all because…"

He moved to her and folded her into his arms. She

sobbed into his shoulder, 'I can't tell you how sorry or guilty I feel for..."

"No"! She broke away and shook her finger at him... "not you, I'm not blaming you, it's not your fault Adam is dead and it's not your fault we're

forced into this position. It's the ones doing this, and I will be damned if I let them take over our lives without a fight."

"Daddy, come look at my drawings" Sophia took him by the hand and dragged him down the hall toward her room. He shook himself out of his dark thoughts and laughed as he said, "If I don't return, tell everyone I perished entering the dark room of a teenage girl, never to be seen or heard from again."

"Daddy don't be so dramatic. My room is tidier than yours, and I'll lay bets. You on? And I'm not a teenager... yet"

Francis laughed and Caroline smirked, "She cleaned it this morning under pain of losing her drawing materials for a week if she didn't before her father got here. Would you like something to drink or eat? I can make breakfast if you..."

"No, all taken care of before we left this morning." They moved to the kitchen and took seats,

"Oh, are you staying with Francis at..."

"No" Francis said, "just met up with him and we had a good drive here and I got to know your husband better as well."

"Ex-husband" as she watched his face. "But we're on good terms now. It makes things much easier for everyone. It wasn't always that way but...events have a way of opening eyes and closed doors."

He watched her carefully as he decided what wound to

pry into and what to leave alone, "I know about the death of your..."

"Adam, his name was Adam, and we were making plans to get married when he was... killed." By the tone of her voice, the wound was still very raw.

"I don't want to stir up any bad..."

"No, it's ok. Sophia and I are almost past the grief and getting to the place where all the good memories still live. We talk a lot about him, and we have such nice photos and trips we took to keep as well." She took a napkin and wiped at an invisible crumb.

"Did Sophia like him? How did she take..."

"Angry, she's angry... and sad as I am, but...she uses her drawing to give her respite and calm. She loved him too. I haven't found anything yet that I can use to ease that loss but I'm trying." The napkin was being folded and twisted.

Francis took the opening "Would you be interested in being somewhere you don't have to feel like a prisoner in your own home and also find ways to get past the anger and learn to protect yourself...and Sophia?"

Caroline took a long moment, silently examining him as he waited patiently. The clock in the kitchen chimed out the hour and still she examined him, patient to the doctor. Then, "It's not a coincidence you came here today, is it? Does Rodane know you had a plan in mind for me...and Sophia? It does include Sophia doesn't' it? Otherwise..."

"It's for both of you and no, I haven't told Rodane because he's about to go on a trip to your country out west and I didn't want him to leave confused and anxious about a plan that might worry him during his...job."

"Tell me about your...plan and what it entails."

"You'll learn martial arts and some tactical skills that would be an advantage if you ever again found yourself in a precarious position. You'd be doing a lot of

training; strength, core building and it's very rigorous. I won't lie to you but it's well worth the effort."

"What about Sophia? She's turning eleven in a few weeks and I worry about her more than anything. They tried to use her as leverage…the bastards."

"The same thing but on a different level, all watched over by trained professionals and in a safe, secure environment." He waited.

"Where is this place?"

"I can't tell you that now, but Agatha or Suri can answer all your questions if you need answers before you agree or reject the offer."

"For how long?"

"That's up to you and Sophia when you feel the time is right. It's open ended."

"Is there a cost… for either of us?"

"Gaining peace of mind, my dear, and a way for your respite and calm. For Sophia…a way to feel she has some control over her life."

"Well, yes, I can see that, but it goes for me too." She grinned at him.

They heard the laughter and the squeals coming from Sophia's room and Caroline's face lit up, "She's still ticklish!" Sophia ran into the kitchen and went right up to Francis "It's a lovely spot sir, and I would love to go. When can we leave? Can Beaker come to?" Caroline smiled and bent down to Sophia while looking at Francis who looked stunned.

"She's still learning to control her 'gifts' and Rodane…"

she looked at Sophia and put her finger over her mouth … "Daddy… doesn't know the extent of your new tricks. We wouldn't want Daddy to go on a trip with that worry in his mind, would we love? Where is Daddy by the way?"

"Went to the bathroom. Sir, can I visit Genie when we're there?"

Francis found it hard not to show his astonishment, "Would you like to? Is she going to be there?" Caroline was open-mouthed but silent.

"Yep, right in the building that's next to me and Mama's. Didn't you know?" She looked perplexed.

Francis shook his head, "Seems there's a lot I don't know but I'm learning. Sophia, how about you and I go out and throw snowballs for a little while?"

"Yes!" She ran to get her snow pants and jacket, light sparking in her eyes. Beaker came running to the door with his tail wagging. He apparently liked snowball fights too.

Chapter 19

Enemies Return

Francis and Rodane had finally put all their visits and chores behind them and were on the way back to Amiens for a good night's sleep. Rodane's phone chimed and he answered to see Raul and Evangela. "Hey buddy, how's it going? Hi Evangela, you're looking good as usual." She smiled.

Raul cut to the chase, "Are you alone? Where are you?"

Francis spoke, "Raul, it's Francis and we're on our way back to Amiens. What's happened?"

"Nothing yet that we know of, but something is going down and we needed to get to you now."

"Should we alert the committee?" Francis looked seriously concerned.

'Well, it directly concerns Rodane, so we tried him first but yes, they need to know."

Rodane shifted in his seat so they could see Francis at the wheel, "We're leaving Caroline's house. Does it concern her? Should we go ba…"

"No Rodane" Evangela added, "Caroline and your Sophia

are safe as far as we can tell. Your trip to Utah, is it still on schedule?"

Rodane was now confused; from Caroline to Utah…? "Uh…no, funny you should ask that. We just had a meeting and…"

"No matter, that isn't the reason we are worried about you."

"Me? What have I got that…"

"Andrew McCarty, you know the name?" Raul blurted out.

Rodane thought for a moment, but Francis was the one to answer, "Nikos and the President, do they need to be alerted?"

"Perhaps yes, but more importantly, Rodane's sister..."

"Cassie or Aldora?" Francis was thinking clearer than Rodane.

"Cassie needs to be contacted and she needs to be aware of a possible threat to her.

"She left for the states two days ago. I'll give you all the contacts I can think of and call their local police."

"Good. We can hit the ground running and hope we beat them to her."

"When did you figure this all out?"

"Today, just minutes ago. We're sorry Rodane for dumping this in your lap so suddenly but we finally have all the pieces and now we are acting on them as soon as we can."

He finally collected his thoughts, "Andrew McCarty, the one who tried to kill us in Spain at the Shrine of St. James?"

Evangela looked at him solemnly, "Actually it was you, Rodane, he was trying to kill. Others were just collateral damage."

"Tell us all you know Raul" Francis had his fingers tight on the wheel, concentrating on driving.

"This is a coordinated effort on the part of more than one person. When we returned to Spain to see why the University was summoning us, they knew nothing about it. We thought at first it was a miscommunication. We handed over the emails they had sent us, or we thought they had sent us, and it was a hack job that bounced around so many towers and used so many shell corporations to hide their origination it took hours to pin it down. We're sure It was done to get us out of the way."

"Which was…?" from Rodane.

"It took us days working with the University to try and crack the username. We ended up with two names from two different countries that were still false anyway." Raul spoke through his anger, "But it did allow us to locate an account where the emails were startlingly coded. Another two days to crack them and it led us to sites that concerned mercenaries for hire."

"Where?" Francis waited.

"Venezuela and Brunei" Evangela added; "Venezuela with an extradition treaty and Brunei where it's difficult to find a wanted person. Both are harbors for criminals."

"When" Rodane was so angry he had a difficult time focusing without their help. "Any word on a specific site?"

Evangela looked directly at Rodane, and he could see the concern in her face, "Two cryptographers from the university math department cracked the code and found all the references to Cassie and her whereabouts in…"

"Pennsylvania!" Rodane spit out. How did they know she was going home? Or did they?"

"We don't know. The references were to their break-in at her house and their anger at a failed mission. There were some code words to a flower or an animal, but we couldn't figure that one out..."

"Flower, the name of a skunk they butchered and then taunted her with, the fucking bastards!"

Evangela was not even shocked, "Yes, for certain. There were references to blood writings on the wall and how this time they would finish the job but... wanted more money. It was more about revenge."

Francis spoke up, "Here's what you do, both of you. Contact Agatha and have her put guards on the compound and Iona Arcos. Contact Cassie directly and see if Iona can give you names of anyone she may get in touch with. Then get hold of Quimby and see if he can get to Pa. sooner than an air flight."

"He can fly without a flight plan and get there sooner than by car." Rodane added his own realization. He was dialing and redialing Cassie's number as they spoke.

"Ok, but you need for someone to try and make it there sooner than an hour or two. If we're right, they are already on route or closer than that."

"There're a few hours difference. Are you sure this accounts for that?"

"Yes, we've taken all that into consideration and allowed for their travel plans through security points and customs.

"Damn it!" Rodane cried out. "She doesn't answer her phone."

"Keep trying Rodane while I get boots on the ground. He addressed his GPS phone system, "Call Agatha Anastos..."

It was going to be the worst two-hour journey of his life.

Rodane Arcos had a lot to lose at this point, but he would make sure whoever was on the hunt for his family had nothing at the end if he could help it.

Cassie woke to the dark night with blackness showing out her window. They were on the mattresses put there the preceding day for the rest of the furniture to arrive sometime in the week. There were no blankets but a sheet and Jacob had a furnace hidden somewhere in his skin, so they were quite comfortable…except for her legs. They were trapped under his and really needed to move and take out the tiny beginnings of a Charley Horse in her left calf.

She wondered why she had awakened if it wasn't from the Charley Horse. Jacob was snoring slightly, and she managed to lift his arm gently and move her arm out from under his. Then she inched her way out of the bed so as not to awaken him. She reached her leg over the mattresses a foot from the floor and stood up slowly and silently. There was water in her backpack, and she drank eagerly, very thirsty.

As she stood up, she heard what she thought was a cat, maybe a barn cat from down the road. An owl's *Scree* filled the air and a rabbit let out horrific screams that sounded like dying. She shivered at the sound and then wrapped her arms around herself, feeling the night breeze filling the house. Then she heard the *'chitter'* of a skunk, a sound she had become all too familiar with for so long.

She went to the window and leaned against the cool jamb when she noticed a pencil of light at the back of the yard, near the tree where a hole allowed for animals to crawl under if they were exploring. She watched it in a sort of trance, reliving the night they came and found her buddy, Flower, in his cage. They proceeded to torture him and finished it off in the microwave. She swore then she would get those vicious people somehow. She backed away from the window and made her way down the stairs as quietly as she could then felt around for her shoes near the front door. That gave her an idea. How about coming at them from a direction they didn't count on?

She went to the closet where her things were stored from the hidey hole and took out the baseball bat. She opened the front door slowly to avoid any creaking and stepped out onto the porch where a night lantern was flickering from the side door panel. She stood still and listened, her ears attuned to anything out of the ordinary which excluded rabbit screams, owls hooting and night crickets chirping. Newly hatched Cicadas from this season, buzzing in the trees like the '*Oom*' of a yoga class, hummed softly. She proceeded slowly around the side of the house until her eyes had become accustomed to the dark shadows playing across the back lawn and her gardens partly bathed in moonlight.

Whoever was here was not afraid to walk normally and didn't seem to mind the soft thuds his or her steps sent into the air. She made it to the raised garden beds and hunched down as far as she could with her bat at the ready. She froze when he, definitely a *he*, suddenly half turned and looked straight to where she was hiding. He began to walk back, nonchalant and seemingly uncaring. When he reached the other side of the garden bed, he looked back and forth and stayed still for at least a full minute. He reached into his pocket and pulled something out. She couldn't tell what it was, but it was shiny and caught a little of the light.

{I hope it's not a gun}

He began to walk away, and she heard him on the phone he had pulled out,

'I don't think she's here. The place is stone silent and no lights anywhere in the house." He listened.

"You think it's a good idea to break into her house? It has a security system and then they'll know we were here, and it will alert them." *Pause.*

"Give me a few more minutes." He looked around again "I'll call you back."

He started toward the house and all she could think of was Jacob sleeping and this man finding him and able to do anything before Jacob was even awake.

{no, it won't happen again, not to Jacob}

She quickly rose and sprinted toward the shadow; bat raised. He must have heard or felt her coming because he stepped out of the way just as she reached him, and her swing met nothing but air while his swing caught her on the side of the shoulder. She grabbed her arm and lost the bat. She went down and he was on her in a second. She kneed him in the balls, and he grabbed them, letting out a hard yell while he flailed around reaching for something. She rose and sprinted two feet to swoop and pick up the bat and grabbed it just as he came toward her. One good swing was all she was going to get. She made the most of it. She rolled down just as he stabbed downward where she had been and got him square on the side of his knee. The '*thwack*" that she heard was accompanied by a guttural '*oof*' as he went down, reaching for her. She managed to get one good punch in the face before he punched her right back and made her ears ring.

He was going for another one and she knew that one would probably put her out. His fist was raised when he heard '*crack*', the unmistakable sound of a gunshot. He dropped his arm; rolled over and hobbled toward the back of the yard to get out of range. He had almost reached the fence with Cassie following close behind when Jacob yelled out, "Cassie, **Stop**!" She remembered and froze in her steps. He reached for the fence and the sizzle of electricity filled the air with the smell of singed clothing and she watched mesmerized as he danced through a series of steps; the marionette on the strings and the night had gotten a lot brighter just for a few seconds. When it was over, he simply slid to the ground, limp and unmoving. Jacob reached her side, lowered his gun and moved over to the prone form.

"Be careful, he might be playing possum" Cassie stood where she was, afraid to move toward them. 'Did you shoot him?" she asked.

"No, just fired it so he would be distracted while I made it to you in the dark and he did the rest. My next shot would not have been a warning." He peered closely at the shape on the grass and leaned down and turned on a pencil flashlight from the man's pocket. "Do you recognize him, Cassie?"

She picked up the bat, gripped it in two hands, ready for her turn at bat. She moved to Jacob's side and leaned closer to look at him. A moan escaped his lips while Jacob rooted through his other pocket and pulled out a card and a phone and almost dropped it as it buzzed. They looked at each other and he showed her the screen; *unknown caller*. He said, "Get my phone quick and we'll sync them. It's on the porch."

She sprinted to the porch, holding her throbbing arm

and grabbed the phone off the step where he had dropped it; ran back to Jacob and held it out to him. He took a picture of the man, called for backup and an ambulance then he answered the call. He waited a second or two and mimicked a man with a gravely, gruff voice, "What" then made sounds like he was out of breath. He put his phone next to the one he was holding out for her to hear as it blinked green. "You didn't call…I was waiting."

"All good" He kept clearing his throat and breathing heavy, "Leaving now."

"Is it done, is she done?"

"Yeah"

"Get back to your hotel. Your flight leaves in an hour."

"Ok" He ended the call. "Shit! We don't know how he got here or where he was staying."

Jacob rifled through his pockets again, hearing an ambulance from a distance away. "Open his phone…your phone. See what his contacts are. Check his last caller." Jacob pushed buttons, checked the readout and was agitated, 'Must be a burner, no IP address. Dammit!"

"I'll go let the EMT's in."

An hour later, they were alone once more. The stranger was taken to the local hospital under police guard, they had checked the contacts on his phone; all two of them and found nothing that could give them a clue as to who he was or from where. "Wait, what was that card you took out of his pocket Jacob? Remember?"

"Hell yes!" He grabbed it out of his pocket where he had stuffed it during their phone call "It's from a bar in town, rough part of town."

She looked steadily at him for a few seconds, got up off

the porch swing and reached out her hand, "Let's go."

"I'm not getting you involved in this..."

"I go or I'll follow you somehow. Either way, I **am** involved, and this is **my** life we're talking about here Jacob. I'm not going to be stopped but I could sure use your help." She remained standing, holding out her hand. He looked up at her, shook his head back and forth and reached for her hand. Her phone rang and she muttered under her breath, "Little late Roddy" without even checking the caller.

Chapter 20

Hiking is for Masochists

Navajo and Reese Canyons are two remote canyons on the *Kaiparowits Plateau* in Utah Grand Staircase Escalante. If you're looking up the sloping trail at a cascade of enormous cliffs and sharp-edged mountain peaks with little greenery or signs of life, it seems as if this could be a hike along a crater of the moon. For hikers, following those mountain chains can be a strenuous, upward trek over very rough terrain that tires you before you even begin to reach the base of the mountains. It becomes a circuitous route with its added elevations up and then its steep descents down. You could just connect with Croton Canyon and the bottom portion of Last Chance. Though that alternate route might be a little faster, it is ever-so slightly longer but not as arduous. Finding a way into the area where the three teams were heading for their proposed dig was still a journey in the planning with no real movement toward any of the routes they had examined for weeks. This was the first of the three teams to make it this far.

Ariel leaned her back against the flimsy door of the hut

they had reached about fifteen miles into the canyon, and no one was there to greet them. She very slowly slithered down the door and landed with a slight 'bump' on the hard-packed dirt of the desert floor. Hard to do when her backpack was in the way, but she managed to make it seem very easy. Richie looked at her with a half grin on his face and sweat rolling off his bandana wrapped around his head like a turban.

"Had enough already? We still have 'miles to go before..."

"If you say, 'we sleep', I'll take out my empty water bottle and throw it at your head."

"*Tch tch,* such nastiness toward your fellow traveler. One would think all this hiking has made you a touch grouchy."

"What's made me grouchy is my throat turning into a parched wasteland and no one here to meet us...as promised." She looked around him down the path they had come up and shaded her hands against the glaring hot sun. "Where's Andy? Wasn't he right behind you?"

"Yeah, he told me to go ahead, he'd catch up."

"Jesus, Richie, don't you ever listen to the talks we get before we are going on a dig in this area? You **NEVER** leave anyone behind, even for a few minutes. What the hell were you thinking?"

"Calm down girl. He had to take a leak and he wanted to do it in peace with no eyes on him."

"Well, then it's the longest leak in the history of piss-poor men I've ever known. Let's go!" She began to lever herself up off her sitting position.

"Where?"

"Christ Richie, do you only ever think of you and you only? We're going to find him."

"I'll wait here."

"No, you won't, and don't give me that look. I'm the team leader and what I say goes, got it?"

Before he got his smart retort out of his mouth, Andy came around the curve of the cliffside and looked up and waved at them. He yelled something but it drifted off into the open space still between them. She watched as the chunky but tall man headed slowly up the hill, his dark beard glistening with sweat and his sunglasses giving off a glare. They waited for him to reach them as Ariel pulled out her satellite phone and held it up to the sky to see if the connection was there and let out a 'Yes" when it showed service.

"I'm going to call and give them a piece of my mind so close your ears for all the bad words Ritchie."

At that moment, Rodane was on the phone with the Lieutenant Governor of Utah and listening to her complaints that could be heard by everyone in the room,

"Do you realize what I had to go through to get you your permits and your requests for teams as well? This is not an excursion that has a tour guide and holds your hands if you're squeamish about heights."

Rodane attempted to talk to her, "We had no idea that there would be incidents here that would require our immediate attention and…"

"**YOU** have no idea what it took to get this all past the planning stage without someone, somewhere, finding out about it beforehand. How can I justify putting all this on hold now? People are beginning to ask questions. The budget office is beginning to…Christ Rodane, how could I let myself get into all this now?"

Rodane spoke kindly, "Maybe because the Governor you work for asked you to?"

She opened her mouth to answer and then took a deep breath and shut her lips in a thin line of frustration.

"Look" he continued, "I'm sorry that things are happening out of my control, but I promise you that in a very few days I will have my crew out there. Your other team may already be there so we can dig right in" and he smiled at her.

"Very funny" but she smiled back, just a little one, but still a smile. "That's two teams, what about the third one?"

"Haven't you heard from them yet? They should have gotten in touch with you days ago." He turned halfway to look behind him at the two sitting on chairs off to the side. They raised their eyebrows but kept silent.

"Not a squeak, can't reach them by phone, text or messaging. Who's the team leader?"

Rodane was worried, "Don't know. They're from the West Coast that's all I know. Their team leader is supposed to be one of the best on paleontological digs in uncharted areas."

"Call me tomorrow early and I'll see if the permits can be changed to allow for more time if you can give me a time that won't change, got it?"

"Yes ma'am. Will do! Thanks for understanding."

"Don't thank me yet, I don't have it done. I can hardly wait to have to tell the powers that be, we need to change things at this point. Thanks for being a pain in the ass!" **click!**

That night, team #2 set up camp against a huge overhang of a cliff that would keep them dry (supposedly) and gave them shelter from the whirling, sweeping winds that so often blew through all those canyons going in different directions. It was a quiet night with no bird song, no critters scratching through the dark, no sound of car or even of planes flying overhead. Their sleeping bags awaited them, but Ariel excused herself to go off down the slope and find a private place to take care of business. She carried a little shovel to cover over her leavings and a flashlight as the night grew darker still. She took a moment to stare up at the clear sky with a million stars and then gazed around at all the mountain ranges to be seen.

The peaks were outlined in the encroaching dark as figurines, with no distinct features, standing like that for millions of years of explosion and erupting earth. When the ground had settled over more millions of years, roaming dinosaurs took over the land newly created; lived, fought, ate, laid eggs and died, covered over by nature burying their remains under tons of earth and layers of sedimentary rock.

She found a spot to relieve herself, covered over her waste and was on her way back to camp as she was struck once more by the awesomeness of the mountains in front of her. She sat down on the ground, wiped her hands through her blond, pixie haircut from sweat and dust, wrapped her arms around her knees and gazed skyward at more stars than she had ever seen before in such a clear sky.

The landscape in front of them had once been part of Laramidia, an island continent that existed during the Late Cretaceous period, when the Western Interior Seaway split the continent of North America in two and the land eventually became broken, scorched and left as a desert to the west of the Appalachian range. More millions of years passed as did Indians walking the land, fishing the rivers, hiking the mountains and traveling the canyons, traveling on to more malleable and friendly land when food was difficult to grow. Bands of Indians of various tribes, mostly Anasazi and Navajo, made good use of the unique region of canyons, arches, plateaus and cliffs; created homes in the walls of the canyons and moved on when the land no longer provided for them.

She lay back on the hard-packed earth and wiggled herself to a soft spot. A satellite passed overhead from North to South, a beacon, beckoning her to the skies.

"What could..." she jumped in her skin and let out a small yelp. "Sorry, I didn't' mean to scare you. I wondered what was taking you so long." Andy looked at her with narrowed eyes, looked down at her lying there, then at her hands and she felt her skin crawl.

{why the hell am I so afraid of him right now}

"Andy, you need to give a heads up or something. I didn't even hear your footsteps" She sat up quickly.

He pointed down at his feet, "Rubber soles."

"Yeah, and I'm about to hang a bell around your neck to alert us."

"You were gone so long we wanted to make sure you were ok. Everything ok?"

She raised herself up, ignoring his hand and dusted her shorts off. She turned on the flashlight and started back to the campsite "Sure, why wouldn't it be?"

"No particular reason, just checking on your welfare."

"I've been taking care of my own welfare for a lot of years. I can do just fine." He turned to her and stopped, making her stop as well, "Did I say or do something to irritate you or offend you?" He didn't look sorry at all, he looked...satisfied.

"She managed a laugh and a wave of the hand, "It's been a long day, I'm very tired and I get cranky when I'm losing sleep. Sorry."

'No problem. We all have cranky days" He then took the lead back to camp and she watched his broad back for … what? She felt very much on edge and wary and it had nothing to do with sleep.

"Did you reach them… anyone?" Rodane was sitting with Agatha and Nikos in the lounge area of the downstairs at the chateau. He had his cup of coffee, the fourth or fifth of the day and Agatha sipped on her water while Nikos drank a beer.

Agatha looked worried and Nikos shook his head in the negative. "No" as Agatha added, "and it's not like them to fall off the grid like this. When did you last speak to Renata?"

"A week ago, when she was still trying to convince me, she wasn't the right one for the job." Rodane scowled at the screen, "You?"

"We haven't heard from her in over a week since she left the training camp."

"Did you try to pin her?" Renata had only recently been found to be one of the 'family' with her biological father being her former parish priest. He had apparently dropped off the face of the earth in the ensuing years. She now had his pin in her possession, the only remnant given to her by him before she left to work for Theras Gallo. She was still adjusting to the facts as they were presented to her by Agatha and still chafing with the remorse she felt, for all those years under the thumb of a monster in a human skin.

"She must not have it in her possession, or she has it but has chosen not to use it. Any ideas?" Rodane was frustrated, "That team was designed to provide security to the real paleontologists and to the two 'family' members, one on each of the other teams. It's been difficult to arrange for them to be on a team in the first place. and if one doesn't show, who might suffer or be in danger?"

"Rodane" Agatha was adamant, "this is too close to fruition for you to be stressed over something that might not even be a problem. Leave that to the others to sort out while we're gone. We haven't heard any bad news so let's not anticipate any."

"My mother, and by the way me, along for the ride, is about to dive in a bathyscape down to the depths of the ocean trenches, be treated for a spreading cancer in a sunken starship from our former world and hope that it works. Nothing to be stressed about you say?"

"We have something we need to inform you of at this point Rodane." Nikos stared at his face, trying to determine how it would affect him.

"Spit it out Nikos, may as well get it all out now and give me time to adjust if I can."

"There will be four of us, not three.'

Rodane looked at Agatha, surprised "I thought you swore never to set foot in a starship again."

"Not me Rodane" She glanced quickly at Nikos as he nodded his head, "The fourth seat is for Eugenie" and she waited for the outburst. Again, he surprised her.

He looked up, happy surprise on his face, no sign of anger

or negative response "That's wonderful. You decided to take her after all?" That was it.

"My boy, you never cease to amaze us" Nikos added.

"Keeps you on your toes, doesn't it?" and he had the nerve to grin.

Back at the camp in Grand Staircase, Ariel sat at the embers of the campfire and avoided the stare of Andy and confusion on the face of Ritchie. She said goodnight and went to her tent. As soon as she entered it, she knew someone had been in there. Not too many choices so she looked for the satellite phone she had hidden under the flap of the tent in the back.

She had placed her tent up against the rock face and had dug out a space the size of a football while the boys had gone to their own porta potty and placed the phone in a plastic bag. She put it in the deep indentation she had made in the dirt, smoothed out and packed the dirt, and put the rock over it. If someone had asked her why she did that, she would have been hard pressed to answer but that she had a gut feeling and they never let her down before. She slept uneasily and lightly and felt tired and draggy the next morning when they woke up. She sat quietly while the two men joked and sparred and finally Andy said he needed to "take a shit" and left for the downward path to the bottom and the back of the outcrop.

"Ritchie, did anything happen while I was gone last night?"

"Like what?" he squirmed on his butt, cleaning his glasses.

"I don't know, that's why I'm asking you." She looked over at him and his color rose, so she knew she had hit pay dirt.

"You may as well tell me because you know I'm going to find out. I always do." She sat quietly and waited him out.

He put his head down and spoke softly, "Andy thinks you're the wrong person to lead this team. He said he should have been the one given the team leadership. That's it. I didn't even answer him, and I wasn't going to tell you because I think he's full of shit."

"Ritchie, did you use my satellite phone while I was gone? I won't mind, I just want to know if you did or not."

"Your phone?" He looked more confused, "Didn't you have it with you when you went uh...down the hill?" he turned redder.

"No, and I don't mind if Andy asked you what we talked about. You can tell him every word we spoke. I'm afraid this will be a rough dig Ritchie. Are you with me?" He looked over at her, gave her that boyish grin of his and said, "All the way girl, all the way!"

Rodane got a call in the early morning before his alarm even went off. Something in Renata's voice was off as he questioned her,

"Where are you and why isn't your team already on the way to Grand Staircase?"

"Didn't anyone call you?"

"No, nothing and why don't you have your pin to keep in contact?"

'It was stolen" Rodane sucked in his breath. "Wait, I don't know who but listen. They wanted to cancel the trip and I convinced them to leave a day or two later instead."

"Why would you do that? What's happened?"

"I must have eaten something that gave me food poisoning. I've been very ill for the last two days and…just wait until I get there tomorrow. Then I'll clue you in." She cut off abruptly, leaving him extremely anxious and puzzled.

Chapter 21

The Dig

There were three teams signed up for this adventure in the deep mountains of Utah. Plans were already being rewritten; finances were at the iffy stage if the Lieutenant Governor could not get approval. Confusion was beginning to show its head in various, expected ways as on any dig and adding those not of the 'family' was bad enough. Now with all the unknowns that could appear without notice, it was looking to be either a great success for them or a catastrophe that unleashed unthinkable results.

Team #2 was already there but no one had contacted Rodane. He had their names, but no files had been sent to him yet, and he knew nothing about them personally. He was mulling over the short conversation that he had with Renata. He was worried about her 'food poisoning' revelation. Over the last two and a half years, he had learned the hard way to be suspicious of anything out of the ordinary. It had saved his life and that of Sabina, his partner, some months ago in Spain.

He had been attacked more than a few times and spent

many hours in pain. He had a new awareness of the situation he found himself in and those he loved as well. His ex-wife Caroline and Sophia had lost a loved one in the stabbing death of Adam. Both had become targets of unknown assailants, some most likely of 'family' themselves. There were rogue men and maybe women who worked to take down all those he had learned about, learned to love and respect and had as much to lose as he himself did. He vowed after Spain and after the attack on Caroline and Eugenie, he wouldn't be caught flat-footed again.

Team #1, with Renata as leader, gave him pause when he considered that one person on that team might be more than they appeared from their files if he ever got them to read. She was ok for now, and many things could happen. She had been in physical training for over sixteen months and only had two months to go but was pulled out for this mission against her wishes. Would he have to deal with her attitude as well?

{she's such a little wildcat when angered}

Team #3 was set up with one of the most revered, renowned paleontology experts in the world, a man he had wanted to meet all his professional life. Professor Wilfred Schultz was well known and respected. Rodane was in awe of the fact that he had volunteered his time without pay when he was approached about joining this dig. He even paid for his own travel expenses just so he could rearrange his schedule to be there. Rodane insisted he be made second team leader if needed, if for any reason, Rodane could not continue. The other team, except for Zoe, as well as most of the volunteers on the list from three different universities and international cities, were totally unknown to him. He did have some of their 'moles' in there but even he didn't know who or how to recognize them. It was a double blind, set up by Agatha and Francis to insure anonymity and safety. In a pinch he could get their names from her or Nikos if he felt a danger was presenting itself.

He rose from his chair and looked out the little porthole of his berth on the *Neptune* where he had been taken two nights ago in preparation for the deep dive to the starship *Mauritius*. It was miles below them off the island they saw from the deck. Agatha was set to arrive here at any time with Quimby as her pilot and Francis, as the pilot of the bathyscape that would dock with that starship. Then there was Emmanuel Duncan and his blueprints. They were transporting Rodane's mother, Iona, and his best friend Eugenie, to do what had never been done before in the entire history of the 'family' here on Earth.

Taking them down to the starship resting on the bottom of the deepest trench in the Pacific was scary enough. Taking them into the interior of the starship and using the lab on board to heal them was something only a sci-fi novel could lay out and produce. He still couldn't wrap his head around what they were about to attempt. It was the only chance to keep his mother alive and to try and return Genie to a functional state and restore her brain activity to allow for a return to normalcy. This was intense, frightening and amazing at the same time.

His mother's terminal cancer was a thing of the present, killing people every minute and taking lives before their time. Too many diseases were still rampant and prevalent in our world of today that devastated families and cut so many lives short before they had reached their potential. The 'family' had helped over thousands of years to aid mankind in advancing medicine, science, chemistry and technology to invent, produce and administer so much knowledge and information. Their one mission was to help us rid whole generations of some of the most hideous and disastrous illnesses on the planet but that came at an enormous cost and danger.

Early on it was easy, since most of humanity was young and still learning small advances such as fire, shards of cut stone used to stab and slice and spears used to hunt and protect themselves. They could only move as fast or as slow as the human population in our time since theirs had developed over time to an advanced civilization in most parts of the Earth. The visitors, going back many thousands of years ago, had assimilated into our world and our cultures. They remained tightknit and had used their advanced knowledge only when it could be inserted into the culture at hand and not reveal their true presence at almost any cost.

If you possessed knowledge far and away more than those around you, would you reveal it to them? Would you give them information that would sound like insanity or delusion without fear of them using it against you or simply laughing at you, maybe institutionalizing or ostracizing you? If there were some who believed you, would it cause a danger to you or those who saw it as a weapon to be used? How much would you reveal that might help them but harm you or yours?

That was the conundrum faced by the star travelers when they began to settle onto our bright blue planet: how to live among mankind in his earliest days and learn their ways and still provide help or creativity to lead humanity farther than they could know or hope to achieve without outside help.

Their main advanced directive was to never interfere in the natural progression of man's cultures, evolutionary gains or their knowledge base unless it was to protect or hide their own inclusion into human's lives. They had few other directives except to use their knowledge to aid that evolution and progression without using their own advanced knowledge and tools to cause occurrences that would unalterably affect all the people on Earth.

It was a tricky, sticky balance on a tightrope that often failed, through no fault of theirs. Those from another world and time found it difficult to prevent humans from sometimes seeing them as gods or goddesses or angels sent to help them and protect them. They incurred anger from priests and magicians or wise men of tribes and factions that made them look like fools or charlatans. They found themselves tortured, locked up for life, burned at stakes, poisoned and otherwise agonizing deaths in many ways when they allowed their goals to overcome their reticence to reveal their knowledge. Then there was the adherence to the directives and their guilt when they ignored some of them.

It worked to man's advantage as well. Starship travelers intermarried with Earth's people and started new generations that were a mix of Earth and their own planet, *Asturia*. After so many dozens of generations of intermarriage, mixed salad populations around the globe and blending of original ethnic cultures and then new 'family' members joining those, it had become almost indistinguishable. Where science and technology were concerned, how much was humanity's enterprises and how much was that of 'family' members? How did they account for their genetic predispositions and uniqueness? How dd they account for all their people spreading rapidly around the globe?

The lines were often very crossed at times and bound to be more so with each passing decade and century. More and more, the directives were forgotten or ignored or simply blurred in the race for medical treatment or cures, new technology that guided whole decades as well as economic safeguards, and fiscal responsibility to protect future generations. There were continually changing cultural impositions of good judgement, new social habits and justice for all those who lived in those times; a lot to consider under any circumstances but especially under their unique ones.

Over one hundred fifty years before this present time, one starship had crashed into the Pacific Ocean and another pod had crashed right before that, filled with rogue travelers; some of *Asturia's* men, filled with anger and hate that their planned insurrection had failed. They had been ejected from their mother ship and sent out to survive or die. There were a few still alive of that group and it seemed like they had conscripted other humans they had joined, to work with them to their own advantage. These were the people they feared the most; those who had nothing to lose and everything to gain in revealing the presence of alien DNA and actual persons alive and working to hide those very differences that made them so valuable. It was power. This trip down to the sunken *Mauritius* was going to be one of subterfuge, complete secrecy and hope that they could do what they were told by their engineer was possible and necessary.

If successful, two women would live, think clearly and function for many years to come. Otherwise, they were faced with their deaths and the possibilities that the trip might be exposed, their 'family' would be in imminent danger and their presence might somehow be revealed as well. Not a positive outcome but one worth the trial and the sweat and hope that went into it. The adage; '*put up or shut up*' was at play here without the advantage of a fun game.

While Rodane was about to embark on a dangerous journey, using tools from another starship planning for arrival from space, to bury a starship in Utah, more were attempting to save a starship in the Pacific and the new tools still there, and begin a new age of enlightenment and technology to spur mankind even farther. Now, how impossible did that scenario sound? He would be here for his mother and Genie, no argument about that. Decisions, decisions! Align the stars, create new light, allow for better life!

Chapter 22

Under the Sea

Rodane stood at the deck of the *Neptune* which was docked and preparing them for the imminent dive with only a few of those present who had signed the consent for total secrecy as a National Emergency. Duncan was not one of them but still there under guard and playing cards below deck with three of the people necessary for running the ship and monitoring the bathyscape *Stellae*, and its four occupants. The captain of the ship had just spoken directly to the president and gotten an all clear for the dive. The *Neptune* was preparing to go out to deeper water to release the *Stellae*. Iona and Genie were placed in the back two seats of the bathyscape that had been reconfigured by Duncan to fold back to a reclining degree. They would be lightly sedated; a minor precaution just so there was no possibility of panic. The *Stellae* would dive thousands of feet down to the deep trench where the starship *Mauritius* had crash-landed so long ago.

He had said his goodbyes to both, the night before. He was almost in tears while holding his mother's cold hands that trembled in his. Iona was pragmatic as always, "Now don't you go and worry yourself about this Roddy. Everything will turn out the way it's meant to be." She looked over at Eugenie in the bed next to hers in the small stateroom below deck. "I know if Genie could tell you, I'm sure it would be the same advice. At least I hope so." She stared sadly over to the still form in the other berth and Rodane wasn't so sure.

Francis was the pilot. Rodane, arguing against him, was still named his second-in-command. The ship was outfitted, the mistakes recognized in the first dive were fixed and the final check had been made the day before in a short dive that passed muster. There was little more they could do other than to just go and hopefully be successful in bringing back those still inside *Mauritius*; either a few at a time over a two-day period, or if one of their landers was still operable, all of them in one with one of the survivors as pilot and Francis piloting the *Stellae* back to the surface with a healthy Iona and Eugenie.

Francis had the key to conjoin with the entry lock. He was hopeful that they would be able to dock. He wasn't sure the key to unlock the docking station would work after all this time but what other choice did they have? Over one hundred years stuck in the bottom of the deep sea was not by choice and their rescue was not even assured but if they were to be rescued, there was little time to waste and nothing to be gained by continuing to try and develop better plans. The filtering systems were almost exhausted, and their oxygen levels had begun to deviate from one day to the next. No, this was it. They either succeeded and brought up seven live survivors and the body of another on this journey or failed and left them to die without ever being able to give them a chance at life on this Earth they had given up so much to reach.

Their continued efforts to reach them by their own communications system had failed. Duncan had attempted to hook into the starship's own signals but apparently it was damaged to the point it was beyond repair. There had been no sign of the one who had alerted them at the port hole by Morse code when the *Stellae* had reached the ship on its first dive with Terrence Gurlow. At least they had not been given that information by Gurlow before he died if he had gotten any. Now it was a matter of luck, time, dependence on the skills of Emmanuel Duncan and the hands of fate in getting them into that ship. That didn't even account for whether they found the medical labs up and running or the means necessary to heal the two going on this journey. If that was successful, could they dare to subvert their own directives and bring up the tools and methods as well as the means to heal both Iona and Genie? What impact could that have on their secrecy?

He gave up on his depressing thoughts and went below to talk to Duncan one more time before their journey began. The card game had ended. Duncan was alone in his compartment, lounging on the bed, reading a comic book.

"Tell me again how we are going to load all the survivors onto the lander if there is one and then bring up all the supplies and tools necessary to heal my two passengers."

A surprised Duncan frowned at him, "I thought you said they were going to be treated down there in their labs."

The tension could be felt in the air between them, "That's the plan but what if it doesn't pan out? What's your alternative for getting them up here with all that they will be carrying?"

"The lander holds how many?" Duncan waited while Rodane thought.

Rodane finally answered testily, 'You don't have to know that."

Duncan remained silent, thinking rapidly to get at the purpose of this seemingly useless conversation. The room was very still until Rodane sighed deeply, "Ok, it can usually hold seven, eight in a pinch."

"Rodane, if you're going to expect me to help you, there needs to be a little more forthrightness in giving me information I need to figure this all out."

"Damn it, I just did. I can't trust you and I can't help that. Now you know!" He glowered at Duncan.

"Yeah, until something else happens and the next time it might be too late for you to reconsider." Then his voice softened, "Look, I know this is difficult with it being your mother and all but…"

"This is not personal, this is me not trusting **you** so let's stick to the script and you do your job and I'll make sure you do, ok?" The seconds slid by while they glared at each other.

Duncan gave first, "If the medical labs can't do what you're expecting, they can put your mom in one vehicle and your friend…Eu…"

"Genie"

"Ok, Genie in the other and then stow the extra seats and redistribute the empty space in both the lander and the *Stellae* to make room for more supplies and parts you intend to bring up. You'll have to leave the deceased traveler in the ship unless you want to make another trip. Much of the supplies can be put onto the racks that have been welded on top of the *Stellae.* That's if they have watertight wrappings or storage units. The water provides buoyancy, so it easily holds more while ascending plus the storage compartments and the claws, all of it done mechanically."

"I never thought of that. You are of some use" and grimly acknowledged that point. He left without another word or nod as Duncan breathed a sigh of relief.

Rodane's nerves were just about shot. He had helped load Iona and Genie into the bathyscape and both were comfortable. Iona was dozing from the sedative given to her, but she held tightly to his hand and whispered "Don't be afraid, Roddy. This is all part of a bigger plan so don't worry. I'll be fine no matter what happens. You must believe that."

"Ok Oma, I'll take your word for it" and he smiled with a stiff expression.

"Liar!" and she smiled back at him, totally at peace and relaxed. He knew it wasn't just from the sedative. Iona was not a church goer, but he realized over the years she had an abiding faith in a higher creator and a greater purpose than just living out a short fragile life on earth. This was not a test for her but an affirmation.

Neptune moved out slowly, with the bright, canary-yellow bathyscape *Stellae,* tied down securely and a guard placed at the opening hatch to prevent anyone from attempting to get in. Francis was driver and Rodane took up the second seat. Both women had fallen into a deep sleep and Iona was wheezing in, and softly whistling with her breath out. Genie remained still and silent, her skin cool and her color heightened to a deeper olive tone. The trip down took less time than the first recorded dive with Gurlow at the wheel. Both men were intent on looking out the small porthole and Rodane took notes on what he saw and watched the depth gauge to alert Francis to any fluctuations.

With each 500 feet, they were alerted by the *Neptune* as to what their oxygen count was, the engine output and the exact speed of the bathyscape. All was going well and soon Duncan announced from the radio,

"You're coming up on the distance Gurlow had reached when he started seeing the ship.

"Roger that" Francis looked over at Rodane, "You ready for this?"

"Would it matter if I said no?" He grinned.

"Nervous?"

'Hell yes! You?"

"Nah, this is old hat even if it's under water." Francis looked over and said sheepishly, "It's damn exciting though to be back in the pilot's seat."

Rodane's eyes widened, "Seriously? You were the pilot from…"

"Yep, I age well, right?"

Rodane didn't answer and Francis could tell his brain was whirling. "I'm old enough to most likely be your great, great grandfather, maybe a lot older."

"How…" Rodane left it hanging.

"All in good time sir, all in good time." He started, "Look" and pointed ahead to the right of the vessel. "Over there!"

Out of the thick, dense grayness, an immense behemoth of metal and rock began to take shape as they drew closer. Sweat broke out on Rodane' forehead and Francis sucked in his breath and guided the vessel closer and closer, then braked. He took out the celluloid plan of the ship and held it up in front of him and compared it to what lay before them in the murky waters. Suddenly, dolphins swam in a circle around them and came right up to the porthole and knocked against it with their snouts, one right after the other.

"Rodane, look at their shape. What do you see?"

Rodane stared at them and after watching them circle once more he said," They're almost pencil thin and…somehow… odd. A new species?"

"I think we're looking at an adaptation that allows them to dive to these greater depths and survive without implosion."

"The pressure at these depths should have caused them to…" he was silent.

"Exactly" Francis stared silently.

Rodane watched him maneuver the controls by slow degrees up, then over, down, then closer still to the upper right of the ship. He stopped and slowly got out of his seat and moved to the back where he took out the decompression suit and began to clothe himself in tight quarters. He looked to Rodane and motioned for him to do the same. Rodane' hands shook as he put on the suit and then Francis helped him to put on his helmet and he tightened Francis' helmet the same way, thumbs up from both. Francis switched on his armband and spoke to the com unit.

"Touchdown fellas! It's a grand 'ole' sight to see." Rodane heard the laughter and cheers from above deck as clear as a cell phone on speaker. He took out the silver tube about 6 inches long and two small wings sprang out of the sides. He turned it around so Rodane could see it as the buttons blinked rapidly up and down the length of it. He spoke into his com unit, "Watch and see how I do this because …if there's a need for one of us to …well, just watch."

Rodane stared at it in total concentration; *yellow, blue, yellow, yellow, green, green, green…pause… red, red, blue.* It let off one beep then two more. The bathyscape began to rise on its own and Rodane felt his stomach take a dive and felt the bile rise in his throat. He took one deep breath, exhaled, then one more and watched as the vessel climbed up then stopped in front of another porthole, almost invisible in the murk. From outside the vessel, Rodane heard a rumble and felt the vibrations as a panel opened from the top of the *Stellae*. He felt the movement as it widened and heard the rumble turn into a rhythmic beeping that stopped when the ship gave off a synthetic voice that chimed, 'Connection complete, waiting for further instructions.'

"You ready?" Francis looked positively giddy.

"What about our two passengers? Can we leave them?"

"Only for a minute, then we have help."

Rodane looked back at two of the most important people in his life and said,

"Ok, let's do this!"

Francis reached up to the top of the cabin and removed the plate fastened by handles to reveal a control panel. He tapped buttons on the panel that mirrored those on the 6-inch silver tool, still blinking in sequence. He watched carefully as the buttons began to light up in faster and faster sequences until they were in perfect sync. A hiss escaped from the rim around the large top hatch, as a latch clicked and the colors ceased. Francis reached up and took the handle of the hatch and twisted it until it began to lower like a vent on a ceiling. Rodane was mesmerized, frightened and exhilarated, all at once. It reached a certain level then swung gently aside and hung silently while Francis and Rodane looked up into an open hatch of the starship, that led into a white lined room big enough to accommodate two or three people. A light was blinking red inside and he could hear a soft klaxon of sorts beyond the door. A ladder was pulled down and Francis began to climb with Rodane right behind him.

When they had crawled up to the open hatch and entered the room large enough to stand upright, Francis stuck the silver tool into the opening to his right with the shape of the wings. He retracted it again and the hiss escaped once more as the hatch clicked and began to slide closed against the wall of the *Stellae's* entrance. The panel in the vessel beneath them remained open. Rodane's nerves were on overdrive, and he was beginning to feel excitement turn to worry. Francis reached out his hand, "Watch the pattern Rodane, ready?" He took the silver tool and pushed a pattern of *red, blue, red, red, yellow, green*. "Repeat the first one to me." Rodane did. "The second one?" Another repetition. "Good man! Remember them. They should realign automatically, but just in case". The hatch closed.

Francis turned around and faced the back of the inner hatch as it opened and Rodane followed suit with trepidation.

{what am I going to find here}

A man stood there with some type of rod in his hand against his side. It didn't look like a gun but what did he know? The figure just stood there, silent and staring at Francis. Francis stared right back.

"Took you long enough. What kept you?"

Francis sounded like a foghorn behind the suit's com system "Oh, almost four generations of people trying to figure whether your asses were worth saving...or not. Not my first choice!"

The figure stepped forward and pushed Francis hard enough to make him skitter backwards. Rodane was ready to get between them. Francis held up his hand, pointed toward Rodane and said, "This man is your new commander so I wouldn't get too frisky if I were you."

The figure stepped back and saluted immediately. "Sorry SIR. Won't happen again, SIR!" Rodane decided to enter the charade, "Make sure it doesn't!"

Francis looked to Rodane, nodded his head slightly. Francis undid his helmet, then went up to the man and grabbed him in a huge hug, clapping him on the back, and Rodane took off his helmet. The three of them stood and stared hard at each other. Finally, the man spoke again,

"Francis, you old devil, how come you're still around to terrorize new recruits and even better, you're still driving after all these years." He looked to Rodane, and said, 'Sir, pardon my being flippant but letting this man drive is asking for a boatload of trouble. We've been here for over a hundred years waiting for another ride and this is who you bring us?" He grinned widely and clapped Francis on the shoulder once again. "Welcome back Commander!"

He turned and swiped his badge over the pad to his left and the door silently unlocked and swung open to a large, brightly lit corridor and what appeared to be a clear elevator ahead. They entered the lift and it rose like a glider, stopping at the first level on the metal panel to his right. As it opened, Rodane found himself faced with the likes of a sight he could never have imagined or been able to describe. It rose so high, he had to crane his neck to even reach the higher levels, not even close to the top.

"Take a look around Rodane; we've got a few minutes before the fun starts. I know you have a thousand questions, but they can all be answered in time. Look around and see what a few thousand years can do for man's future, if we manage to make it there."

The suited man raised his eyebrows and looked at Francis who winked at him and they waited quietly while Rodane did just what he had been invited to do. The lift apparently rose all the way to the top but off to each side were ramps that extended to both halves of the ship like corridors leading to other sections. They were spaced evenly apart with clear glass or some other material that allowed for entrance into closed off partitions and open spaces where a beehive of activity was going on.

There were three men working on one closed panel with welding torches or something akin to them but with no flame. Halfway up, there was a sort of gyroscope surrounding the lift that turned slowly and he could feel the thrum under his feet. He realized it was a gravity conduit that allowed for normal gravity. Two other men were loading supplies of some sort and carrying them to the elevator where they looked down and saluted at the three below them.

Rodane realized he was at a disadvantage, "What's your name if I may ask?"

Francis spoke, "Where are my manners? Rodane, I would like you to meet Lieutenant Cliff Stanoff from the Engineering department. One of the finest engineers I know who got us out of more than a few scrapes on our journey to your world."

Cliff's color heightened at the praise and offered his hand to Rodane to shake. "Glad to meet you, Sir."

Forget the 'Sir' Stanoff. I'm Rodane from here on out."

'Yes Si…Sure Rodane. Glad to meet you, you don't know how much."

Cliff proceeded to point out the levels of the ship and the functions of each level, "There are sections along each side that divide into further sections for crew quarters, dining halls, entertainment, kitchens, Hydroponics and passengers," he swept his arm from one side of the ship to the other, "sick bay and hospital as well as nursery, labs, engineering, transport, more passenger's quarters and all the other parts of keeping people alive on a journey from one star to another. I would take you on a tour, but time is of the essence I believe?" looking at Francis. "For now, I want you to meet the rest of the crew and you can give them instructions as to what you need to get us out of here."

Francis grimaced, "I have some news from above and I don't know how you'll take it, but it has to be dealt with immediately." He proceeded to lay out the case of Iona and Eugenie and those above waiting to see if they could establish communications to see them through it. Cliff listened intently, nodding his head with folded arms and Rodane realized all sounds from before had ceased and he looked up to see five men poised on level two above them, just waiting.

"There, that's the gist of our concerns and our needs. What do you think?"

Cliff shook his head, "Never thought I would be glad and

disappointed at the same time, but my men have been waiting for…"

"Understood and I know how much this is to ask but…"

"No, not disappointed at your request, just disappointed we couldn't have done this sooner and brought you our technology faster for all those it might have helped. Of course, you can ask, that's why we came here, wasn't it? What are a few hours or even a day to do what we've waited to do for over a century? How many of our people can say that?" He gave instructions to two men who immediately took the tool form Francis to open the bathyscape and went down to the elevator and the *Stellae.*

Rodane found himself choking up with a lump in his throat. All his arguments against them being here or doing what they came to do dissolved in that moment and he knew just what a boon these other star travelers were. He was a part of it. It made him feel…humble…ashamed it took him so long to realize. He still had questions, doubts, fears but it was nothing to the realization and pride he took in making an entire planet strive to do better and he was to help them find the means to do so. That was going to be his duty and his responsibility in the future; act more civilly, treat others with the respect they wanted for themselves and help everywhere. So, he had to man up!

"Ok, let's meet the others and get started on your preparations." Cliff pushed a button on the elevator panel, and it whisked them to the upper reaches. One of his men went to sit with Iona and Genie until it was time to act.

Chapter 23

More help Coming

Grand Staircase Escalante might be a shock to those who see it the first time. Some might be extremely disappointed it doesn't look like Zion or Bryce or the Grand Canyon or Arches. But after a few days there and traveling from one canyon to another, most are entranced and dying to go around the next bend or hike through the next slot canyon. They then realize it would take them weeks to get to know the entire canyon, if then. A once in a lifetime trip would begin to look like more than one trip to most people. It is in amazingly good shape, few footprints from man or animal, no litter and sights that lead to extraordinary hikes many might think they could never accomplish.

Those there now, taking part in a dig, surprised themselves at the resilience they felt, the exhilaration they had coursing through their veins watching a sunrise from a tent or sitting on a high rise looking at an awesome sunset, drinking lukewarm coffee from their almost empty supplies. They were absolutely mesmerized, except for six people slogging through muddy trails left over from the flash storm they had the night before.

It blew out their tents, upturned their supplies in the aftermath and left grit and sand in each person's mouth that caught them unawares. The half-track vehicle carrying all the digging equipment had its own troubles, getting stuck on the steep inclines and heavy mud, causing them to slide and skew sideways at precipitous overhangs on very narrow trails. They made it to camp with everyone complaining about the trip and the women in the group telling tales of scary, slippery bends in the road where one simpered and whined, **"thought I was going to die!"**

They unloaded the half-track and the driver left to return to town. He would return in a week to resupply them with food and drinking water. They proceeded to whine about having to sort, catalogue and prepare for the group meeting in three hours that would assign them their tasks for the next two weeks. Renata looked around her and raised her eyes to the heavens which she addressed in a low voice removed from most of the other people there, "Why did I ever agree to this? How stupid was I to leave right before I was done?" She folded her arms around her and ducked her head into her lap.

She jumped at the voice, "Yeah…I was thinking the same thing. No amount of money is worth this aggravation for what, some old bones?"

She turned her head slowly and looked over to a man at least in his thirties, tanned, rough-shaven, chugging from a soda bottle, looking at her with interest.

"Want a real drink?" He offered and she smelled it and realized it was anything but soda. She was about to tell him he would be in big trouble if they found out he had alcohol on this dig but decided to keep it to herself.

"No thanks, I'm good" and pulled up her water bottle.

He put out his hand, "I'm Cosimo, like the Italian Medici. Glad to work with you."

An alarm bell went off for no discernible reason other than she had met many men like this over the years, hitting on someone they saw as interesting or a possibility of a little fun on the job. Better not to alienate them from day one.

She chuckled a little, "Well, at least you're not one of the Borgias, all a bunch of bloodthirsty scoundrels."

"Oh, I see we have a historian here, I'll have to watch my step."

"Well, it was nice meeting you. I better get cleaned up for the meeting in a short while."

She rose, dusted off the sand and dirt from her shorts and waved her hand at him as she walked toward the common tent. There was a shower set up with recycled water from a barrel connected to the pipes, cold of course and a curtained off area for privacy. As she entered the tent, ducking her head, she looked back surreptitiously and saw him still standing there watching her. She didn't stop and kept her head down in one move. She realized he hadn't asked her name.

{huh! one to watch}

They spent the better part of the evening checking lists, being assigned their posts and reading articles about the site they were about to tackle. Question and answer period took them to almost ten and Renata was tired to the bone and eager to go to bed. The next morning would start at dawn. Just then, Cosimo came up to her and stood too close and still smelled of alcohol. She stood waiting for him to make the first move. "First, I realized I didn't get your name and second, would you like to have a drink with me before bed?" He leaned close to her and she found it hard not to step backwards but held her ground, "No, I'm dead tired from today and I think I'll pass on the drink. It usually leaves me with a headache when I drink at night. Thanks, anyway, see you tomorrow".

{there, didn't turn him off or challenge him by ratting him out}

The next morning, she went to the common tent, used a porta potty, took an apple for midway through the day and went back to her own tent and washed up, then dressed in the same clothes as yesterday. It was going to be a long two weeks if their plans didn't work out.

Rodane had told her the bare workings of their week and he was of the opinion things could go even quicker if they soon contacted the starship. He was going to try and be here by mid-week if all went well with his mother and Genie. She stopped and thought of herself and Genie. They hadn't seen each other since Spain and before that, they were enemies. That changed when they both spent time at Rodane's mother's house for healing and planning. In the end, they had been 'frenemies' and that wasn't half-bad really. Maybe when they both had returned home…

{no, best to leave sleeping dogs lie}

She was up at dawn and took the opportunity to get breakfast in an empty main tent and wash quickly at the showers. As the others slowly came in, some were bleary-eyed and flinching from possible hangovers.

{serves you right for partying and drinking until past midnight}

They started right in after breakfast; measuring and 'stringing' areas for digging, handing out tools and assignments, taking attendance with a short 'meet and greet' and two hours of reviewing documents of previous finds in this part of Utah. That kept everyone's interest. Pictures were passed around of artifacts previously uncovered to give them an idea of what they were to look for.

Most were volunteers; students of Archaeology or Historical Pre-history' undergraduate or graduate students of various disciplines. Some were never a digger before or even a secondary cleaner or helper and a few were there simply because they knew someone who knew someone. They would drag them all down and waste time, but some got lucky and surprisingly, enjoyed the experience.

Renata didn't have any previous digging experience, but she knew how to use a shovel and she also knew how to size up people while she got the lay of the land. Everyone had heard through the grapevine; the grapevine being Orson and Claudia, her teammates, that she arrived late because of food poisoning so most were concerned and very solicitous. They kept her from lifting heavy equipment and told her to take water breaks more frequently which she was glad to do in the baking sun. By mid-afternoon, they all felt the heat and the strain on otherwise strained muscles and backs. She kept her ears open, listened to conversations while she was taking her 'breaks' and watched all the young people socializing and scoping each other out. That thought made her smile since she was also one of the 'young' people, but she felt anything but that.

"How can you smile when it's this uncomfortable? What's your secret?"

She turned and found herself staring at Cosimo with another man standing next to him with dark glasses examining her. The other man, having a chunky build but muscular, and a heavy, dark beard, stared. She felt the heat rise in her face and the shiver that went down her spine. She felt like a bug on a tray; pinned down and preparing to be an experiment.

She looked directly at them, "I've been waiting for this trip for months and it feels good to be here, heat and all. Why are you here if it's this uncomfortable?"

She looked at both in turn and waited for a response. The other man shifted from one foot to the other and remained quiet. The beard threw her off for a few seconds but then she realized who she was looking at and the shiver became a pit in her stomach and a foggy haze over her eyes for an instant of panic. She wanted to throw up her breakfast but put her hands under her and took in shallow breaths.

Cosimo smiled but left her cold. "We're gluttons for punishment and we've been looking forward to this for almost two years now. We'll adjust and the trip will have been worth it all, don't you think?" He tilted his head at her. She gathered her courage and jumped up from her spot, "I'm Renata and you are?" She stared at the other silent man."

At this point Cosimo jumped in "Oh, I didn't even get your name last night. How stupid of me and discourteous. This is Andy, a friend of mine from college, many years ago."

Andy reached out his hand and clasped hers firmly and muttered something indistinguishable. She could not help herself; she pulled her hand away and backed up a step.

"Well, my break's over so I'll leave you two to bake in the sun. Nice meeting you Andy. Maybe we'll run into each other." She walked away in the opposite direction and refused to look back. She would not give either of them the satisfaction. She knew without a doubt, this was a planned meeting, designed to see if she recognized Andrew McCarty and what her reaction would be. This was the second time Cosimo had come up on her and she hadn't realized he was there. That had to stop.

There was a huge white tent set up with baskets outside for people to take if they thought they had found something of worth. There were runners assigned to each area to fetch baskets and take them to the tent for 'panning' and labeling if there was something there. She headed in since no one was allowed in except the leaders of the teams and their resident archaeologist who still had not arrived. She drew the flap open and hurried into an unmovable body, stumbled and grabbed the hand offered to her and looked up to see a young woman well-known to her and blurted out, "Zoe!"

"*Shh!* It's *Ariel* and you don't know me! She put her finger to her lips and looked toward the tent to make sure no one could have heard them. She pulled

Renata over toward the back corner of the tent and spoke quickly,

"Meet me tonight at the showers. I need to talk to you but make sure no one realizes we know each other…and bring your pin" She turned and left the tent before Renata got over the suddenness of their meeting.

Renata's eyes followed her and listened to any noises approaching. She went over to the large table and grabbed some small tools and headed back out only to run into one of the members of her team, Claudia. The woman was striking, dark-haired of Middle Eastern heritage and was one of the smartest and most knowledgeable historians Renata had ever met. They quickly became friendly, and Claudia was the one who stayed with her when she was so ill that she couldn't get up from the bathroom floor the night she had been sick. She brought her weak tea, made sure she was able to navigate on her own for the two days she was still somewhat ill afterwards. They talked well into the night right before they arrived at Escalante and learned about each other's likes and dislikes including preferences in men.

"Who was that who just left here?" Claudia went over to the table and chose a shovel with a pointed tip and a stiff apron to try and keep dirt to a minimum on her own clothes.

"One of the other team leaders that's been here for a while."

"What did she want?" Renata's antenna went up,

"Why do you ask?"

"No reason, except the scowl on her face when she hurried past me, was something I tuned into. Was she upset with you about something?"

Renata decided to tread carefully, "Not with me. I think maybe she was tired and a bit grouchy. Maybe she was one of those that stayed up late last night and are now paying the price."

"Huh! I think most of them are sorry they even came at this point. They must have hangovers. Wasn't alcohol on the list of no-nos?"

Renata chuckled, "Can't argue with stupid, can you? They'll always find a way."

They left together and started back toward their assigned area and met up with two volunteers that would carry away the dirt and take the sifted residue to the examining tent for closer look. They spent the height of the day steaming in the heat and made little inroads into the depth they were aiming for. Afternoon break was for water, fruit, and a review of everyone's efforts. Team three had finally arrived and they were hard at work trying to play catch up. Their leader was an older man, heavy- bearded, very overweight and wearing a Panama Jack hat that allowed for shade. He was sweating profusely and had a hanky in his hand to wipe away the sweat pouring down his face. Renata walked over to him and extended her hand,

"Professor Shultz, I presume? I'm Renata Kappos, Team One. It's good to finally meet you. Can I get you some water?"

"Well, thank you Renata, I'm just thinking if I stand here in the sun and sweat, I might lose a few pounds." He looked at her and waited. She was taken aback. After a few silent seconds, she answered him, "If that's a proven method, why are you not extremely rich and famous?"

"Who says I'm not?" Then he grinned to break the ice.

That night, after sandwiches and salad outside for some breeze, Renata excused herself, went to her tent and gathered towel, soap and shampoo and headed for the showers. She made sure everyone saw her carrying her things and waved to those who looked over to her. She ducked her head under the tent opening and put the sign on the outside of *'occupied'*. The tent was big enough to fit a tall or heavy person under the one spigot that gave five minutes of timed water. They were lucky if three people could wash before it turned cold but still, better than nothing. She waited for a few seconds and jumped when a voice came from back of the tent against the rock walls.

"Renata, if you can wash, dry off and then head for the "latrines" down the path, meet me there in five minutes. Did you bring your pin?"

"No, it was stolen while I spent the night over the toilet."

"What?"

"Tell you about it when I get there. Is it just us?"

"Unless someone wants to crash our party and that wouldn't be wise for them."

Renata enjoyed getting a fresh spurt of warm water and quickly washed her hair and body and toweled off in less than three minutes. She gathered her things and went out the tent opening, turned the '*occupied*' sign over and headed toward the portable latrines. She rounded the corner of the pathway and a hand snaked out and grabbed her arm. She was about to punch out when Ariel whispered, "*Shush*! Step over here."

There was thick brush that covered an open space and veered away into a dense undergrowth at the base of the mountain. Ariel led her some yards away zigging and zagging until they were out of sight completely, about 100 yards and were totally removed from sound and sight and the mountain loomed behind them, rising to heights that seemed to touch the graying, low clouds. Dusk was settling in slowly and bird noises were dropping away as they headed for their perches and nests.

They sat on the dry ground, while both took in deep breaths as if they had run a distance. Ariel spoke first,

"Tell me about your pin being stolen. Any idea how it happened or who it could be? Think it was just because it's a pretty piece of jewelry?"

"Whoa, hold on Zo…Ariel…one question at a time. No, I have no idea who or why, but I don't think it's any coincidence. Not when we know there's a chance there are moles here and they have their own agenda. Tell me about your team."

"Well, Ritchie is a dear, last year in college studying for Forensic Science and eager to be part of a dig and get his hands dirty. He's kind of naïve and very pleasant but makes some rash decisions."

"Wow, you've had him under a microscope, seems like. The other?"

"Andy's a little harder to figure out. He…" She stopped and the expression on her face was one of being perplexed and irritated. Renata waited and when she got no more from Zoe, she asked, "What aren't you admitting to me or maybe yourself as well?"

Zoe looked surprised, "It's that easy to read me?"

"Only when you consider how much we've been blind-sided lately and the need for both of us to be brutally honest, even with our own feelings. The other? What do you get from him?"

"Arrogance, distrust, secrecy and dishonesty."

"Well, that about covers it, don't you think?"

"One more thing; he makes my skin crawl."

Renata leaned back on her butt and clasped her hands around her knees and rocked back and forth, keeping her silence. Zoe watched her closely.

"You know something don't you Renata? Spill!"

"You only saw him once and that was while he was moving fast. I don't expect you to remember while all hell was breaking loose…"

"What are you talking about, who was moving, what hell was breaking loose?"

"Shrine of St James, the accident on the road that was

no accident, Sabina and…" Zoe's eyes widened, "Rodane? You're talking about the attempt on their lives in Spain? Who…no…you can't mean…"

"Andrew McCarty is here, and his name today is Andy, full beard, mustache, about 30 lbs. more on his frame…perpetual sunglasses…the same."

"We've got to call Rodane or Agatha or…" She jumped up and spat out, "that slimy bastard! No wonder I never trusted him from the beginning. All this time…did he know who I was or that we're here to…"

I don't know but I'm not going to try and find out from him. That would be too suspicious if we started pressing him for background, especially if he knows who you are."

Zoe began pacing back and forth and Renata grinned at her and said, "Sit down Rodane." Zoe's neck swiveled, "What?...

"That's what Rodane does when he's thinking or stewing."

"Does it work with one pin? I'm new at this." She dropped down to a sitting position, legs crossed and pulled out her gold pin with cut out mountains and jungle at the edge of water.

"Let's find out." Zoe took her pin off her shirt and handed it to Renata who sat it on the ground and turned it so that one point was stretching to both seated. Nothing happened so they joined hands, shifted their seats so they each had a point facing them. The air glimmered, dust particles floated in front of a wavy, expanding shimmer of a figure taking on shape and substance.

"Hello girls. Is there something that needs immediate attention?" Agatha hung in the air, floating about two feet off the ground.

They spent about thirty minutes going over all they had been through in the last few days and Zoe had read her in on all the doings of her team. Then Renata told of her days of food poisoning, the theft of her pin and the realization of the presence of Andrew McCarty. Agatha looked at them over her spectacles perched on her nose and grinned despite herself,

"You've been terribly busy for the first days of the dig. I guess I need to get used to you two getting into mischief whenever I put you both together, yes?"

Renata was about to respond when she closed her mouth tightly and waited to gauge how serious Agatha was being. One thing she had learned quickly, from working in this 'family' was patience, and thinking each thing through before responding.

"You were right to contact me girls. I'm going to pass this on directly to Rodane and he will either get in contact with you at the first moment he can or...show up...as he often does. Anything else?" they shook their heads slowly, "then I will be going and ask you to keep your head down and your eyes open"

Zoe murmured, "How can we spot anything with our heads down at our feet?" and she giggled.

"I heard that young whippersnapper!" as Agatha too, grinned.

Chapter 24

Healing Hands

Iona was awake and involved with one of the men who would be treating her, asking myriad questions, yawning every so often, still groggy from the sedative she had been given for the way down. Here they had put her on a sled that gyrated in any direction and strapped her in while hauling her up from the *Stellae*, then repeated the maneuver bringing Genie to the upper level of the Starship *Mauritius*. Genie lay there still, while the trained engineer examined her and put her through a test or two, using the smallest equipment Rodane had ever seen for medical testing, a tiny phone in appearance, with lights.

Iona was entranced by the 'gadgets' as she called them and lay focused and alert as possible while everything was done with efficiency and expertise. The persistent pain in her gut was silenced with an intravenous drip of unknown medicines but it was doing the trick, so she wasn't questioning it, just enjoying a few painless moments in a very long while.

"We'll be finished here in just a moment." Cliff turned to

the two of them and nodded his head toward the exit door. Rodane looked at Francis and shook his head '*no*'. Francis shook his head slightly to Cliff who frowned at them and continued the testing.

Iona spoke so quietly they hardly heard her," You two can run along now like good boys and let the doctor do his magic."

"Mom, I didn't come all this way to be shut out. I can handle this. You know I can."

Cliff answered, "You can't be in here while I use the proton gun. The radiation is too high for anyone, even me. I work from the outer room in full hazmat suit."

Rodane squared his shoulders, "Then explain it to me if you want me to leave her here. Otherwise, find me another suit."

Francis looked annoyed, "Now Rodane, we've gone to enormous lengths to do this. It isn't the time to…"

"No, it's exactly the time…I should have done it an hour ago."

Cliff put down his gloves, turned to them on the stool where he was seated and motioned to the two stools on their side of the bed.

"As a cancer treatment, proton therapy allows for the treatment of multiple, different types of tumors. It's performed with a specific machine that often weighed more than 100 tons when we first developed it."

"Still does" said Francis "at least on this planet. When did it develop to that extent?"

"As long as I've been alive, it's been gradually getting smaller in size but larger in results." He pointed to the corner of the room and motioned to a machine the size of a large double door refrigerator with a panel set into the left-hand side door and had a row of blinking lights back and forth. "We had almost managed to make it even smaller right before we set out on our exploration and settlement. I would imagine it's even smaller now." his tone, one of nostalgia and wistful.

Iona spoke more clearly now turning her head to Cliff, "Explain it to me in simple terms if you can"

Cliff looked at her, "Proton therapy, also known as proton beam therapy, is a form of radiation treatment used to destroy tumor cells. Instead of using x-rays like regular radiation treatment, it uses protons to send beams of high energy that can target tumors more precisely than X-ray radiation. This is preferable to older methods of non-invasive tumor treatment like X-ray therapy because it allows doctors to target tumor cells while doing minimal damage to surrounding tissue."

Rodane asked abruptly, "Like what?"

"X rays, as with radiation, can include hair loss around treatment sites, digestive issues, headaches, possibly some diarrhea and mild pain. But for most people they're not severe and very brief." Cliff looked at Iona.

"So… how do you know how much to blast or bombard or whatever you do…?" Rodane was not satisfied yet.

"Precision is a major part of proton therapy treatments. We can home in on your tumors and the surrounding tissue to an almost miniscule degree. Your medical team has already done all the groundwork in gathering images of your tumors prior to treatment. You were required to undergo several medical imaging procedures, including CT or MRI scans. That's saved us a lot of time and helped us isolate the areas we need to protect.

"Many patients go about their normal daily lives after a session. Most patients require multiple sessions of proton therapy treatment to see results, which doctors track using medical imaging technology. We can thank your doctor here for making that possible by having you wear a monitor that tracks the radiation levels and the factors to look for like blood counts and pressure levels. Proton therapy is the most technologically advanced method to deliver radiation treatments to cancerous tumors available today on your planet or ours. You will be one of the lucky ones to have it delivered to you."

Francis spoke up in surprise, "How would her doctor know…"

"You'll have to answer that one yourselves. I just know the files you gave me included all the information I would need to build the monitor and our lab is working on it now while I perform the treatment."

"If it doesn't work?" Iona surprised Rodane with the first negative remark she had spoken so far.

"Well, I'm no magician but I can almost guarantee it will work. A lot of it depends on your state of health and right now, it's very stable and remarkably strong. Your doctor must be very…"

"My doctor is invariably one of you! That's a guess but she knows Nikos well and that's a sure sign if nothing else is." Iona grinned at Francis and Rodane. "How does it work?"

"As simply as I can make it, both standard radiation therapy and proton therapy work on the same principle of damaging cellular DNA. The major advantage of proton therapy treatment over standard radiation therapy, however, is that protons slowly deposit their energy as they travel towards the cancerous tumor and then due to a unique physical characteristic called the Bragg Peak, deposit most of the radiation dose directly into the tumor and travel no further through the body. This means healthy tissues and surrounding organs don't receive unnecessary radiation and that reduces unwanted complications and side effects.

X-rays will continue traveling through the body until exiting out the other side resulting in the delivery of unnecessary radiation to healthy tissues and organs. So, it's a win-win for us and you. It's very quick; about a half hour to an hour."

Iona turned her head to Rodane, "Are you satisfied Roddy? I know I am. I told you I was willing to do this and I still am. I'm even more sure now that it might be the only chance you get to have me around to pester you a little longer."

"What happens after? How do you know it's been successful?"

"Here's the magic." Cliff leaned in, "After the proton blaster has done its work, the nanobots are sent in to clean up any debris left from the disease and that speeds up healing in hours so that we can get results by the time we reach the surface and get you to a medical facility that has the necessary machines to test with blood samples." He looked very proud of himself. If what he said was true, he deserved to be as they all did.

Rodane looked at him steadily as if to ascertain if he was being perfectly honest and confident or just trying to quiet his fears. His mom seemed at peace with the explanation so he leaned over his mother to kiss her forehead and he murmured, "I'll see you soon. Love you." Cliff told them he would send for them when she was awake. Francis led them out of the lab and closed the door behind Rodane. "Let's go and watch from the outer lab if you want."

"I don't think I'm ready for that. How about we get to see the rest of the ship. It will most likely be my only chance… ever."

Francis looked delighted, "Let me show you the upper deck and the control room….and the hydroponic gardens and…" he was like a kid in a candy shop.

The second day of the dig was hotter than the first and that was an accomplishment. They all sweated through the early morning hours when the temperatures were only 95-103 degrees by noon and slowly rose to another five degrees in the next four hours. Everyone took a siesta in the late afternoon with fans going and ice crushed in plastic bags at their heads and feet. They had dug over fifty wheelbarrows of dirt and still had found nothing but more rock and dirt. Not even any bones new or old to be found.

Renata had met up with Professor Schultz and they had spent an hour discussing the area and the possibilities based on the other digs that uncovered the Lythronax, first discovered by BLM employee Scott Richardson in 2009. This entire area had now become one of the most inaccessible regions of the United States: Kaiparowits Plateau of southern Utah. On Oct. 23, 2013 – A remarkable new species of tyrannosaur has been unearthed in Grand Staircase-Escalante National Monument. At 80 million years old, Lythronax became the geologically, oldest tyrannosaurid dinosaur ever discovered.

This vast and rugged region, part of the National Landscape Conservation System administered by the Bureau of Land Management (BLM), was the last major area in the lower 48 states to be formally mapped by cartographers. There was a rub to finding that particular specimen. Renata and her fellow workers were digging into what might be a calamity of unknown proportions if they were to stumble across what was buried at this very site they were now digging up, with each wheelbarrow of earth.

Ten thousand years earlier than the present time, an entire expedition of 'family' members had crash-landed their starship into that mountainside, and it had subsequently been buried under tons of rock that formed the present mountain, due to a horrific earthquake and landslide. Before the ship was totally buried, the survivors had managed to retrieve much of the tools they needed to survive and supplies to keep them alive. They had then continued to live there. The terrain was ice-covered in many areas, bone numbing cold and frost for most of the year that gave them chilblains when they left their warm tents and distant caves.

Finally, after many deaths, possible starvation and disease in that final year on the Kaiparowits Plateau amid the canyons of the Escalante, they voted to move Southeasterly toward gentler lands. They had heard about those lands from other tribes of indigenous people. Before they left, they took all the instruction disks, tools and written journals they had kept in the ship and blew up the remaining portions of the mountain hanging on by a few hanging cliffs and watched as their last link to the stars was gone from them forever under more hundreds of tons of rock and dirt.

Now, descendants of that 'family' had been sent by them to finish the job and rebury the ship that was only a few hundred feet under the surface. They could not afford to let the ship be discovered by anyone, much less the paleontologists and scientists begging to be given licenses to scramble over the hills, dig into the side of the mountain and possibly… even likely, discover the ship.

Renata and '*Ariel*' *(Zoe)* had located a small hidden stand of dense bushes behind a rock pile which they could scurry to in the dusk. They needed to discuss what had to be done next. They were both weary and dehydrated yet eager to get this over with. The fact that Andrew McCarty was now here, and recognized Renata made the task even more dangerous and difficult. It all depended on the instructions from home and they were not forthcoming. It was three more days until they would be driven out to town and allowed to roam free for a couple of hours and use landlines to contact their people.

"Ok, when are they supposed to enter our solar system? It's been almost a week. Weren't they supposed to be out of the Black Hole by now and headed for…?" Zoe was frustrated at the timeline.

"*Phobos*, they were leaving *Triton* for *Phobos* but weren't sure how long it would be if anything went sideways. I think no one has heard anything."

"I can hardly wrap my head around all of this. Did you ever think you would be…"

"Nope, not in a million years…though now it seems it's more than that." *Sheesh!*" Renata also chaffed at the delay.

Chapter 25

Mountain High and Sea So Deep

Rodane was pacing outside the closed corridor leading to the medical unit. It had been two hours and he was getting more antsy by the minute, watching the beehive of workers from his perch on the upper level. He had about five coffees down and was ready to go for more when Francis stepped out of the double doors that '*whished*' behind him. They both moved to the clear glass and peered down at the brisk work going on down below.

"You know they're packing up and loading their tools and supplies? Francis peered at him, "Your mother is doing just fine and already coming out of the anesthetic. They'll be moving her to the recovery area in a few minutes, but you need to go and see for yourself how she is."

Rodane didn't need a second invite. He went through the double doors and a med tech met him at the end of the short corridor. "Sir, you need go through the contamination tube. I'll meet you on the other end and provide you with your mask and suit. You need to strip down sir. Just leave your clothes on the floor, they'll be cleaned and returned to you."

"He didn't question it, didn't argue, just followed instructions, put on the suit and mask as he left the tube. The tech was waiting outside a door with an X marked on the door to his right with, **No access Without Tech** on it. Inside, Iona was lying quietly on snow white sheets, face at rest, a peaceful expression on her face. When she heard the door open, she opened her eyes and smiled at Rodane and reached out her hand to him. "Well son, as you can see, I'm still here and you can tell Cassie when you see her, it was a piece of cake!"

"I'm going to let you be the one who tells Cassie when you see her." The *whish* of the door had him turning and seeing Francis and Cliff with grins on their faces. Cliff stepped forward and addressed both, "I'm happy to tell you, there are no signs of the cancer that was spreading in your body. We'll take another look in a few hours and if all is as it should be, we'll be ready to release you for the return journey. I can follow up with you in a few days after we've arrived at your destination."

He grinned at Iona, "I can't tell you how excited my crew is at the thought of taking you up with them far better than when you arrived here." Francis signaled to Rodane, "Could I have a few words with you please?"

Rodane kissed his mom on the forehead, "I'll be right back." He looked at Francis askance, "What's up? Is something wrong?"

"Not wrong, Rodane, just worrying. They've been testing Genie or trying to test her with a scan before they attempted to invade her unconsciousness. They can't get through."

"What do you mean they can't get through? Through what? Her brain, her scull?"

Francis rubbed his face with both hands and put his

hands up in the air and breathed out in a *whoosh*! "I've never seen anything like this, and I have seen plenty over the years. She's blocking them from entering, from even letting the machine show us her outer skull, much less her inner brain. It's like a fog over the screen."

"What are you saying, that's she's doing this? Maybe the machine is..."

"The machine is fine, we tested it on two crew members, and it's working perfectly. But not on her. She's blocking it."

"How is that possible? From what I know, Genie is an awesome protective service detail but has no links to the actual 'family'. She has no special skills or abilities."

"We all beg to differ. She has an enormous amount of skill and amazing ability to shield herself from whatever seems a threat to her." One of your trade secrets that might have been latent perhaps?"

"Can I see her?"

"That's why I'm here. We thought if anyone knows her, you do, and time is of the essence unless you want us to leave and ascend to the surface with her in her present state." We can do that, but I can't guarantee what her state will degrade to under pressure in the bathyscape coming and returning since we can't get a read on her."

"So, it's my call?" Rodane now held his head in his hands and let out a huge breath. "Ok, let's do this." They walked toward the other end of the walkway leading to the opposite side of the ship.

She was also lying in a bed with snow white sheets but with a tech seated at her bedside while a blood pressure cuff was reading her signs. The sound of pressure rising on her arm and the beeping of the monitor at her head were the only sounds in the room. Rodane sat down where the tech had been and reached for her hand. It was cool and flaccid as he rubbed his fingers over each of hers. He didn't say anything, just sat there looking at her. Her fingers stiffened and she slowly pulled her hand away and placed it under the covers. His face registered surprise and curiosity, "Did she make any moves at all with either of you?"

"No", they both said in unison. "Nothing at all."

He thought for a moment, "Genie, do you know who I am?" He waited and she didn't respond. "It's Rodane, Genie, can you hear me? Do you know where you are? Genie, you're on the *Mauritius* and in the medical unit. They're trying to bring you back to us Genie, do you understand that? We…I… need you back with us. Won't you help us?"

The silence was deafening as she remained still, now tight-lipped and her body was stiff. Rodane leaned over and whispered something in her ear. Seconds went by and she slowly lifted a hand from under the covers and Rodane picked it up and held it lightly. They remained like that for minutes and tears leaked from her eyes and ran down her cheeks. He took a tissue and wiped them from her face and tightened his hand on hers. He looked once more at her face and whispered once more in her ear. Then he stood up and signaled to Francis, "Have them try again" seeing Francis' face, "Just once more and if it doesn't work, we'll prepare to move her back to the bathyscape and we can begin the return trip."

Francis began… "What's different, what if…"

"What have we got to lose at this point?" Rodane just cocked his head and waited. Francis gave the signal, and the tech readied the stretcher to return to the MRI-CT Scan cubicles. The monitor continued beeping as they went out the door.

The sky was a cerulean blue with hints of purple and pink, the soft clouds wafting across the mountain. Rising high to the East, a breeze somewhat mitigated the heat of the coming hot day on the dig. Not too much had been accomplished with a soaking rain two days before. They planned to make up for it now with all teams awake and active. That was a good thing for Renata and Zoe, since it had given them two days of inactive digging.

Zoe had a gift. Give her a math problem and in seconds she could predict day and time to the minute if nothing went wrong on the other end. Agatha had given them the coordinates of the *Asternum II*, and *Phobos*, the second moon of Mars. Zoe predicted an arrival in two days which would bring them to tomorrow if all went as planned. The further collapse of the mountain they were digging into would be hours away.

Now they needed to come up with a reasonable excuse to halt the dig right before that. It was a slim margin for error and if people continued digging, they could be in danger. If it was halted and the *Asternum II* met any hindrances, it would be for nothing and soon it was almost certain to reveal what was under the original collapse; a starship from thousands of years ago buried under those tons of earth and rock. Cosimo and Andy had kept their distance but also kept their eyes on both Renata and Zoe. It was unnerving but at least the two women could know what both men were up to.

As with any mystery in real life, the options needed to solve their problems were limited and depended on the expertise and the knowledge of those trying to solve it. Agatha was sitting in her own room at the compound, trying but failing to come up with a solution to so many problems with this scenario. Her head was spinning and her patience was almost exhausted. No one dared to interrupt her and time was running faster than she could think. So many things had occurred in the last two weeks that she was not sure where to begin to sort them out. She ticked them off in her mind, from what she considered the most important to those items not in jeopardy at this moment.

a. Prepare for the arrival of the survivors of *Mauritius* from the ocean and the crew of *Asternum II* when they came through their Black Hole to Phobos.
b. Get Rodane from his mother's bedside to Utah.
c. Get information from Cassie about the attack on her home and Cassie herself as well as Jacob, without reading him into their 'family'
d. Find the pin stolen from Renata and the culprit as well.
e. Notify the President of the trip down in the bathyscape and the ship from the planet *Asturia.*
f. Find out what Eugenia was keeping from them for her healing to begin.

She thought she had them in order but that didn't mean something couldn't become more pressing that she wasn't aware of at this moment. The knock on the door almost had her jumping when she had said no intrusions. She answered,

"Enter". Suri came to her and spoke gently, "Agatha, The *Mauritius* is now at the surface and Rodane needs to see you if possible. He claims it's urgent."

"Sure he does! Everyone here thinks their problems are the most urgent and require my immediate attention." Suri remained silent as Agatha listened to herself and flushed. "I'm sorry Suri, that was uncalled for. Of course, tell him I'm available now." A minute later, Rodane came in and sat down, not even a 'May I?'

"You're back! Good to see you." Agatha waited. "Agatha, I need to go to Utah and I can be there by tonight if you allow Quimby to fly me there. He has already agreed and is getting his plane ready as we speak."

{*well, that takes care of having them in order now*}

She tried not to lash out at him as she felt all this unravelling before it even started. Maybe it was time for her to plan on retirement sooner rather than later. She was not in the mood for making a hasty decision that might gum up the works.

"I'm surprised you would want to leave so soon after having your mother go through her surgery and treatment and your worry about Eugenia. Do you think that's a good idea? Have you talked this over with Cassie?"

"Renata and Zoe are in a pickle with Renata's pin being stolen, *Asternum II* is not yet here and no telling who is behind the glitches that seem to be more than accidents or one-time problems of happenstance. Time is running out and they need my help. That about covers it."

"I won't stop you but I ask that you keep me informed on the hour if possible. That's about all we have now."

He left quickly and she rearranged her list in order of

importance. It might just last for an hour or two if she was lucky. Items b and d were now Rodane's concern and she could concentrate on the rest. She felt some stress easing, her tired muscles and her brain whirling just a little slower. She rose to go and check on Eugenia in the Medical center of the compound. She felt like she was going into battle with this one.

The moment she saw her, she sensed a difference in Eugenia. She looked over at her still form and made her way slowly to her bedside. When she pulled over a chair next to her bedside, Genie stirred and murmured so low she could not be sure she had done so.

"Genie, I know you like that new name of yours, if you have something to say dear, please say it so I can hear."

"Sorry" Genie murmured and then turned her head away.

"That's all well and good my dear but...sorry about what?"

Genie clutched the edge of the sheet and Agatha reached over and gently put her hand over the twisted fist. Genie relaxed her hand and Agatha took her fingers and rubbed them slowly until they were relaxed. She looked at her for a few moments and her expression changed to one of wonder.

"It's true then, you do have a *connection* to our 'family'? Did you know? I hate to put it this way but is that why you are *hiding out*?"

There were moments of calm and Agatha continued reading her as long as Genie would let her. The conversation would have looked all one-sided if anyone had noticed, but to Agatha it was mind bending and slightly shocking. Nothing too much in this life of hers was too shocking after all the years she had been here.

"Do you think it might be time to face your fears? I'll be with you every step of the way."

More minutes passed and Agatha was ready to leave when Genie turned her head and opened her eyes. She looked directly at Agatha for what seemed like too long but then a small, shy smile reached her parched lips and her fingers tightened around Agatha's hand. Agatha went over to the bedside tray and brought over a cup with a straw and lifted it to Genie's lips where she took small sips. Then Agatha said, "I'll return in an hour or two and we'll talk, would you like that?"

Without a word being spoken, Agatha nodded her head and then went to the door and placed the DO NOT DISTURB sign on the door handle and left silently. Genie closed her eyes and let out one sigh that relaxed her tight, tense muscles and she slept, at peace for the first time in months, maybe years.

Chapter 26

Mountain Not so High

The dig was still in progress and Renata's timetable and her watch showed her that the laser beam from the *Asturia II* was only hours away. She and Zoe had not spoken since their last encounter and the heat had driven everyone to agree that a trip to town was due to alleviate the dehydration by going to a pub and spending the late afternoon getting real showers, getting a good night's sleep in the motel and making calls to home or anyone else they wanted to reach. She declined the invitation and a few others wanted to continue working but with short trip to town and then a later return.

She walked down to the base porta-potty and was coming out when she was clouted on the head, first saw stars, then blackness. She awoke to find herself behind the toilet and down a few yards behind a tangle of bushes. She found herself hog-tied and gagged and the taste in her mouth was one of blood. She almost gagged but controlled the urge to avoid swallowing and possibly choking. No sound, no voices, no indication she was alone.

{what the hell now what}

"Sorry for that but you are entirely too close to be ruining our plans and you left me no choice" Claudia stepped behind the bushes and bent down over Renata, "I wish things could have been different."

Renata wanted to scream or at least kick out but she was unable to move more than her eyes. Claudia must have seen something in her eyes because she took a step back and raised her hands in the air, 'I'm not the baddy here, well...maybe I am but not the only one." Renata saw someone coming from behind her and saw Cosimo, hands in his pockets, smiling and putting his arm around Claudia, who winced. Renata noticed. Claudia moved away from him and looked around, "Make this quick, we don't have much time."

Cosimo motioned to her, "Get it out and we can get started. Claudia reached in her pocket and brought out Renata's pin and smirked at her, "I thought for sure you would be guessing who by now. When your little friend came, I was almost certain you had begun to figure it was me. Ah, well, glad I was smarter than you after all."

Cosimo came over close to her face and Renata tried to turn her head but he grasped her chin and forced her to turn to him. His hand tightened until she let out a muffled expletive. He breathed into her face and stroked her cheek then moved his hands down to her breasts and drew even closer.

"It's a shame I don't have more time to devote to showing you I can be fun." As his voice lowered and he spoke softly into her ear, his hands were reaching farther and farther down as she squirmed from his touch, "Your pal Andy, will be along in a few moments and then we can get started. What? You didn't think we noticed your reaction to his appearance?

We thought you were so cute trying to be so evasive."

Claudia walked over and smacked him on the shoulder, "Hey buddy, we're here to do a job, not play handsy with her. I suspect that's not in the plan either."

He turned abruptly and grabbed her by her hair and twisted until she cried out, then slapped her across her face. Her cheeks flamed red and she had abject fear in her eyes.

He spit out, "I don't tell you your business and you don't tell me mine, got that?" He raised his hand again and she blurted, "Sure, got it. Sorry."

He dropped his hand and turned back to Renata."I'm going to take out your gag and if you make one sound, I'll clock you again, even harder. You might pass out but we'll get what we've come for in the end. Make it easy on yourself." A noise had him begin to turn away and two others came around the bushes, "Don't make a move unless you want me to use this."

There, stood Professor Schultz and Zoe. The professor had a small gun in his hands and when Cosimo moved a step, he aimed at his crotch and cocked the gun. The *'snick'* it made had him stop in his tracks. He raised his hands. Zoe moved to Claudia and held out her hand, waiting, "Slowly girl" the professor said quietly. "I'm a good shot and I can turn this on you and just as quickly turn it on your sleazy partner-in-crime." His face showed he was not bluffing.

Claudia opened her closed fist and handed the pin to Zoe who put it in her pocket and then brought out a small roll of duct tape. "Something to use in a pinch before the rangers get called." She shoved Claudia around and swept out her foot and took her down to the ground in one swift move. "You poisoned my friend?"

Claudia was silent. After trussing her up and removing

Renata's gag, Professor Schultz motioned for Cosimo to get down on the ground. Cosimo looked like he had swallowed vinegar but dropped to his knees. Professor Schultz went over and pushed him down to the bare earth with his face pressed against the loose dust, then clouted him across the side of his head with one short stab of his pistol. Cosimo was down and out for the count.

"Somehow people think a fat man cannot have muscle and strength, especially when they are my age. We love to prove them wrong, on both counts." He smiled benignly at both women. Zoe taped up Cosimo with pleasure.

Renata spoke after taking a big breath, "Thank you Professor but we still have Andrew McCarty to handle. He's not who..."

"Don't worry my dear, Quimby and Rodane have him well in hand. We only need to worry about *Asternum II* right now." He saw the look on their faces.

"It seems I have managed to gob smack both of you without even trying. You really don't know anyone for sure, yes? He reached in his pocket and brought out another pin. "Does this make you feel more secure?" Both women stared at it for a few seconds and then smiled broadly. They pulled out their pins and got down to business. Agatha would be very pleased to finally hear of their well-deserved break.

Zoe, Renata, and Professor Schultz were all sitting on the ground two miles south, away from the site, knowing a few diggers could arrive back there at any time. This was crunch time and if something else happened to disrupt it, there would be no going back to try a do over. The rangers had responded quickly to the request made by Professor Schultz on his satellite phone and had taken the two lowlifes away after taping the report of both Renata and Zoe and checking on the background of the professor. He had an impressive background.

Now they were hoping Quimby and Rodane could get back from the regional airport, after taking Andrew McCarty to the plane and having their security watch over him. They calculated it would be twenty minutes to the first laser attempt in over 300 years to cause a landslide of epic proportions to the mountain still reaching high in the sky. All their hopes rested on a slow return to the site of all those in town and accuracy of the *Asternum II's* crew.

The sky turned hazy with a brown tinge to the clouds that looked like the beginnings of a dust storm. Clouds quickly became more cirrus than dark cumulus and then seemed to roll quickly toward the mountain far in the distance and the ceiling seemed to have dropped instantly. After five minutes of them holding their breath intermittingly in anticipation, they heard and felt a rumble. The ground around them shook like a herd of animals were galloping near them. They saw headlights in the distance moving toward their vehicles, weaving slightly on the dirt packed road from the strong wind around them that came from the mountain area. They moved to the side as the vehicles approached, then waved them down. The dust had risen to great heights and blocked out the remaining sunlight until it seemed as if night was beginning to creep in on the entire area.

They explained to those coming back from town how

they had scooted out to this location when the land under them began to shift and shake. The two jeeps pulled up next to theirs and they all waited, watching the clouds change color and shape and heard the rumbling in the distance like a large storm brewing. They watched together when minutes later, the rumbling became louder than thunder and dust started turning into a wall, reaching farther and farther out.

They all retreated to their vehicles and closed the windows as the dust swept closer and closer to them. In the next instant, the noise became so loud, they put their hands over their ears and watched as a cloud of debris tore across the land in front of them, making its way to their supposedly safe southern side, with chunks of rock and pebbles hitting the vehicles so hard, one windshield cracked. They were astounded when they saw the mountain shrink in size as the thick dust continued pelting their vehicles and were startled by a shovel that flew into the side of a four runner and drove a hole right through the side panel as they ducked below the windows.

Seconds later, Renata gaped wide-eyed, as she saw a large wooden box used as a soil-sifter, coming straight toward them. "Duck" she screamed over the noise. It flew right over the jeep and kept on going.

"Whoa, get down!" shouted Renata and all three left their seats and tried to find space on the carpeted floor as far back to the windowless area as they could all scramble. After what seemed endless minutes, the cars stopped their shaking, the dust around them slowed and dissipated quickly. It now sounded like a shower of hailstones clinking against the car on three sides. After more minutes of it all subsiding, they got out of their vehicles and looked at each other with both fear and trepidation.

"What's happening" one of the diggers asked. He looked like he was a deer caught in the headlights. Professor Schultz went over to him and put a hand on his shoulder and said as gently as he could,

"We're ok, it's all over now, I think. At least it seems so. Is everyone all right?" He looked around and saw others crawling on their hands and knees, afraid to lift themselves up to a possible skewering.

Slowly, each person looked around, shell-shocked, looking for someone they knew to give them assurance they were not going to be pelted with deadly rocks or smothered by a dust storm. They all rose and two girls began crying, grasping each other for comfort and releasing pent up fear. All the vehicles had dings and small holes all over their sides and one taillight hung, dangling from the back bumper like a lighted lamp giving direction in a cave entrance. Silence around then now, except for softer crying and heavy breathing from one or two still feeling their heart rates slowing down.

"What the hell did we just witness?" One man looked around him, judging whether he should run or not.

Renata answered," It seems as if we just experienced a collapse of our dig site. Nothing else could explain this. What do you think Professor?" as she turned to him, her eyes sparking and her voice steady. He looked at her, tried to hide his satisfied smirk and addressed all of them,

"I think it's fair to say our jobs might just have become expendable for the near future but you can be thankful we weren't there at the time. He turned slightly, smiled at '*Ariel*' and looked up at the noise above them coming closer. The rest of them seemed poised to run…anywhere but there.

"I think our rescuers have arrived, not a minute too soon." He waved his hands to point in the air to attract attention. A helicopter gilded about one hundred yards away and was making a soft landing. Two National Guardsmen jumped out, followed by Quimby and Rodane as a ranger was driving up in a state vehicle. He exited the car and asked, "Everyone here, ok?"

The next half hour was used to bandage some cuts and scrapes from flying glass and other unknown objects. All those not injured helped with that and Professor Schultz radioed for a tow truck for the most damaged, undrivable car. Quimby and Rodane checked out each person individually. Before the ranger left, he asked, "You folks feel pretty lucky? You were far enough away from this event as you could be to witness it without being hurt. What were you guys out here for? We got the call and headed out right away but the road was too shaky to make good time. We got here as fast as we could."

Zoe looked around, "I think we'll chalk this one up to happenstance and fate. How are all of you doing? Something to write home about?"

"No way. If my parents heard about my being in the thick of this, I would be grounded from digs for the rest of my life" one of the girls added happily, "which thank heavens, I still have. I might tell it in a memoir but that will be *waaay i*n the future Maybe in a pub or bar if I'm half drunk" she giggled at the laughter surrounding her. It broke the tension and they all headed for their vehicles and doubled up on passengers as Renata, Professor Schultz and Zoe hung back. They left a dust trail that all those driving behind them stayed a good distance away.

The two guards stood at attention, awaiting orders. The ranger asked them if they needed a ride back to town. They told him they had orders to stay at the site until a crew arrived. He left and the guardsmen took up positions.

"You can talk now fellas" Renata turned to them. "what's next Rodane?" Quimby spoke first, "You know you missed that blast by about a football field of distance, don't you? Cutting it kind of close, weren't you? He looked directly at Renata with a stern look on his face. She was puzzled by his attitude but chalked it up to relief that they had succeeded in their efforts but feared for their safety.

"I'm just thankful it went off almost as planned. We happened to be a little busy at the time. We couldn't leave the site until we were sure no one would be there from town. It all worked out." She looked still puzzled at him but he turned away and walked toward the helicopter, still with the rotors turning. "Let's go" and he turned his head and addressed her directly, "Like the thrill of danger, do you?"

She was about to whip out a response to him and was getting angry at this criticism, "Listen fella…you don't know a thing about…" Professor Schultz walked up to her and placed his hand on her arm.

"My dear, I think we all need some down time from our 'experience' and I believe we've successfully achieved our end results. We're all tired, running on adrenaline, I dare say stressed, so maybe a glass of wine or two and a good meal in town would help us recover from it?" He smiled at her and winked his eye. Rodane walked up to her and whispered, "Take a deep breath Renata. We've still got a lot of cleaning up to do and hashing out our next moves. How about we do it in a more…restful way?" He turned his head back toward Quimby and then to the now gearing up helicopter. "We can address his concerns later, much later."

"Sure Rodane, we're all tired and edgy. A good meal and especially some good wine will do the trick. Then I think I'll sleep for a couple hours."

"That's the ticket." He steered her toward the helicopter and Zoe brought up the rear, considering what Quimby's reaction told her in her gut. She smiled to herself and thought

{aha more here than meets the eye I think}

Zoe knew the next hours would be crucial to their possible future moves against those who were continually trying to do severe damage to their families all over the globe. This was a warning, a very clear warning to them, that they were in for a fight. They needed to show them who was going to win and perhaps get them off their game. They **had** to find out who was in charge now. Gallo was dead, the failed attempt to wipe them out as leadership had shown them new problems, ones they had either been unaware of or non-existent until…. she stopped in her tracks right before she headed up the steps to the helicopter.

{this has all started for real when Rodane was brought on board}

Chapter 27

The Secrets out...or Not

The entire Hilo flight back to the plane at the Regional Airport outside town was one of relief and conjecture. They had flown over the collapsed wreckage of the mountain which appeared to be a complete success. Nothing remained of the dig or any evidence of any tents or equipment. The money needed to first clear out the damage and then put a team together, much less apply for permits and all the paperwork involved would be enormous for any new dig. It would be too much for any one state to handle alone. That plus the fact that they now had time to figure out a plan to end the entire process until later in the future.

Quimby returned the helicopter to its assigned shed and went to prepare the small plane for take-off. Once in the air, Rodane addressed all of them,

"First. I guess you all know by now that Professor Schultz was placed on this dig not just because he is well qualified but one of our own" he nodded to the Professor, "and he's the reason this whole plan didn't go down the tubes."

"So why didn't you tell us he was the one to be trusted?"

Renata was still on edge. "It would have made a big difference, don't you think?"

"Anonymity, remember? You were the one that agreed that would keep things more open to better investigation. I didn't know myself."

"Well, that was before I was poisoned and had my pin stolen and Andrew McCarty showed up. Don't you think plans needed to be changed by that point?" Renata was still peeved, he could see.

"Well," Rodane took a second to answer, "I happened to be in a bathyscape miles under the ocean attending to … other matters. Sorry for the missed opportunity."

Renata realized what she had just said and why he was unable to warn her. She felt her face flush and she cringed, "I'm sorry, that was uncalled for. It's true we are under a lot of pressure and I shouldn't take it out on you."

"Did you not have any idea your pin had been stolen by Claudia and she was in cahoots with …"

Quimby spoke loudly from the cockpit, "This might not be the best time to discuss these issues. Maybe we'd be better served deciding what we say when we get home and what happens with the Governor of Utah when he learns he's lost a lot of money and an entire mountain?"

They all giggled. They decided to curtail any more discussion until they were back at the compound and met with whatever other members of the committee might be present and awaiting their return.

"That's **enough!**" The muttering, complaints and the loud murmurs had been going on long enough and Nikos had to bring this under control. He stood up and gestured to the door, "There's the door if you want to argue this out because we have work to do and this isn't going to accomplish anything except more rancor and disagreement. We're better than that!" He slammed his hand on the table, looked up at all of them one by one and waited for a count of ten. No one moved and all the noise stopped, the silence golden to his ears.

Agatha looked around at those present, "Let me see a show of hands as to who wants this to be tabled for now."

Not one hand went up so they sat quietly. Evangela, Raul, Suri, Sabina, Leander, Alyssia, Acacia, Rodane, Quimby, Nikos and Willow made up more than the quorum of their committee to cast votes and argue the points put forward. The number of committee members had been 15 just two years ago and it quickly became evident over those two years they had been severely under attack and had lost quite a few people. Egan was …somewhere, hadn't been heard of in months and no one had an idea how to locate them. Kieffer was in jail for fraud and cooking the books. Petrus was retired with a heart condition. Cloe, though just appointed to replace Petrus, had not been able to get away from D.C. and Tegan was asked to the meeting but was not allowed a vote as of now. He looked confused as he took a seat across from his mother, Willow. This might be the only chance they might get in the coming days to figure out how to prevent chaos and a world scare while still trying to uncover the mole in their ranks.

Events were unfolding faster than they had plans for

controlling them. In the last year, members were spread all over different countries; attacks were more evident and more pronounced. Nikos stood up and went to the Whiteboard at the front of the room. The events were listed with solutions listed from a to z.

"We now must come up with a plan to house and supply all the survivors of the *Mauritius;* decide which of our candidates for new teams is most able to serve immediately; not to mention make a unified decision on whether or not to give all the information we have to our President."

Leander snidely remarked "Oh, is that all?"

"Ok Leander" Nikos said, "You've been against this since the beginning. Let us know your thoughts."

Leander looked about to refuse, thought better of it and began, "Well, my advice may not be palatable to some of you. You all know my reservations about bringing up the survivors of *Mauritius*. You also know I don't trust any leader of this world today with the information you are willing to give them…"

"Now wait a minute here, Leander" Raul almost rose out of his chair. He looked around the room, took a deep breath and sat back down. "We've gone over and over this and forgive me, but weren't you the one who said we needed to make our presence known to the world? Did I miss something here in the last two days?"

Rodane was watching carefully from one to the other. Then he glanced at Evangela. She nodded her head slightly up and down at him but waited. Leander looked at Raul, scoffed at his words,

"I said **we** should make our presence known, not the President. Two different things. It's time we were in charge, well past time." The murmuring in the room got louder and more concerned. Evangela looked over at Rodane and spoke,

"Leander, did you know that we have monitored all our conversations, all of them, for the last three years since the attack on the compound?" He looked confused,

"So? What has that got to do with..."

"So, did you also know that included phone calls made from here in the compound or any of our residences as part of the committee protocols?" She turned slightly to Rodane, "Were you aware of that Rodane?"

"Yes, you told me, once I had been admitted into the committee as part of my 'initiation' into the 'family", that monitoring was always there."

She turned back to Leander, who at this point, was flushing and beginning to sweat. "Leander, is there something you need to advise the Council of concerning your conversations or your phone records?"

"I'm not the one to be questioned here. How dare you t..."

She stood up quickly, put her hands on the table, took a breath and spoke loudly, **"YOU** have much explaining to do concerning your phone calls to those we know are our enemies or paid informers to our enemies." Across from her, everyone turned to look at Willow who sat with a look of utter sadness on her face and tears coursing down her cheeks.

Tegan got up and without a word, walked around the table, went to her and leaned down close to her and put his arm around her shoulders. Her soft crying filled an utterly quiet room. Leander didn't even glance their way. His face was white with rage, fists clenched. Raul left his seat and offered it to Tegan, next to his mother.

Evangela flicked open the file in front of her and then used the controller and posted them on the Whiteboard. A list of phone records was shown with many marked with yellow highlighting. Below them were the records of conversations had in the compound for the last four months, the time starting from their arrival there the first morning as a committee. Leander was shifting in his chair; his face twisted into a scowl and he jumped to his feet and tried to exit the room.

When he flung open the door, there were two armed guards outside who barred his way. He turned back with a look on his face of pure hate. All those present witnessed a complete and total transformation from the Leander they thought they knew. The silence in the room was only slightly less than the hard breaths and grunts coming from Leander. No one spoke for the next two minutes. Leander finally glanced over to Willow and his expression of disdain and disgust did not miss anybody's attention. Agatha entered the room with Francis.

The two guards led him to a seat and stood over him. They both had stunners in their hands. He sat quivering from his anger, refusing now to meet the eyes of anyone in the room. Evangela spoke, "You'll notice from the records of phone calls, he makes them to the same numbers on some occasions. Others are of a different nature. All of you are aware that your phones are open to any of us on the committee, correct?"

They all nodded assent. Evangela looked over at Leander, "You realize this Leander?" He stayed silent. "We can do this with or without your help. You can be placed in holding and then brought to us to make your appeal. Which would you prefer?"

He stared and then spat out, "You're all a bunch of cowards and fools. You have no right to be here and make decisions for us."

Willow said softly, "Leander, please don't do this. Try and see this from a legal viewpoint. What if you were appointed with defending these charges for a client?"

"You should be defending me, not bellying up to all these…"

"Stop! You can see what's on the board just as we can. How can you defend that?" Willow took a deep breath and looked to the rest of them, "I'm so sorry you feel like you had to do this. I understand why. Leander and I…" she paused and tears began again, "We haven't always seen eye to eye on many things but I believed he was a good man and just airing his frustrations and anger."

"Don't speak for me woman! We haven't seen eye to eye since you turned traitor to me and opposed me at every turn. I can't stand the sight of you anymore than I can stand the sight of all these hypocritical fools seated here."

Tegan stood up, "Dad, that's no way to talk to…" Leander scoffed,

"Oh, shut up you coward. You've taken your mother's side on any arguments I've had with her over the workings of this damn, inept committee that acts like God. I wrote you off a long time ago Tegan. You have the spine of a jellyfish."

"I'd rather be that, than an angry, foolish traitor to all we stand for." Leander lunged from his chair and the two guards grabbed both his arms and forced him into the chair. Evangela walked over to him and said, "You'll have plenty of time to air your arguments after we've seen what you have incurred in the last months and who you've been in contact with Leander. Or do you want to go now and let us continue with our…"

"I wouldn't miss this clown show for the world. Go ahead and show us all the lies you have accumulated."

Evangela turned to Agatha and then Francis. They nodded and she turned to the guards, "Please take him to holding and await our call to return him here."

He jumped up and the guards held him while he was writhing and pulling at them both, "You can't do this. I have my rights; I'm part of this committee. You are fucking cowards!" He was spitting out his words and his face was twisted into a mask of fury. He screamed obscenities all the way out the door.

After a few minutes of calm and quiet, they turned to Evangela as she continued, "I guess it was foolish of me to hope we could do this without all the rancor but…"

Suri stood up and went to the board, "Don't apologize for doing your job and don't feel bad for us. We had some heads up in the last few weeks. Something was building in Leander and he was not the person we knew from all those years of protecting our family. Let's continue if everyone feels the need?" Suri looked around and all heads nodded in unison.

"We've broken down all Leander's communications to phone calls, bank transactions, emails, credit card expenditures and travels he has had in the last four months. That seems to be where all this started. Or at least for now with what we have found. We've identified all the people we could and hope to get more with his computer records and text messages." They switched to camera. Each sleeping room had been renovated and outfitted with a computer system of its own to allow for personal use during night hours and if ill or confined for any reason. There was a central control panel where one monitored it.

"Alyssia, your head supervisor, oversaw all the passwords, IPO's and files for emergency connections and review of sensitive information. She has been tracking Leander's movements right after he made a phone call as soon as we arrived here at Amiens right before our first breakfast.

"What made her suspect him?" Suri asked.

"Our new system of security automatically logs any phone calls; alerts the supervisor and they are recorded as well. The camera shows his phone to his ear, leaving the hallway and making his way up to his room. There is a phone record of that morning that goes out to an unknown we will tell you about in a moment"

Alyssia switched to the next record on the board, "You'll see that same number is listed more times throughout the three months we've been tracking him. We set up an algorithm with Alyssia's help to alert the cyber team whenever that number was called." She pointed to at least three recorded calls and four numbers that were identical. Next to that was another column of emails that were highlighted with time and date. "I'll give you a few minutes to look at all the emails and then we can listen to the recordings."

Tegan spoke up, "Excuse me, but I have a question?"

"Of course, Tegan, what is it?" Agatha spoke for the first time that day.

"I'm…not sure if I sound like I'm arguing the point, but isn't privacy needed for…"

"You're asking the very same question we asked ourselves. Yes, there is generally a need for privacy. All our committee, before you joined us, were asked to come up with a plan to use in case we were suspicious of someone in our own committee or among our people. It's been a long debate and a longer time trying to achieve transparency without breaking confidences and privacy."

"But..." Tegan looked embarrassed, "Can you accuse someone if they had those confidences broken without their knowledge or consent?"

Sabina spoke, "Tegan, our compound was attacked and a mole was never found among us, yet information kept getting out and attacks kept happening. We all agreed that it was a necessary evil and there is no confidentiality when all agreed that this mole had to be found. Otherwise, we could never exist in peace and safety. We aren't held to the Miranda warning. We are protecting an entire planet and an entire people that need to be safe and protected from the likes of Theras Gallo, Andrew McCarty and all the others who wish to destroy us and our generations to come. But we did have the permission of the White House and the CIA."

"Sorry, I don't mean to be arguing, but isn't privacy something we all need to defend?"

"Yes, it is" Sabina answered, "Until that privacy uncovers attempts on our lives, our families' lives and the safety of all of us. When you have studied all the facts laid out, you will see where this is coming from. If you could be a little patient?"

Tegan took his seat but it was his father, after all. Day turned into late afternoon, and they read all the emails between Leander and Senator Gorham as well as those he sent to Andrew McCarty going all the way back to the car accident and the injuries their own team sustained in Spain. They perused the various calls, listened to them as recorded and names were attached to voices.

The algorithm allowed for interpretation of voices that elicited anger or resentment, lying or fear. It uncovered contacts such as Andrew McCarty, Senator Gorham from DC, Dr. Ardsby in charge of Eugenie and Marian Papadakis at the clinic, a mercenary without a name yet, and a woman from Greece named Solana Pappas, paid by Senator Gorham. Bank records were then examined with invoices from Leander himself as well as a Senator Hitchens, now deceased. Millions of dollars were spent in weapons purchases and the warehouses were searched with weapons recovered, then confiscated by DEA.

"Leander has been allowing Senator Gorham to run the show as he has all the money needed to pay for all the mercenaries and those hired as hit men." Suri changed slides and showed all the attacks on various family members, Cassie Arcos, Iona Arcos, Renata and Caroline Arcos, Attempts made by an unknown hit woman in Az on Renata Kappos and Zoe Martin with dates and times that synched with calls between Leander Barbas and Senator Lindley Gorham.

"We're still uncovering others as well." She put something down on the table. "This is the listening device we found in Leander's room and we have camera footage of every inch of the search for corroboration. He has been listening to many of you from the vents in the floor and the various rooms. It was how he knew that Cassie was traveling to Pa. and then he sent out the hit man paid by Senator Gorham. We have a good lead on who destroyed Cassie Arcos' home, and we're pretty sure it was Andrew McCarty. The handwriting of the note left, matches his. We found Egan Filbert in Utah...but also Az from his travel itineraries."

That statement elicited loud murmurs and a few gasps. She continued, "Egan is the one responsible for putting the dig in jeopardy and…" the murmurs turned to loud epithets… "Yes, I know, I was as surprised as you. The two agents Francis sent to investigate, identified him from camera shots inside the offices. He was hired with fake resumes and used his office to stall the dig permits. He's changed his appearance very much as you can see." They all took a moment to gaze at one of their own who had turned when he worked for Theras Gallo.

"We have two more items to show you. I think everyone is very tired and weary at all the evidence piled on you so quickly. Would you like to continue tomorrow? Can I see a show of hands?" No one wanted to adjourn.

She continued, "You'll notice that these recorded conversations take us back as far as two months ago, when we were planning the intervention of *Asternum II* and you can read them for yourselves." She gave them a few minutes.

"You see here, the financial records of Dr. Ardsby from the clinic and Aldora's trip to Greece to locate Melodia. Thank heavens Aldora was able to lose the woman following her in the crowd. All travel expenses for the Pappas woman hired to locate and follow Aldora were paid by Senator Gorham's campaign funds as well as the unknown person who attempted to silence Cassie at her home in Pa.

We are still assessing whether further funds were paid to Leander to connect him to one of the persons on *Asternum II.* Agatha will fill you in on the knowledge we gained from recording Leander in our secure offices that connect to the *Asternum II* with dates and times." Everyone was glued to the screen.

"The next item we finally put together with corroboration from Francis and Agatha, was the trip Leander took to the cabin with Rodane. We assigned him that trip on purpose. Francis gave him an opening to come clean about the supposed emergency Leander was able to plan for Raul and Evangela to travel. He had hopes of getting information from Rodane or maybe even worse."

She noted Rodane's expression, "Sorry Rodane but we couldn't alert you to this or you might have been so angry you'd have given us away" There was a recorded camera shot of a white car that followed them out the next morning. "We had someone who was there in case of need, but your trip was a ruse to allow for Leander to get to Cassel to obtain more information on the *Asternum II.* It worked in our favor." Agatha got up and went to the board and showed them a conversation between Leander and the man named Cassel,

"The last piece of the puzzle was when we found out there were communications with the *Asternum II* that didn't involve any of us except Leander. Until we realized from recorded calls that Cmdr. Haller had let us know about their coming trip forward, we had no knowledge of it. Leander is the one who had the assignment to connect to the Space program and their supervisors. They've been alerted."

"Did you suspect he had kept information from you?" Suri was tense and angry.

"Alyssia had been put on alert for any movements or contacts from Leander. He came back to Amiens that night and made a beeline to the safe room and contacted Peri Cassel. We have it on camera. Many lives could have been lost if we hadn't gotten everyone away from the site before the mountain collapse. As it was, we almost lost Renata, Zoe and even

Professor Schultz, who was one of ours."

The murmuring started again. Francis rose and said, "We have some people in custody and are preparing to go and investigate and question them. I think that's about all we can take for now and I, for one, am very exhausted emotionally with all this spy work and espionage among our own people. How about we meet tomorrow, after lunch? That way those who want to sleep in and recover somewhat can do that. Show of hands?" All hands went up and most retired to their own rooms to review the last hours spent, in their own separate files on a memory stick. Left in the room were Agatha, Francis, Quimby and Sabina with Willow and Tegan. It was a very tense silence. Then a conversation began that lasted well into the night.

Chapter 28

All Hands-on Deck

The following day, in the Communications room, there was little space for all of them from the night before in the Committee Room but they squeezed in a few more chairs and made the best of it. There were three screens up on the walls: all live and active. Agatha sat with her hands folded, Francis was peering at the second screen where members of the *Asternum II* were looking back and forth at each other in stunned silence. Finally, Cmdr. Haller spoke: "You are sure …what's his name…?"

"Leander Barbas" answered Francis "and we are still assessing any possible others but…"

President Dwayne Harper was walking back and forth on the third screen, hands in his pockets and he turned, facing the camera, "Pardon the interruption but I want to tell all of you here that in the efforts of complete transparency, we've begun a deep dive into this man and…" he looked at those from his vantage point, "I can tell by the looks on your faces, you're not happy with that but just be patient while I explain, if I might?"

"Of course, Mr. President" Francis motioned for him to continue.

President Harper took a deep breath and continued. "Please remember I'm new at this, all of it; from recently becoming the next president to learning about…how do I put it… all these new and alien happenings now on my watch." He cleared his throat and continued pacing, "My lasting responsibility is to protect and defend all my people and follow the laws of our country as well as international law. That requires me to make sure I am sticking to our laws as well as global and the interests of all the people, which now seem to include the entire population of the Earth."

He looked over to the screen which showed the leaders of the *Asternum II* who also didn't look all that happy with his words. "Gentlemen, I promise you that at this time, this will go no further than this room and you can quote me on that when you meet with my cabinet." He heard gasps from many on screen.

"I was obliged to inform them of any threat to our safety or to the people. They are under the strictest secrecy that we can expect or demand. Each cabinet member has been thoroughly vetted over and over."

Captain Devin Socrat spoke up but with a tremor in his voice, "Sir, we can understand that but…with no intention of disrespect, I've studied your world for a very long time and we had plenty of that on our voyages here. I know a lot about how that 'strictest secrecy' you speak of is a very dubious thing, especially in the last few decades." He let out a cleansing breath.

"Captain Socrat, is it?" President Harper sized him up." I totally understand where you are coming from, well… not where you are coming from but where you ...never mind, I'm still adjusting to shock at all this in such a short time." He looked at both other screens and took a moment to collect his thoughts.

"Let me assure you that the treason act is at play here and all are aware of the consequences if they so much as leak even a hint at your presence on your temporary homesite. In effect, they've literally signed their lives away if anything leaks from any conversation, held by all of us." He motioned around all three screens. "Commander Haller, excuse the interruption, please continue."

"You've alluded to what I was going to ask. If you are already in the position of searching for any others who might wish to do us or your own people harm, then can you tell us how you propose to keep that secret? You need access to files, codes, statistics, personnel and an organizational search of epic proportions, yes? So much could fall through the cracks or be hacked."

Voices began to mutter and then conversation began among all the people present, with emotions rising and the sound increasingly anxious. Agatha cleared her throat twice, then slapped her hand on the table and all those restlessly muttering fell silent.

"If I may, President Harper, could I answer part of that?"

"Of course," the president looked relieved and gestured to her.

"To all of you who might not know, we've established a large committee of our personnel that are investigating lists of possible 'family' members, previously unknown to us and we hope to have a list for all of you in the next few days. We've sped up the search through necessity as you can guess.

That also includes any we find that might be a risk to us, or someone who has previously had a record of stirring up hostile acts or movements. If they are known to us as 'family' but suspicious by their actions, there will be further investigation and President Harper has agreed to use his resources to uncover them."

Willow spoke up, emotion playing over her face, "I understand the need for secrecy but how will we protect those found from any indiscriminate investigation or what could be seen as denying them their rights? Don't we have to protect them as well?"

Sabina thought she knew exactly what Willow was going through. This whole situation was still raw and hurtful from her own husband being found to be one of those traitors. She reached across the table and took Willow's hand,

"Would it help if I told you that Melodia is taking over the committee that is overseeing our search and her team is handpicked by her and all of us? Our committee with any opposing views would then require more research before exposing their identities."

Willow took quite a few seconds to absorb this and then she smiled faintly, "I couldn't ask for anything more. Thank you for that."

Quimby asked, "Cmdr. Haller, can you give us all insight into your passenger that might help us understand the latest events? We're all anxious to discover how we might tighten our protections."

"Captain Socrat, your help here?"

Devin Socrat was uneasy, "Mr. Cassel was seen in a search of our camera feeds after we had installed a safe device that alerted us once the first three instances of leaked information were confirmed. He left a very distinct footprint. We questioned him and he was more than anxious to 'out' himself so to speak. He has always been somewhat..." He hesitated.

"Arrogant. Don't be afraid to admit it or speak it," Cmdr. Haller grimly acknowledged what they all suspected.

"He was proud of what he considered his 'family' duty. We discovered he was the 21tx, great grandson of one of the family members here from many centuries ago..." he looked at the tablet in his hands and said, "a man named Deshares, supposedly one of our travelers who was considered hundreds of years ago as a god among the natives. Oh, and a woman named Amber Windom that was the 20tx great granddaughter of our traveler that was named...let me see... An Italian woman named Parsia in your world." he heard the collective gasp from all those seated. "Sorry, is that a sore spot?"

"Not at all, just a little history unearthed and now the name of the person involved." Francis was surprised, his voice ended almost in a whisper.

"Well," Haller looked down again, "Oh yes, and a man recently in your government that was named...let me see... yes, a man named Lindley Gorham. He was determined he could track down any descendants and convince them to join him in his attempts to gain some control over what he saw as an inferior species. He and Cassel had been in contact several times but we couldn't locate him from your records".

They continued speaking for another half hour and then closed connections until the next afternoon to give them time to discuss all the new information they had been given. When the dust was settled from yesterday's secure meeting, three things stood out. They needed to be sure of the route they would take to pursue them.

One was the ongoing research into family members not yet identified or recently unearthed. There was a time crunch to install a safety measure they could use to identify them and then contact them. All genealogical sites, no matter where, could now be securely accessed by Melodia and her team. They were working in a Faraday cage, under the basement of an unknown site that had been built in the last few months, after the crash of the Communications in the US and other countries as well.

The second pressing point was how to let those President Harper was mentioning, into their secret of over 120,000 years and how could they rely on their discretion not to reveal something that could start a worldwide panic or upheaval.

Naturally, the third issue was finding a way to uncover all those the likes of Lindley Gorham, to see how far into the worldwide communications breakdown he, and those connected with him, could be hidden. Those could likely be solely responsible for the global attack. How to put a stop to it and any others was still a question to be considered by all those involved, once the reveal was a fact.

They had not even arrived at discussing a different issue of having to give shelter and safety to the members of the *Mauritius* that had been rescued from the sunken starship. All survivors were still being evaluated for deep sea pressure and PTSD. That was to be expected because of all the time spent in dealing with imminent death. They were also being vetted for any changes on their home planet *Asturia* before the *Asternum II* had launched. Those changes were many. Now, someone unexpected was coming to their aid.

When the last presidential election was held in the US,

Former President Sheamus McAndrew and his wife, Lori were incredibly happy with the idea of having a more normal life and spending time with their family. It was not to be, not at the present time. President Dwayne Harper had turned to his former boss to help him unravel all the pieces of the spider web in which they found themselves now enmeshed. Since President McAndrew had been aware of the 'family' dynamics and their members for his entire presidency, Dwayne was given a heads up by Sheamus before he even took the Oath of Office. He promised to be there if needed.

President Dwayne Harper had been instrumental in helping recover the *Mauritius* and knew of the starship traveling to *Phobos,* a moon of Mars, to help with the starship crisis in Utah. That was enough to make his head spin. He was sure no other president found himself in these types of situations.

Taken one by one, these problems were solvable. Together, it was a basket of snakes, just itching to sink their teeth into anyone available. It was time to make a few extreme moves within the family circle. The Committee met early on a Saturday. Rodane was co-chairing for the first time with Agatha and Francis; Sabina was replacing Kieffer O'Brian and Cloe was now replacing Petrus, who had been most eager to return to the island and resume a more quiet, simple life, however many years he had left.

Francis began the meeting, "It's good of all of you to travel here at a moment's notice. I am sure we all appreciate it…" he nodded to Agatha and Rodane. The rest all agreed. "We've been eager to let you in on all our news as we present you with the information you see on the screen." They spent an hour discussing all the information gleaned from their previous meeting.

"All of you know her by reputation, but I would like you to meet her in person." He looked up at the door when Agatha entered with Melodia.

She came over to a round of applause as her cheeks reddened and she bowed her head. They all got up from their chairs and surrounded her and chattered among themselves while Francis looked on with patience and a smile on his face. As they took their chairs again, Melodia used the whiteboard to lay out her plans for unearthing and connecting to family members yet unknown, and perhaps even unaware of their ancestry. She asked them to write down any family members they thought might be helpful in the search. They scribbled names and contacts for a few minutes; Melodia collected them. Then she and Alyssia left the room to begin research.

As the room grew quiet once again, Rodane rose and addressed them all. "I think you know how resistant I was to my inheritance and obnoxious." He looked directly at Agatha, then at Raul, "I ask for your forbearance and apologize for the trouble I have caused for all these sessions. I made an asshole of myself." The twitters from most, filled the room, "No, I'm perfectly serious. I understand your reluctance to trust me and I am going to work so hard to gain that trust, you will get tired of hearing from me."

He sat down as they remained quiet until all at once, they clapped and Raul whistled. Then Agatha stood up and spoke, "Well, you have been a pain in the ass but you've also risen above even my expectations in such a brief time and we all recognize that. Now, everyone get out of here and go to your appointed teams to figure out how we are going to address the fact that we might not be living here on this planet in secret very much longer. Out, all of you, get food and drink and get to work!" When they had all left, she connected to the starship *Asternum II* and began the most important conversation in her lifetime.

Chapter 29

Loose ends

Far away, in a small back country of Eastern Europe, a bearded Lindley Gorham, a former Senator of the USA, was dressed in lavish robes, living in a secure gated compound, fit for only the wealthiest of business leaders and officials. He surrounded himself with soldiers, mercenaries and all those charged with his comfort, secrecy and ease. The meeting with many of his followers was about to begin. His chosen adjutant commander brought him a letter which he opened and read quickly.

When he reached the end of the letter, he reacted by swiping the entire contents off the long table and listened as glass shattered and food was crushed by his boots stomping over and over across the entire mess. e yelled for his right hand man and

He yelled for his aide and screamed for all those attempting to clean up the mess to get out. They fled within seconds. No one wanted to reach out to him when he was this irate. No one wanted to become the subject of his rage and violent anger. His plans had been wrecked in the last few months and he was eager to find someone to take the fall or feel the retribution he could unleash.

This was not the timid, quiet, nerdy, unpolished Senator who had played the part for years. This was the man who wanted to have his army, men and women just like him; paid for, enabled, trained and with total loyalty to him, ready for the Armageddon he was sure he could unleash. All he needed was time, more money, and more people he could convince it was time to get their claws into the entire government of every free country he could pay for or get firsthand.

There were already plenty of them in this compound and others spread across many countries and more coming every day and week. He barked out orders to bring him every tech engineer, electrical specialist and software genius they could pay or command. They would see how much he could accomplish with all those who hated just as much as he did. They fed off it, they breathed in the fetid air and the stink of rage and revenge. They beat it into their own people and watched as they cowered and caved. He was eager to see how the world took it when all their communications and big businesses crashed once again and this time, it wouldn't be caught or stopped until he decided to end it with his own demands.

Tall, lean, holding onto the hat on his head, hunched into the raincoat he wore in the heavy downpour, he stopped at the corner, looked around on three sides and made an abrupt turn into the alley. He went behind a dumpster and slowly counted to ten. He followed the trail of trash and broken glass to the other end and then turned right again. Anyone watching him would think he was lost. When he reached the next street, he doubled back to the first street and moved quickly to the crosswalk.

The edge of Georgetown in the late hours was not very crowded. There were bars open however, on just about every block. After ten minutes of walking and rerouting a few times, he arrived at a corner, where the lights were flickering over a tilted sign for the tavern he knew was open until 2 in the morning.

Walking in, he saw it was just crowded enough to miss his entrance unless anyone was watching. The conversations were muted and convivial. The man at the booth in the corner had his back against the wall and muttered, "Bout time you got here, I was ready to leave."

He took off his damp coat and laid it next to him on his seat, "Just careful."

Soon, a pint was placed in front of him without a word. The place gradually emptied out as they discussed pleasantries, their jobs and family. Both were men recently approached by the former President, Sheamus McAndrew, to join his new non-profit organization. Sheamus had lots of clout, more of wealthy investors and a great deal of savvy and sway to get things done without being a bully about it. He worked well with others and played nicely in the sandbox of both finances and politics. He had hit them with a humdinger of an offer.

Gerard Fowler and Joe Jordan had been approached by Sheamus just weeks before he had even left office. That December was a cold, rainy mess of famous Washington winter weather. Sheamus had entertained them in this same tavern after closing time, with printouts and figures amassed over a period of months by his own wife Lori, and her friends. It was at her suggestion that he meet with them. Only the bartender had been there for that first meeting. Now he was busy wiping counters, arranging the top shelf and going back and forth from the kitchen to the cellar. He knew all of them quite well.

Sheamus's wife and her friends still amazed him, yet they all scared him if he would acknowledge it. They were devoted to his wife, who was very astute in judging any hurdles she faced, coming back into private life. The two men now sitting in that booth without him, had also amazed him at the time. He couldn't put his finger on it, but it was the same feeling he got when his wife's friends came to him with either warnings or suggestions or information to ease his frenetic mind, when faced with an issue that he had trouble solving. They never missed.

Sheamus had asked both men to consider a job they had personally never worked at before, espionage and intelligence. They were well versed in those two practices, familiar in both their careers.; Joe as a high-tiered accountant on Wall Street and Gerard, a former Navy Seal, now detective in the Md State Police. All three had been fast friends from college and Grad school. Sheamus knew them from college sports, late night tutoring sessions and many nights on beer runs and parties. They had stayed connected for all the years after, not regularly, but enough to keep the bonds tight among them.

Now, here by themselves, they felt a little daunted by his request. They had considered his terms, discussed it for weekends by themselves and with Sheamus McAndrew at their shared cabin in Upper Western Maryland. Their families were close, they were godparents to each other's children and they also shared the same mindsets concerning sports, politics and only left religion to those who felt the need. Now, they had to decide. Sheamus McAndrew was gearing up to begin his company in public and it was start now or keep doing what they had been doing for decades until retirement.

Even though the tavern was empty except for the two seated there now, Gerard 'Gerry' as he was known by all those he knew well, whispered and hunched over the table, "You can't imagine what I have been going through for the last few weeks."

It was catching. Joe leaned over and whispered back, "If it's what I've been doing, my wife thinks I'm about to go off the deep end and she may be right."

"My God" Gerry ran his hands through a short haircut, "did you ever think we would be part of something like this?"

"Not in my wildest dreams" Joe sat back and breathed long and steady. "How do we keep this from our wives, have you thought of that?"

Gerry sat back and took a long drink of his beer, "I can honestly say I have never kept anything important from Grace in our entire marriage. I'm not sure if I could lie to her with a straight face. Look Joe, I've been racking my brains all week and I've come up with a plausible story for you, that is mostly true, in a sense."

Joe grinned, "I've seen and heard your *plausible* stories. One might call them 'fish tales'. Think Grace might see it? I know Claire is pretty good at reading me if I have the faintest sniff of 'doubt' about me."

"Here's the thing. You're a whiz at finances, Claire knows that. If you tell her Sheamus wants to hire you part-time to handle all his business investments and Lori recommended you to him, would she buy that?"

Joe mused for a minute with curled lips and a frown on his upper forehead, "Yeah, I think she would. But...how can Lori..."

"Lori knows. She's..." he now pursed his lips and thought how to deliver his news, "She knows everything. She's a big part of it."

"A part of what?" He looked hard at Gerry who stayed quiet, "She's... one of...them?"

"Yeah Joe, she's one of them. Christ, I'm beginning to believe half the world is *them*."

A silence descended for at least the five minutes they were digesting this. Joe looked out the window at the rain still falling and Gerry looked at his phone to see if any calls had come in from downtown. He was on day duty but could be called if a death occurred that was suspicious. It was happening more and more frequently. Joe looked over at him and asked, "What excuse have you thought of that you could use to tell Grace?"

Gerry turned his beer mug around and around while looking down into the remaining beer as if it was an eight ball that could provide an answer for him. He looked up at Joe and smiled,

"We've been talking about my retirement some, and I thought I could use that to lever into an actual 'second career' which would totally keep me busy. Working for Sheamus could avoid any possible doubt in Grace's mind, as to my next move and she'd likely appreciate me not interfering with her schedule." He grinned more widely now. "Grace would be ecstatic with my retirement. She's been really stressed lately with the amount of work I've been doing and all the night calls. That raise in salary wouldn't hurt either."

Joe looked at him with a frown, "Easier for you than for me. I can't retire and I've got two kids in college. The new money is great but what about the security? You know Sheamus was very upfront and truthful about the amount of danger we, more you than me…might face. What about the kids?"

"I know, Gerry answered, "that's' what I haven't figured out yet. I've got to find a way to let Grace know that it's top secret and we might need more security. She might flip at that, seeing we've always had those problems before. She might not want to consider also having them now."

"Yeah, but Gerry, it's almost foolproof. What better 'second career' than one you've been so good at all these years? It's the perfect cover, even for those who might be wondering…or…looking." He grimaced, "Sorry, but you've got to consider that too. What about the increased travel that might be necessary?"

They continued into the late night, watching the rain finally drizzle away, drinking their beer and musing over the task they now realized they had already decided to take on. Talking it out, they had discovered they both were thinking along the same lines without even admitting they were already invested. The bartender came over, collected their empty mugs and nodded at them. Gerry shook hands with him and turned to Joe,

"Time to go home and face the music. When do you

want to tell Sheamus?"

"Wanna bet he already knows which way we would go, Lori too?"

"Nope, not losing money on that one."

They went in different directions to head home and there was a lot to think about. Some scary stuff as well, for the next few…months, years? Gerry found himself sweating even though the night was getting chillier on his walk to the train. The bartender followed them out and kept watch from a distance until Gerry boarded the train home.

Three thousand, eight hundred and twelve miles lay between Washington D.C. and Amiens France, as the crow flies. The time difference had her pacing the floor in Amiens France, around 9am in the morning light, while the two men leaving Georgetown were going home about 3am in the dark's misty, early morning. She had gotten about three hours of sleep, fitfully tossing and turning. She had her suitcase open on the bed but hadn't done anything to pack. She was at a crossroads.

Sabina Carter was a thoughtful person, usually levelheaded and most often very circumspect with her emotions and her skills. Today, her mind was a quagmire of indecision and stress. The night before was not only a revelation but a quandary, the likes of which she had not experienced since she was perhaps three or four years old. She wished she had not gone to Alyssia and Melodia. It wasn't their fault she was in this bind but the information they had relayed to her, made it very difficult to think straight. She had heard, *"A little knowledge is a dangerous thing"*. Well, she certainly felt she was in danger and that was silly, wasn't it?

She had a choice, in fact, many choices; follow up on the information they had discovered, ignore it and continue in her present situation, seek out advice from Suri or Francis, share it with Rodane Arcos and swear him to secrecy....so many others she was batting back and forth in her confused mind. She stopped, flung herself across the unmade bed, put her hands over her face and let out a "*Arghhhhhh*" so loud the puppy at the end of her bed '*yipped*', jumped off and fled to the corner.

"I'm sorry Archie, come here pup" and put out her hand. He jumped on the bed and started licking her face, while trying to snuggle into her bones. She lay there for a minute and then sat up against the headboard. She thought out loud, "What would Rodane do?" That did it. She would do the exact opposite. She put her suitcase back into the closet, put Archie into his crate and headed out to the lower floor of the compound.

She walked into the dining room and saw a few people still eating breakfast even at this late hour. It was Sunday and many slept in before the tasks of their offices had them running circles around their inner clock. Spying Francis, sitting alone over at the window, she walked over purposely and sat down without even asking if he was free. He looked up, seemingly perplexed, "Good morning, Sabina, how may I help you if you would be so kind?" He smiled to take the sternness out of his voice.

'I'm not going to beat around the bush, Francis and I'm not going to ask you to apologize for..."

"Not telling you sooner?"

'*Whoosh*' That took the wind out of her sails in a heartbeat. "What? You knew all this? How could…"

"You notice Sabina, I asked how I can *help* you, not what can I *do* for you?"

She sat quietly while the hands on the clock above the large serving counter, snicked the seconds loud enough to hear from her seat. She put her head down, a tear dropped down her cheek, and she looked up at him. He saw her confusion, her heartache, her fear, all in one rush of emotion she usually kept so close to her, out of hurt's range. He reached across the table and took her limp fingers,

"Sabina, my dear, I'm too old to play games and I knew you would be coming here soon. I wasn't sure in what state. Let's just say I was prepared for any state that meant you were trying to digest this puzzle that has been unleashed on you unexpectedly. Are you ok?" He thought about what he had just said, "Now that was a very silly question. Of course, you're not ok. Let's rephrase that, are you going to be, ok?"

"Did you know before Alyssa and Melodia?"

"Yes child, I did. Recently, it's my job to be made aware of anything that is in the least suspicious. This was most certainly that."

"Did you…I don't want to simper but…did you know long ago?" She waited; unaware she was holding her breath.

He took too long to answer, "What **did** you know, so I don't have to wonder if you're lying to me now?"

Francis took a deep breath himself, "When Suri found you, it was in a hovel of a so- called house, with those who were watching you. I can't say 'taking care of you' because it was anything but. She didn't bring you home that day or for a few weeks. She took you to one of our safe houses and stayed there with you."

"Why didn't she bring me to her home right away?"

"I think she was trying to uncover any memories you might have had concerning who and where your parents were."

She interrupted again, "Why couldn't she do that here, or...where **was** her home?"

Again, he took too long to answer, "Was there something wrong with me that she didn't want the others to see or know?"

"I don't think that was the reason but no, there was nothing wrong with you."

"Then why..."

"I'm going out on a limb here and I don't want to put more doubt into your mind but..." He reached for her hand again, "I will admit I was afraid to find out why she kept you there and later, I never found a good way to ask her. You had been settled into our 'family' so long, it seemed like a needless inquiry."

"Was I able to shine any light on where my parents were or why they left me there?"

"The doctor that examined you when you were finally at Suri's house believed you were traumatized by something that had happened to you but he couldn't get any information from Suri or you when he questioned you."

"What about the people that had me in their house?"

"Well...now, that's another mystery. When Suri with Agatha, went back to question them the very next day, they were gone, no one saw them leave, and there was nothing in the house to show you even lived there." He sat back and waited.

Something occurred to her, "Who watched me while she went back to question them?"

"That I don't know. Something to ask her?"

"Ok, we'll let that one alone for now. If I wasn't responding and the people who had me were gone, what did you find out?"

Francis looked at her, "Do you want to get coffee or breakfast? You're pale as a ghost and your eyes tell me you haven't slept much last night."

"I need go get Archie and let him do his business. When I come back, promise I won't find you unavailable or missing in action?"

"Come to my office whenever you want. I'll be there and it will be a little more of a private conversation." He studied her, "Do you want to ask anyone else to join us?" She thought about that and decided, "I think one on one is good at this point if you don't feel uncomfortable with just me."

"He rose from his seat, "I'll let Rodane know…"

"No! You can't tell him…"

"Easy Sabina. I was going to say I'll let Rodane know I can't meet with him for our appointment until later." He now studied her, "Is there something you're not telling me about Rodane?"

She was flustered and her cheeks reddened, "It's just that until I find out more, I want to keep this just between us… and…and…Archie here…" her face was flaming now, I… trust Rodane but I can't be sure of anything until I've figured this out."

"Of course. You know where to find me." He rose and left the dining room while Sabina poured herself a strong coffee and grabbed a muffin as she left. One thought was coursing through her brain,

{did Agatha also know}

Then she remembered; of course, Agatha knew; she was with Suri looking for her parents. Then who watched her while they were gone? If she could discover that, she could ask that person for information before she went to them. Then she paused on the stairs. She had now realized,

{I don't trust them! That makes a big difference how I do this}

She continued upstairs to take care of Archie, then she knew exactly who she needed to talk to, and soon.

Chapter 30

New Beginnings

AsternumII was settled in on the dark side of *Phobos.* If earth's telescopes could home in on any moon of Mars, they would not be able to view *AsternumII* from any vantage point. But if a rover were anywhere near…?

On board, events were heating up quickly and the two chief officers were ready to declare everyone confined to their quarters. It was a drastic step but Piri Cassel had tried to outfox them and in so doing, had jeopardized their very existence in this galaxy. They had searched the entire ship many times. Either he was somewhere they hadn't yet searched or…someone was hiding him who they hadn't considered. Whispers were growing louder, children were noticing their parent's stress and the parents were noticing the officer's stress, affecting all levels and all teams. The coms switched on; Lt Forbes spoke: "Sir, we did inventory as ordered, there is a space pod missing."

Cmdr. Haller spoke, "How can that be? Didn't you just do a check a week ago?"

"Yes sir, but one was in for maintenance in the secure

zone. Uh…we didn't check that area sir. It was off limits."

"You dolt, off limits to most, not to a secure check!" Track it down, **NOW**!

"Sir, we can send you the co-ordinates of where it was heading when it ejected, if that would be helpful?"

"if that would be…" He took a breath, "Lt, send me anything you have no matter how insignificant you might think it is. Understood?"

"Yes sir, right away sir."

Genie was asleep, her dreams filtered through her mind like strands of fairy hair, golden in color, flowing and seemingly under water. She watched as a person gradually materialized into a solid shape and then, as all dreams do, turned into a place she found herself without knowing where. The ruts in the path were deep like horse and carriage had been through here many times. She looked around and saw the countryside with fields of stubble and a few spindly cows that looked emaciated. Ahead of her was a gate at least 6 or 8 feet high. The voice was hard and stern, "Don't go in there. Don't even let them see you."

She moved quickly over to the side of the path and hurried behind the scraggly bushes. Then she heard a cart coming from the other end. She tried to go further into the bushes that scraped her shoulders. Thorns bit into her hands and arms. Blood seeped from her fingers and a different voice said, "You need to get to the cellar or all is lost." The voice became trembly and she realized she was already in the cellar in front of four cells. She was frustrated she couldn't stay in one place.

"Get the keys, you know where they are, get them and hurry! They're coming, go out the other end. Run!"

She woke up with her legs twisted in the sheets from running in place and her sweat was running down her face. Or was it tears? Her heart was hammering and her breath was shallow gasps. A knock on the door had her jumping,

"Are you ok Genie? Do you need anything?" She didn't recognize the voice. She looked around and…where was she? How did she get here? There was one mirror, nothing on the walls, no pictures, no sign of anything to let her know where she was. The knock was harder this time,

"Genie, are you alright?" She thought fast, "Can I see Sabina?"

"She's not here right now. She'll be here later this afternoon. Can I get you something?"

"No, I'm fine. I'll be up in a few minutes. Thanks anyway."

"See you downstairs for breakfast?"

"Yes, I'll be there soon. Thanks"

Now she had to think and think fast. She didn't know who the voice belonged to and she didn't know where she was. But she had thought of the name *Sabina* in a brief second while her mind was whirling. She eased herself out of bed and put her feet on the carpeted floor. She put clothes on from the drawer and the closet and they seemed to fit. The sneakers by the bed fit. She had better come up with a reasonable plan for trying to identify anyone here…wherever *here* was. She stood up and carefully walked to the window.

{I can walk and I can speak that's something but what?}

Her fingers trembled as she pulled back the curtain and

saw the mountains in the distance, reaching high into a gorgeous blue sky, with snow covering the top.

{Now where the hell am I? who is Sabina}

A knock on the door had her jumping, "I'll be there in a few minutes!"

{God almighty these people are eager to get me out of here}

A deep voice had her jolting back a step, "May I come in?" She didn't recognize it, but then she didn't know what or who **to** recognize.

"Wait a minute, please." She went over to the door and stood undecided. She looked around for anything she might use for protection, took a breath and walked slowly to the door and opened it a crack,

"What do you want?" Her voice opened with another crack, "Do I know you?"

"Well Eugenie, if you let me in, and we can keep the door open if you like, we'll see if you know me." He waited.

She squared her shoulders, breathed deeply and opened the door. He stood tall, more than 6 feet and she tilted her head, squinched her eyes almost shut while she gave him a hard look. She began to close the door, "Genie, I was hoping to get at least a few minutes to talk to you. I can go get someone else to be with me if that makes you more comfortable."

"You called me Eugenie and now I'm Genie? Who are you?"

"I'm Phillip."Time to cut bait he thought, "Phillip Barbas. You used to..."

"I don't want to talk to you, I'm mad at you." She pushed the door closed a little more.

{Why am I mad at him? I must know him}

'I'm very sorry about that. We were just getting to know

each other better but I understand if you don't want to talk to me." He began walking away…

"Wait" She felt very foolish, "Do you know why I'm mad at you?"

'If I had to guess, it's because I got you to listen to me and you did something you very much didn't want to do. I guess I might be mad too."

She peered out the door into the hall from front to back. No one was there and the sounds of breakfast came from downstairs. It was still as a tableau and just as silent. She opened the door a little more, "It's not just you, it's… someone else I can't see. She closed her eyes and fisted her hands after a few seconds. "Do you know someone named… Adelaide? Or…" she shook her head, trying so hard to jog that wisp of a memory.

"Agatha? Does that ring a bell?"

"Yes, that's it, I'm angry at her too. But…I don't know why."

"Do you think if we talked for a little, you could begin to put some of the pieces together?" He took his hand off the railing, keeping his distance.

"Come in, I can always throw you out the window." He laughed a little and then became sober again.

"I'm hoping our conversation won't lead to that." He entered the door and pushed it back against the wall.

"You don't have to do that. I think I trust you. Did I trust you, before?"

"I'd like to think you did but then we really haven't talked yet, have we?"

Her face lit up a little, "not really talked but…you told me things would be ok if I just let my guard down." She looked perplexed, "But…we didn't talk, we…thought…Am I going crazy?" her shoulders slumped. "Agatha did the same thing and I'm angry that I changed my mind. I didn't want to. She made it sound so easy. It's never been easy to… I don't want to talk about it. You wouldn't understand, I don't understand."

"Do you remember any of the time you were in the hospital?" He took a big gamble, "Or on the bathyscape?"

She put her hands over her ears and rocked back and forth, "I didn't want to go there but…I promised Agatha I would try. I didn't say YES!" She moved to the window, "Where are we?"

"Where do you think we are?" Phillip didn't move from his spot, afraid to lose his small victory even getting into the room, "Look out, is there something you recognize?"

"I…trained here for a long time, I think. My team had…" She whipped around, "Caroline, I remember Caroline and… Helena" She lightened up and her face finally had a smile on it; small, hesitant but a smile.

"You're beginning to remember and that's a good thing but it may scare you somewhat to know what brought you here." She walked slowly over to him and looked up into his smiling face.

{I know him…how or why}

It brought a warm feeling into her body and she trusted him. No, she more than trusted him and…

{he knows it. He just thought it.!}

Phillip moved to the window and she stood next to him.

Down below, people were beginning to come out into the field. Carts were rolled out with all types of gadgets, gear, boxing gloves and long wooden sticks that looked like…

jousting poles.

She put her hands on the ledge and spoke even though her throat felt closed and her heartbeat faster, “I wanted things to be the way they had always been. I didn’t want change; my life would not be the same. But…it’s happening anyway, isn’t it?” Tears slipped form her face and he turned her to him. She resisted a little but then slumped into his arms and cried. He let her. The hiccups came next and she took the tissues he offered her and blew her nose and walked over to the one chair in the room. He sat on the edge of the bed. Genie looked over at him as he felt her hesitance and she said,

“I must tell you about my dreams because I think they mean something and I think it’s important because something is going to happen that is very bad and dangerous to all of us. I think it’s already started.”

He considered her words, “Who do you mean by ‘all of us’?”

She clasped her hands together, almost whispered the words, “The ‘family, ’shit! really, all of us here from beyond and the ones already here” She sighed, “Holy mother, it feels so good to admit that to myself, finally.”

Phillip rose from the bedside and put out his hand to her, “Let’s go have some breakfast and Sabina should be here by now.”

“There **is** a Sabina, I wasn’t just making up a name?”

“There most certainly is and she will be delighted to see the new you.”

They headed down the stairs to a new day and a new Genie. She felt excited and leery, all at once. They reached the dining hall and when she entered, everyone rose and started clapping. Her cheeks reddened and the first step was a doozy but she took it and Phillip led her to a table. He stood in thought,

{We're in it now, no turning back Genie and I couldn't be happier.}

Printed in the USA
CPSIA information can be obtained
at www.ICGtesting.com
CBHW080444130224
4195CB00003B/4

9 781977 256614